Kathryn
Quarry Hall: Book Three

Michelle Levigne

M Zion Ridge Press
Books Off the Beaten Path

www.MtZionRidgePress.com

Mt Zion Ridge Press LLC
295 Gum Springs Rd, NW
Georgetown, TN 37366

https://www.mtzionridgepress.com

Copyright © 2013 by Michelle L. Levigne
ISBN 13: 978-1-962862-60-8

Published in the United States of America
Publication Date: February 15, 2025

Editor-In-Chief: Michelle Levigne
Executive Editor: Tamera Lynn Kraft

Cover Art Copyright by Mt Zion Ridge Press LLC © 2025

Chapter One

Wednesday

Kathryn pulled her cobalt extended cab pickup into the parking space outside the motel office door. Then she checked her cell phone. It was habit. She didn't expect to get a signal, let alone any messages. Driving through this particular section of the mountains meant scanty cell phone reception at best, and depending on motel room or public library wireless to get onto the Internet.

Which was exactly why she had come here, ten hours of driving away from Quarry Hall, for her time of retreat and contemplation.

Bea, her near-black Akita companion, whimpered and leaned over from the passenger seat to nose Kathryn's hand before she finished pulling the phone from her jeans pocket.

"I know, it's a waste of time, but—" Kathryn blinked, staring at the list of missed calls.

Somehow, her phone had picked up bits and pieces of signal long enough to register the missed messages and calls, and Finnegan Roberts' name topped the list.

She hadn't come out here consciously to avoid Finn. More accurately, to avoid calling him and having "that talk" they needed to have since learning of her illness. Yet if she was honest, Kathryn knew coming out here, where tiny communities clung to the mountainsides and modern technology failed more often than not, was doing exactly that. Avoiding him. Even if she had been too busy to keep track of how long it had been since Finn's last phone call, her subconscious knew. He had been emailing her at least once every week to come look at a ministry desperately in need of the Arc Foundation's sponsorship and her leadership, each email adding new information on the people, the community, the churches barely hanging on by their fingernails.

When he called and got through to her instead of leaving a message, Finn got more personal. That made her hesitate to respond via anything other than emails. He admitted he wanted her to be close to his new job posting with the FBI, so he could *finally*—his word—get serious about the relationship they had begun in college. Since the days when she had consciously slid away from the faith her mother had raised her in, and Finn had worked to drag her back up the slope before she went too far.

"Now isn't a good time," Kathryn murmured, and scrolled past Finn's name, to make mental note of when Vincent and Joan and Jennifer had called. Their messages hadn't come through, naturally. Just the notation that they had called.

Bea whined, nudged her hand, then took the Chinese knotwork of Kathryn's key chain in her mouth and tugged the keys out of the ignition.

"All right, all right." She sighed, consciously turning the sound to laughter, and tucked the phone back into her pocket. "We're getting out and we're getting a room. Are you happy?"

Bea licked her cheek. Kathryn sputtered and wiped her face, and hit the door latch with her other hand. Her smile faded by the time she had one foot down on the ground and turned to face the motel office.

A little more than a year ago, she would have thought nothing of finding a secluded spot along the mountain road with a lovely view, unrolling a sleeping bag, and camping under the stars. With the gray seeping across the sky, threatening showers by nightfall, she would not have minded spending tonight's storm curled up in the back of the cab with Bea, cozy and warm, lulled to sleep by the drumming of the rain over her head.

Not tonight, and probably not anymore. Nowadays, her knees and elbows ached without warning, no matter how good the weather, no matter how much exercise she got. Sometimes when she spent more than two hours straight behind the wheel, she had a bruised sensation through her legs and back. She didn't get breathless spells or dizzy and need oxygen or a wheelchair, like her Uncle Harrison, but that didn't mean anything. All those symptoms waited to pounce on her, one of these days.

She had learned to listen to her body. When the slightly achy, bruised feeling whispered over her muscles, she got off the road and found somewhere comfortable to lie down and rest as soon as possible. If she didn't, when the spells of exhaustion hit she wouldn't be worth anything. Just four months ago, she had ignored the warning signs to run an errand to Pittsburgh. At a gas station on the Ohio/Pennsylvania border, one whiff of fuel fumes sent her to her knees, dizzy and retching.

The symptoms were different, but she was dying just like Uncle Harrison. And just like him, Kathryn had no idea how fast or slow the process was. She took each day as it came, and lived a little more cautiously than before. No more pushing herself to the limits of her endurance. No more testing to see how far she could go. It wasn't good stewardship or faith to ignore common sense and then expect God to bail her out.

That meant a hotel room instead of camping out, and stopping before dinnertime, instead of driving past nightfall.

"What do you think?" she said, glancing up and down the neat row of cookie-cutter doors and windows, ten on each side of the door of the motel office.

Someone had painted the doors and window frames different jewel-tone colors, graduating along the spectrum in matched sets. A crimson door and window frame, followed by a rich orange set, followed by a shade like ripe pumpkin, then sunny, lemon yellow, and on up through a deep, royal purple, and then crimson starting the cycle all over. Kathryn considered the curtains that matched the window frames, and the smell of fresh coffee coming through the open door of the office. She might just stay here for her retreat and contemplation time, instead of continuing south to the bed & breakfast that Joan and Sophie had recommended.

Bea looked around, then glanced at the wide curve of mountain road only ten yards from the motel's walls. The big Akita sniffed, snorted, and headed for the office door. Kathryn laughed and watched for traffic. Nobody passed in either direction by the time she reached the open doorway. That suited her just fine. The less traffic, the better.

As she signed the credit card slip and let the whisper-thin, white-haired owner talk her into accepting a plate of fresh-from-the-oven cookies and two apples to take to her room, Kathryn heard the first rumble of thunder. She glanced over her shoulder to the open door, drawn by the chilly curls of breeze that reached through. The sunshine had faded to sullen gray.

"Oh, don't you worry. This old place has been sticking fast to the mountain for the last eighty years," the woman said with a chuckle. "No matter how hard a downpour we're supposed to get tonight, we won't get washed away."

"Oh, I'm not worried about that." Kathryn picked up one of the business cards in the twenty-slot display rack on the motel counter. "How good is the pizza? Worth getting drenched?"

"Don't get drenched. Ricky delivers. And it's incredible. I've been to New York, and they don't hold a candle to what his family makes."

"Sold." She laughed and tucked the business card for Ricky's Pizza Emporium into her pocket.

Yes, definitely, this was the place to hole up and rest and do some thinking. She just had a good feeling about it, like when she obeyed one of her vision-dreams. This was where she needed to be.

~~~~~

Lightning crackled and thunder roared, nearly drowning out the drumming of the rain through the thick walls of the high-security building settled deep into the mountainside. The flashes came closer together, until the lightning strikes seemed to hit on the other side of the thick wall of ancient pines that hid the laboratory and luxurious house attached to it.

"You don't belong here." Dr. Reginald Malvern struck a pose in the
~~~~~

doorway leading from his living quarters into the laboratory. His icy blue eyes flicked from side to side, tracking the movements of the six dark-clad men as they walked slowly through the long, sparsely lit room.

The man leading the group glanced around, flicked one hand to his left, and the man behind him swept his arm across the counter, clearing it of racks and tubes, beakers and sample dishes. Dr. Malvern let out a choked cry of offended dismay. Liquid splattered and trickled into multi-colored piles of granules and powders, sending up sparks or puffs of smoke. The leader flicked his right hand, and a man on his right did the same with a worktable, sending a blizzard of papers and booklets and tablets and pens across the floor.

"What do you—" Malvern stopped short as the leader raised his left hand. He closed his mouth. The other man lowered his hand, nodding.

"You don't learn as quickly as my employer would want, but faster than most," the leader said.

He and his men stayed in the shadows. They were tall, wide-shouldered shapes in dark clothes, softly glistening from the storm they had passed through before they entered the building. They were nearly identical in their hooded jackets with no markings or decorations.

"The guards are gone." A blond, jeans-clad young woman stumbled into the lab from the hallway, coming in behind the six men. She met Malvern's gaze and her eyes widened, visibly stunned.

"Regina—" He flinched as the leader of the six men raised his right hand again.

"You know what we want," the man said, turning to Regina.

"She doesn't know anything," Malvern blurted. "I don't even know what you want."

"Don't be a fool, Doctor." He chuckled coldly. "I'm sure your daughter knows far more than you think. We hear she's a genius, despite what you think of her. The question is if she'll give us what we want to save your life. You're not much of a father. As an employer, you're even worse."

"What do you want?" Malvern said, voice strained, cracking.

"What you've spent the last eight years perfecting, of course. Regina, darling—" He beckoned, and two men reached out and caught hold of her by her upper arms, hurrying her to the front of the group. "You know where it is, don't you?"

Regina stared back at Malvern, stone-faced, no emotions, no sign of fear or anger or even recognition of the man who faced her.

"She knows nothing about it," Malvern insisted, lowering his volume. "I never told her about this part of my work. She doesn't have the brains to understand what I've been working on, or what you want."

"Liar." The leader laughed, the sound sucking warmth from the air and deepening the shadows. "We know everything we need to know. We have many kinds and ways of persuasion, Doctor. You ought to know that by now. You use quite a few yourself. Even on your own daughter. You've been a very, very bad boy."

More laughter. Regina closed her gray-blue eyes and turned her head away. Shoulder-length hair hung down to hide her face. She rubbed her long-fingered hand against her jeans, stopping their visible trembling.

Malvern's lean, aristocratic features paled as Regina stepped through the debris and wreckage on the floor, over spilled containers of white and gray and black powders and shattered test tubes and smoking, bubbling liquids. She approached him, and when he reached out a hand to her, she sidestepped, putting a worktable between them. Regina didn't meet his gaze as she reached for a set of keys hanging from a peg under the lip of the long worktable down the center of the room.

"No!" Malvern shouted.

He reached to stop her as she crossed the room to a cube refrigerator tucked under another worktable. He raised his other hand, clenched in a fist. Two men leaped, caught him by both shoulders, and spun him around. He lost his balance and fell, hitting his forehead against the countertop. Blood spatters joined the other stains and spills on the floor.

Regina's hands shook as she bent, inserted a key in the lock, and opened the refrigerator. She hesitated and glanced once at her father, who stared, his face losing more color as blood dripped into his eyes. She flung the door open, exposing a dozen clear plastic cubes sitting on the skinny shelves. Each box was little more than two inches on a side and contained an iridescent white powder.

"Good girl," the leader said. "You ought to take a lesson from your daughter and cooperate for a change. She's saving both your lives."

Malvern shouted and lunged across the room, evading the men who reached to stop him. Regina let out a shriek and stumbled backward, falling under the table and against the refrigerator. Four cubes toppled off the little shelf, jarred by the impact. She flinched away from the wide spray of glistening powder as the plastic shattered on the tile floor. As the two men converged on her father again, she looked around the room. No one watched her. Her face twisted into momentary fury like the lightning that continued to flash outside. She snatched one cube out of the little refrigerator, turning her back to the altercation, tucked the cube into her jeans pocket, and tugged her sweater down over the bulge.

She slowly hauled herself to her feet. The leader came up behind her and pushed her out of the way. Regina grappled for the refrigerator as she stumbled away, pulling it over on its side and out from under the table. Every cube spilled out onto the floor, the plastic shattering with high-pitched snaps, sending powder in all directions. Malvern erupted in a tornado of fury, but couldn't break free of the men holding him by his arms. He kicked and swore. Iridescent powder spread across the lab floor, disturbed by the movement. Trickles of liquid from the other side of the table touched the powder. Flares of phosphorescence, sparks, and spurts of smoke erupted from the combinations.

The leader stomped through the knot of struggling men and swung, backhanding Malvern hard so he flew backward, his head slamming against the nearest worktable. He stalked over to the sparking, fizzing, sparkling puddle of melting white powder and shattered plastic and glared down at it for three heartbeats.

"Well, Doctor, what are we going to do now?" He narrowed his eyes and turned to Regina, who pulled herself to her feet, shoulders hunched, sniffling, the fury in her eyes bright through the curtain of her tangled hair. "Why do I think you did that on purpose?"

A radio crackled, loud with static, a voice nearly indecipherable. One of the men who hadn't been fighting Malvern pulled a slim black box from his belt, looked at the tiny screen that gave off a dim green light, and handed it to his leader.

"We're just going to have to convince you to make more, aren't we? Bad news, Doctor. This storm is going to slow down those reinforcements you were waiting for." He laughed when Malvern went pale at his words. "Yes, we know you decided to renege on your deal with our employer, and you called the Feds for help. Very bad decision. It's a good thing nobody is going anywhere for the rest of the night." He gestured at the door into the living quarters. "Let's make ourselves more comfortable and have a little talk, to convince you of the error of your ways."

~~~~~

Kathryn had a relaxed evening, using the motel phone to call Quarry Hall and check in. Vincent and Sophie were on the road, taking care of a security consultation with people only identified as "old friends" of his. Jennifer had no idea why Vincent had called Kathryn. She promised to call and let him know where she was. Kathryn gave her the motel number, because she didn't plan on leaving her cozy room for at least three days, and the cell reception was absolutely wretched.

"Of course, for all we know, part of it could be blamed on the incoming storm. In the morning when everything clears up, it could be nice and sunny," Kathryn remarked.

"Let's hope not. You need a low-tech vacation just as much as the rest of us."

"Is that what you call it when Sophie has left her nest of gadgets and Internet toys?"

"We're not that helpless," Jennifer retorted. Her voice sounded tinny over the landline.

After catching Kathryn up on the latest news, including the lack of
~~~~~

progress on tracking down Joan's half-sister, Nikki, they made their farewells. Kathryn checked her cell phone, just in case Finn's message had made it through the dead zone and landed in her phone. No such luck. She sighed and contemplated the apple fritter she had ordered with her pizza, then reached for the motel phone to call Finn. She wasn't ashamed to admit she was being a coward.

Ten minutes later, after leaving a message explaining the situation with being in the mountains and bad reception, she stretched out on her back and contemplated the swirling pattern of the plaster ceiling. Kathryn couldn't decide if she was relieved that Finn wasn't available, or if she should worry. Maybe he was out on a field assignment right now? Maybe that was his message—something had turned sour and he wanted to ask her to send up some extra prayers on his behalf?

Bea whined and climbed up on the bed, to sprawl half across Kathryn's legs. Blinking a threat of tears from her eyes, Kathryn smiled and reached down to give her companion a good, hard rub.

Thursday

Kathryn ventured half a mile down the curving mountain road to Kimmy's Diner for breakfast. The motel owner assured her Kimmy wouldn't mind Bea coming in and sitting under the table, and she was right. The owner/cook even offered a big bowl of meat scraps for Bea's breakfast before Kathryn could ask.

The rain pounded harder, the thunder boomed louder, and the lightning strikes came closer together, threatening to touch ground on the mountainside. It was a good day to curl up in the comfortable old brass bed under the colorful quilts, with Bea snuggled next to her, and read all day. If anyone tried to call her, they didn't get through on her cell phone.

She slept through lunch, and decided to indulge in another pizza, delivered, for dinner. Kathryn was more than happy with where she had landed, and even if the weather hadn't been so wretched, she wouldn't have wanted to leave anyway.

~~~~~

A thin rivulet of storm water traveled in ripples down the curving asphalt mountain road that night. Lightning flashed, turning the dark stream silver, outlining pebbles and branches and wind-torn leaves in stark relief. Then darkness enveloped the road, hiding the steep slant of shattered rock and mud and moss on one side, the clumps of trees and drenched grass on the other. Thunder barely made itself heard through the screaming of the ripping wind.

A tiny avalanche of mud and sludge and sharp wedges of rock
~~~~~

slithered onto the berm. The wind slowed a moment, as if to hear the gasps and whimpers coming from a battered young woman slithering down the slope on her muddy hands and torn knees.

Regina fetched up against the rusty guardrail on the inside of the curve and huddled in the minimal shelter, choking on the rainwater and mud streaming across her face. Coughing, she struggled to clean her hands so she could wipe her face. Mud obscured the rips and tears in her jeans and sweater, and sealed the bloody scrapes on her hands and knees. Her hair ran with muddy water, washing blood from the cut on her right temple almost as quickly as it oozed through her makeshift handkerchief bandage.

Lightning crackled across the sky, extending tines in every direction. Regina watched it, too tired to feel frightened by nature's violence. She clutched the guardrail and hauled herself to her feet.

Two more lightning flashes illuminated the road, showing where it curved to the left as it went up the mountain, and to the right as it went down. Regina leaned against the guardrail, blinking away water, looking down at her legs and the guardrail, bracing to climb over it.

Light flashed. But not lightning. With a strangled cry, she went to her knees behind the guardrail, nearly putting her face down into the muddy torrent cutting a trail across the gravel. A dark crimson Jeep skidded up the mountain road, gleaming in the pelting rain and its own headlights. It hugged the curve, splashing water over the guardrail before it passed by.

Regina let out a choked sob. Her hands shook as she grasped the guardrail to pull herself to her feet again. She gritted her teeth and gave one poisonous glare at the fading red taillights. Legs shaking, she climbed over the rail and stalked across the road.

The plastic cube full of iridescent powder fell from her torn, soaked pocket when she was two-thirds of the way across the road. Regina didn't hear the sharp crackle as the plastic shattered and the white powder spilled onto the roadside. It bubbled and hissed faintly and sent up steam as the water traveling down the road's asphalt surface enveloped it.

Chapter Two

On the other side of the road, Regina paused before lifting her leg to climb over the next guardrail. She brushed her hand across her jeans pocket and let out a wail as her fingers caught on the torn cloth. Her wail turned to fury and she tore the sodden cloth free. Feet slipping in the mud, she turned and retraced her steps.

A flash of lightning illuminated the bubbling white puddle in the road as she put one foot into it. Regina staggered back, gasping, and hurried to wipe off the side and sole of her dripping shoe. Tears joined the dirty water streaming down her face. She stood over the broken cube and the slowly melting powder and clenched her fists, terror fighting with anger on her face. The faint flash of headlights coming down the mountain around the curve startled her. With one more terrified glance at the white puddle, she headed back to the guardrail and threw herself over.

Her foot slipped. For one precarious moment she balanced in thin air with her other foot hooked on the guardrail. A harsh scream broke from her lips as she went down, tumbling head over heels, digging up muddy divots with her elbows and knees and heels. She crashed through a low bush at the base of a massive tree. Her forehead slammed into the trunk and she tumbled into the cover of the bush.

Regina struggled for two seconds, gagging on mud and muddy water, trying to tear free of the tangling branches. Then her eyes closed and she collapsed.

A dark green 4X4 crept around the curve in the road. Hi-beams played over the clumps of trees on the outer side of the road, the tangles of bushes and wild flowers and rivulets of mud traveling down the mountainside. The two men inside leaned close enough to the windows to fog the glass with their breath. They spotted nothing besides storm-tossed bushes and trees and muddy gouges where storm water carved new trails down the mountainside.

Staying in the outer lane of the road, allowing the men to see as much of the slope as possible, the truck's right side wheels crunched over the broken cube. The plastic shattered into tiny white fragments like snow. The powder had ceased bubbling. The tires mixed the white syrup into the mud and gravel.

The 4X4 continued down the mountain road.

Two miles further up the mountain, inside a maze of switchback roads and gates and steep slopes, the luxurious laboratory home built into the rock face went up in a churning inferno, despite the gusts of icy, rain-laden wind.

~~~~~

Cameron Harper demanded the best from his associates. He set them a strict example with his own mannerisms, style of dress, exacting precision and attention to detail in every aspect of his life. Nothing was wasted, ever. Mistakes had to be transformed into opportunities. If the mistakes of colleagues and opponents gave him openings to wound or control, all the better. Emotions, he considered a waste of energy. He kept his in control and channeled the energy to other areas. Only people who had worked long and closely with him could see through his elegant, icy demeanor. There were very few of them. Everyone else, especially those in disfavor, saw anger ready to lash out, and disdain in his every mannerism. He approved of that, because a fearful subordinate was one who paid closer attention to detail and worked doubly hard to avoid or rectify mistakes.

Like the one that troubled him now.

Slowly, he put down the tablet holding the newest report from the two agents coordinating the field team. His manicured hands framed the device lying flat on the inlaid wood table. A slight jouncing of his upholstered chair and a rumbling of engines intruded into his thoughts. Harper didn't spare one moment of annoyance for the storm that tried to throw his private jet through the skies like a rubber ball. What couldn't be affected was not worth the wasted energy of worry.

Silver-streaked black hair gleamed softly in the subdued lighting. Onyx eyes sparked with disgust. He set the tablet on the table next to his notebook computer and closed the lid.

Standing before him, Lisa McCain watched and waited with the quiet poise that had earned her employer's approval and trust. Slim and tall, so she appeared to be all leg, she wore her sleek black business suit and pumps like a military uniform. The slight dropping and weaving of the plane in the storm didn't alter her stance. Hands crossed behind her, she held herself in perfect readiness.

Harper slid his computer across the table. Lisa stepped forward and caught it, continuing the movement to deposit it into its carrying case. A twist of her wrist closed the case. He sipped at the brandy in its heavy, felt-bottomed glass and sat back in the thick, navy blue cushions, lips pursed and eyes half-hooded.

"Phone?" Lisa suggested.

"They didn't lose that, along with the sample and young Dr. Malvern? Amazing." The faintest hint of a sneer touched Harper's lips and his voice oozed chill. He didn't wait for her response but held out his hand.
~~~~~

Lisa slid his cell phone from its pocket in the computer case, opened it, and handed it to him.

Harper pressed the speed-dial button. The screen flashed, indicating a connection had been made despite the storm. When a man's voice came through the speaker, she settled back into her place at the end of the cabin. Her workstation surrounded her with three computer screens. With a portion of her attention always focused on Harper, she went back to checking networks, changing information, hiding information, and the dozen other duties he bundled under the label of "computer magic." Lisa was the best and she knew it. She also knew she had to stay the best if she wanted to keep her job, and possibly her life. Harper's people had no retirement plan; it wasn't an option.

"Just lovely," Harper said, his voice rising enough to be heard over the jet's engines. "Oh, *now* you think she didn't trust you? Maybe something happened to make her second-guess our deal? You are seriously eroding my trust in you. The little fool was ours from the beginning. This loss is on your watch."

Another pause. He leaned back into the plush upholstery and raised his glass for another sip.

"I don't care how her father's death changes things, or what interference the authorities offer, that drug sample is ours and we will get it back. Along with Regina Malvern's head, if necessary. Do you understand? I don't care what you have to do or who you have to kill."

~~~~~

On the stormy mountainside, the strengthening wind formed a momentary gap in the half-sheltering cover of the trees. Regina roused partially as water battered her face. Eyes blinked away the blood-mud that had started to thicken in a mask across half her face. A low moan escaped her. One hand pushed ineffectually against the mud and leaves. She raised her head a few inches, and the white pain that shot through her from her battered head to her toes yanked the air from her lungs. Her eyes fluttered closed. Choking on a moan, she slid back into unconsciousness.

In the darkness of her mind, gunshots roared and her father fell with a red flower of blood blossoming in his chest. Again and again and again.

Friday

Kathryn woke with the dream still swirling through her mind. She lay perfectly still in the motel bed and kept her eyes closed, holding onto the fragments of the dream. Some details stood out perfectly clear, illuminated by the flashes of lightning.

Thunder rumbled far in the distance and she jerked, startled to find
~~~~~

the storm had followed her out of her dream.

A blond tumbling down a muddy mountainside. Falling into a stand of trees. Smashing her head on a trunk. Trucks flying up and down the curve of the mountain road. Obviously searching — for her? To help? To rescue? To hurt?

The fragments didn't fade as she sorted through them, trying to find some meaning, but drowsiness wrapped around Kathryn within a few minutes. She sighed and rolled over, dragging the blankets up over her head to go back to sleep. Maybe clarity would come if she gave the dream a chance to resume. She still hadn't opened her eyes. A few more rumbles of thunder penetrated the blanket and returning sleep.

Kathryn jerked at the chirping ring of her cell phone. She groaned as she climbed out of the well of warm, comfortable, well-earned sleep.

It couldn't be her phone—she had tested it several times during the day, on the off chance the constantly retreating and attacking storm had cleared the atmosphere and reduced interference. Nothing.

The phone chirped again as she struggled free of the tangle of thick, clean white sheets and faded quilt, with the green thermal blanket from her truck thrown on top. She stubbed her fingers on the nightstand and dislodged her pack of colored pencils, the Concordance, and notebook before she found the slim shape of the phone in the darkness. A twist of her wrist snapped it open in the middle of the fourth cascade of chirps.

"'Lo," she mumbled, voice thick.

"Please tell me you haven't been having any weird dreams," Vincent said.

"Weird for normal people, or weird for me?" She grinned, even as she rubbed her eyes with her fist.

"Don't ask a lot of questions, sweetheart, because I can't give you any answers."

"Friends from the old days calling in favors again?" She bit her lip against asking if his shadowy friends from his dark and dangerous past had the kind of technology that let him ram a cell phone signal through dead zones. Only some perilous emergency warranted that kind of effort.

Please, I'm on rest and relaxation time...

Kathryn reached for her notebook with her free hand and promptly sent everything on the nightstand crashing to the floor. Somewhere in the darkness, Bea snorted and grumbled and the springs of the other bed shifted and groaned. She leaned over the side of her bed, trying to find her notebook in the darkness. She didn't want to turn on the light—but she had to now.

Vincent didn't answer her question, and that was enough of an affirmative to wake her the rest of the way.

Kathryn's fingers ached from frantic searching and stubbing by the time she found the push button for the bedside lamp. She winced and tried to ignore the aching in her eyes from too much reading before bed and not enough sleep. She leaned over the side of the bed and snatched up her notebook with the pen jammed into the spiral wire binder. On the way up, her head hit her new deluxe Greek and Hebrew parallel study Bible that hung over the edge. It crashed to the floor. She scooted back against the brass headboard.

"Right now, just keep it at search and rescue," Vincent said, his voice quiet but clear through the scrambling and crashing. "One person can be invisible and move faster than a team. There are multiple opposing forces running in circles in the mountains near you. They're so busy avoiding each other, you'll be able to get in under their radar. There's a woman on the run who needs your help. Keep your head down and start praying before you take another step."

What else am I supposed to do on a stormy wet night? Kathryn mused. She nodded compliance, even though no one could see her but the massive, silent Akita curled up and watching her from the other bed.

"My friends aren't exactly asking for help — yet — but they're willing to take any help we might want to offer. Since you're close by… My recommendation is to get in there, work under cover of darkness, find the woman and take her out of the area. Far and fast. Don't get anyone local involved, and don't let them notice you. The further away you can get before contacting anyone, the better. Seems to me Finn Roberts is the closest authority I would trust in this kind of situation."

He paused, and Kathryn wondered if she had made a sound at mention of Finn's name.

"Any reason you wouldn't want to see him?"

"Of course not." She grinned at the flutter in her chest. Finn hadn't responded to her call, making her think once again he might have gone out into the field for something important.

"Once you talk to the woman and determine the situation, go as high as possible in the food chain. If you can't trust Finn, then go over his head. Just don't trust anybody within a hundred miles of those mountains. My friends aren't sure how much local law enforcement has been compromised. Since first indications are an inside job, meaning a mole or a traitor, we don't trust anyone but the people we know."

"Must be bad if they're asking — no, they didn't ask, did they? But for them to let you help has to mean it's delicate-bad."

"Got that in one. The timing of allthis … There has to be a reason why you're the closest one there," Vincent admitted, his voice taking on a slight touch of gravel.

"Or that anyone is nearby at all?"

"I shouldn't even be here, shouldn't be inside to see the fireworks go off. I'm officially acting as escort for Sophie. Some big hush-hush job for

Joan's friend, Sidarkis." A momentary bark of laughter escaped him. "She's going nuts over the sci-fi quality equipment they've got here."

"I thought Sophie could wrap the Colonel around her little finger."

"She can and does, but when things started going nuts, we got separated. I ran into some old friends when whatever is happening went down on the mountain. That's why I'm not giving you much data. Don't have much to give you, and don't want to get them hung out to dry with their superiors by overstepping." He sighed. "Be careful. There are people going in, and they'll provide cover if you need it, but we'd all be better off if you didn't need it. The less disturbance you make, the less noise, the less stopping for red tape, the better. I'm not telling them anything about you, either. The less anyone knows, the less chance of compromise and betrayal."

"Got it. Just get in there, find the woman — what's her name?"

"Nobody's sharing that much intel. We need to act fast and quietly. That's the main reason they're letting me contact you to make a try. The door could close just as fast as it opened here."

"Got you. Get in, find her, get her out and as far away from there as possible, as fast as possible."

"Before somone decides you might be a liability."

"Uh huh." That solidified just how precarious the situation was.

Kathryn had learned long ago to trust Vincent, his knowledge and training and instincts. If he didn't think she could handle the situation, if her life would be placed in too much jeopardy, he wouldn't risk her.

Bracing for confirmation of what she had seen in her dreams, she yanked her pen free of the notebook, tugged the cap off with her teeth, and dropped it on the blankets. "Where do I go?"

"The woman was last seen running through the forests on Mill Road, about ten miles above Millersburg."

Kathryn made notes as Vincent gave the details of the situation and what witnesses had reported of the ruckus on the mountainside. A woman fleeing for her life. Gunfire. Park rangers reacting like Nazis had invaded. Explosions and a fire in a section of the mountainside where rich people built exclusive retreats dripping with security, and local rumors speculated on government laboratories or witness protection safe houses. People dead. No name for her subject; no background; no explanation of why or how. Only a description of hair, eyes, height, the clothes she wore when last seen fleeing a fire in the middle of a killer storm and a rain of gunfire. Vincent could only give a general idea of where the woman had gone. Meaning no one really knew.

"I've never been in Millersburg," Kathryn said. "Why does it sound familiar? Not that it's an unusual name."

She closed her eyes, visualizing the sightseer's map she had taken from the motel office, showing all the antique and specialty shops and tiny cluster communities all through the mountain chain. If she remembered correctly, Millersburg was the next major town along the winding mountain road, heading east. Meaning it had more than twenty houses, a service station, and a general store.

"Doctor Jeff West is there, in a fairly new clinic. He joined up about three months ago. One of Jennifer's contacts, from her Air Force days."

"That says a lot for him."

The fact that Jennifer Deverall, another daughter of Quarry Hall, had either recruited or recommended him, meant that he was reliable, dedicated, and someone she liked enough to keep in contact with him despite the painful associations of her former life as a military brat.

"That's all I can tell you, little bird. Make sure you pray hard before you head out. My next call is home, just in case the lid comes down and we go incommunicado. If there's anybody else in the area, and they're freed up enough from their assignments to help, I'll send them your way."

Kathryn shivered, and a moment later silently scolded herself not to look for trouble where there wasn't any. Yet. Just because Vincent was ready and willing to call in reinforcements for her didn't mean the situation was more dangerous than he would admit. And it didn't mean he was starting to coddle her, expecting her body to betray her at any moment and put her in a wheelchair. He didn't work that way. Caution and being overly prepared was just common sense.

Bea slid off her bed, down into the gap between the two motel beds, and up onto the mattress next to Kathryn. She rubbed her big, furry head against the hand holding the pen. A fond grin twitched Kathryn's lips, despite her recent thoughts.

"We'll all be praying hard," Vincent added.

"Like, duh. What else would anybody be doing?" Kathryn tucked the phone between her shoulder and ear, freeing a hand to stroke the dog's thick, dark fur.

"Every prayer, every thought, until we get word you're free and clear. You're the only one available within one hundred miles. I don't call your positioning or my being here to know what's going on a coincidence."

"No, neither do I," she murmured. *Okay, God. Whatever You have waiting for me, make me ready.* "I'm on my way."

They estimated when Kathryn would be clear of the mountains and her cell phone would be reliable again. Much of that schedule depended on finding the woman lost on the mountainside, and then evading anyone who might be searching for her. Vincent arranged the next time they would make contact. Hopefully he and whoever was trying to help the missing woman could meet up with Kathryn and her assignment would be over. Then he cut the connection.

"Hunting time, Bea," Kathryn said with a sigh. "Did you think we were going to be bored here?" Bea let out a soft *woof* and licked her hand. "Nope, neither did I. But we can always hope, can't we?" She closed her eyes and pressed both clenched fists against them. After a few seconds, she lowered her hands and looked around the room, blinking hard as her eyes adjusted.

The clock on the nightstand read 5:08 a.m. Her mouth twitched in an attempt to smile. She was on vacation. The word practically demanded she sleep as long as her body wanted, and not move from place to place while out on the road, with different accommodations each night. She would miss the mismatched furniture and creaky, antique brass bed and the glorious view of a gorge filled with blackberry brambles and overgrown grass and wildflowers.

The fragments of her dream pulsed through her mind for a few seconds. Kathryn shivered a little. Such "coincidences" of being in the right place at the right time had been happening with increasing regularity, even before Joan came to Quarry Hall, in answer to years of prayers. Kathryn doubted she would ever get used to them even if she lived to be over a hundred years old.

The pleasant shiver turned painfully chill, sending a throb through her that was more emotional than physical. Ghost pain from exhaustion and oxygen starvation that made all her muscles feel bruised washed over her, just for a few seconds. She hadn't had one of her spells in months. She refused to have one now, especially since none of the warning signs of an impending spell had shown up yet.

"Get behind me, Satan," she whispered, and pressed her palms against her eyes as she prayed hard, shoving away the anticipated physical illness with faith and force of will.

Chapter Three

Enemies had used her as a vehicle to deliver creeping death to her Uncle Harrison. In a sense, they had been used by the enemies of the Arc Foundation to stop her from whatever God had planned for her life. This flare-up, even if it was mostly in her imagination, was a sign to her that Satan didn't want her out there, finding that missing woman.

Which just meant she was going to pull on the armor of God and head out with even more confidence. Anything that had the father of lies attacking had to be important. Evil would always stand against something God wanted her to do. So that meant she *would* do it.

Kathryn finger-combed her long, straight brown hair a few strokes, then started braiding it. Nudging Bea with her knee, she slid out of bed and padded across the room, feet bare, dressed only in an oversized green t-shirt. It hung like a tent on her lean frame. For a moment, she thought maybe it was a little larger than when she bought it for a nightshirt. No, Brooklyn and the specialists who had examined her the last time she was home at Quarry Hall said she was holding her own against the degenerative illness that didn't even have a name yet.

Holding the waist-long braid with one hand, Kathryn searched amid the clutter of empty pizza box, a net bag of apples, beef jerky wrappers, and cracker boxes, until she found her hair twisty. Three twists of the dull green elastic band secured her braid. She padded into the bathroom and snatched up her toothbrush.

Lord, this is starting off on the wrong foot. Help me get my balance fast, please, she prayed as she scrubbed at her teeth and avoided her bloodshot hazel eyes in the mirror. *Whoever she is, this woman needs help, and for some reason You've brought me here to help her. I'm scared. I'm always scared before the job starts. Work through me, please.*

She stopped short, barely managing to avoid spraying toothpaste all over the mirror when Bea dragged her hiking boots into the bathroom by their long laces and dropped them at her feet.

"Thanks, furball." Kathryn wiped her mouth and dropped to one knee to hug her companion and bodyguard. "Can't find anything in the dark, you know? We'll have enough daylight by the time we get there." She sputtered when Bea licked her face, taking a last trace of toothpaste off her cheek.

Within twenty minutes, Kathryn had taken a quick shower and

dressed in a black t-shirt, jeans, boots, and her blue plaid flannel jacket. Her suede jacket was still damp from her mad dash through the rain from the general store across the street from the motel. Yes, she had ordered pizza delivery, but she had a craving for cream soda, and Ricky's Pizza Emporium didn't carry it. She cleaned her few changes of clothes from the top dresser drawer and jammed everything back into her duffel bag. Bible, notebook, and study books went into her computer case.

She mentally made a list of what she would need, for however long the search would take. Apples and crackers went in her backpack. She would take her first aid kit from under the seat of her truck and put it and her flashlight in the backpack. A short coil of rope might be helpful, and a blanket, just in case the woman was injured and unable to move when she found her.

"I hate thinking like the Rescue Rangers," Kathryn muttered. Bea cocked her head to one side and whined, prompting a snort of laughter from her. "It's okay. Just my usual grumbling. Let's move it, okay?"

She stopped in the motel's tiny diner and had the cook fill her economy-sized thermos with coffee; double cream and double sugar. Kathryn preferred hot chocolate, but the place was out of it. Anyone who had spent the night out in a storm would appreciate something warm to drink, no matter what it was.

~~~~~

Kathryn thought through the bits of dream during the fifteen-minute drive down the mountain-hugging road to Millersburg. She kept her strategy simple: find a portion of mountainside road above the town that matched her dream, and then look for the fleeing woman. Why else would she have been granted the dream, if not as a clue in finding the fugitive before she got into further trouble? The problem was that if she were fleeing for her life, at night, in a storm, Kathryn wouldn't have taken the road at all. It was too easy to get caught that way. Facing unfamiliar territory was preferable to open spaces where headlights could pinpoint her, and where sheer drops would keep her imprisoned at the worst possible moment. It was similar to the damsel in distress who chose to run out onto the train trestle to escape the moustache-twirling villain. It was inevitable that the train would come before she could get to the other side.

Millersburg was a tiny, rustic spot on the map that, according to the tourist guide put together by a team of six chambers of commerce, existed mainly as a jumping-off point for day-hikers, hunters and campers. One side of the town pressed up against steep rock faces and slopes, while the other side got as close to the edge of the downward plunge as was safely possible. In her second pass through the town, she counted four gas stations, all within eyeshot of each other. Four stores handled camping supplies, two storefront operations offered guides, and a stables on the
~~~~~

edge of town rented horses and three-wheelers for the truly adventuresome. She spotted two fast-food restaurants, both with their lights off at this time of the morning. What did that tell her about business traffic around here? Would that be a help or a hindrance in her hunt?

She made note of the four small strips of shops. Between four and six units, with stores on street level and offices or apartments on the second floor, with no third floor. Lights came on in two diners, nearly straight across the street from each other, as she studied them. Drawn by the lights, she looked down a side street and saw the brightly lit sign for the sheriff's office. How had she missed that before? Especially with all that activity — a little too much, for her taste — in front and the parking lot on the far side, and on the streets all around the building. Lights were on, inside and out. People scurried in and out, so the door practically stayed open. Trucks came and went, eight just in the few seconds she drove past it. That much traffic, just after six in the morning, was better suited to the larger towns further down the highway. She thought about what Vincent had said about not trusting the local authorities. Even if he hadn't given her that warning, she wouldn't have thought it wise to attract attention or do anything to help people remember her.

Kathryn finished her second pass through town, turned around, and came back. She found a place to park off the road a few hundred yards past the business section of town, where unlit streets went up and down the mountainside at odd angles, creating the residential section of Millersburg, before sloping down to the river. By flashlight, she compared all the maps she had of the area, planning her route. And more important, planning where she wouldn't go.

Bea kept watch, and Kathryn made mental note of how many cars went past her, either by the sound of tires on wet pavement or headlights glancing over her truck. After the third set of headlights, her safe period had run out. She wouldn't be anonymous after this. Whispering a prayer that she had found what she needed, she folded the maps and tucked them under the flashlight, stroked down Bea's back to thank her companion, and got moving.

At the first ranger's station, half a mile up the first road off the highway, she had to stop. Kathryn had planned to simply drive by. Two rangers manned a roadblock made of sawhorses and boards. She decided it was too early in the morning to even try to pretend harmless curiosity. Anybody who was a stranger, out on the road at this time of the day in such rotten, heavy, gray weather, had to have a reason for being out and about. She said a quick prayer no one would ask her any questions requiring her to lie.

She considered the chance that locals were involved in whatever sent the blond woman fleeing in the storm when she faced the two rangers manning the roadblock. Why did they have to just stand there and look at her truck? After a few seconds, visibly conferring, they split up. One approached her. He didn't rest his hand on the holster at his side, and that just wound the tension filling her a few degrees higher, instead of letting her breathe easy. The ranger who didn't approach her truck ducked quickly out of sight. He had a heavy-duty rifle in his hands, with a wide scope of some kind. Kathryn didn't know enough about guns, she didn't *want* to know enough, to be sure if it was a night scope or telescopic viewer.

Had she been on the mountain roads at higher elevations at all during the last two days? No, other than on her way here. No, she hadn't gone to any higher elevations yet. Had she heard or seen anything unusual in the vicinity in the last day or two? No.

Dreams didn't count. She knew from experience not to talk about her dreams to anyone but her family at Quarry Hall.

The ranger gave her a map with red lines marking roads the public was not allowed to travel. Before Kathryn could ask how she would know the roads if there were no signs, he smiled thinly and told her there would be road blocks similar to his as markers.

Kathryn asked what was going on, because anyone without inside information would want to know. Not asking would just make him suspicious. As expected, the ranger told her there was no danger, as long as she stayed on the roads and didn't leave her truck except at designated stopping places. He said some people had become lost during the storm. There were landslides in a few places, and a fire where a house had been struck by lightning, but nothing to worry herself about.

If he called her a "little lady" and slipped into a good old boy drawl, she would have Bea knock him over and sit on him. Yet again, she wondered how much easier life would be if people told the truth, instead of thinking they were protecting innocent bystanders by hiding details.

She thanked him—what else could she do?—and waited until he pivoted the boards out of the way to let her pass down the road.

What had this missing woman been involved in last night? The fire and whatever else had emergency workers out in the storm? That didn't matter at the moment. The job was to simply get in there, find the missing woman, and get her to help. Fortunately, someone whom Arc trusted was nearby. *If* Kathryn found the woman.

She glanced at the map after she went around the second bend in the road after the roadblock. All the forbidden roads spider-webbed out from one central area. The fire and dead bodies were most likely in the center of that web. She wondered if Vincent and his friend were there already, or heading in that direction.

"Not alone out here," she murmured, staring through the wet

windshield at the road that glistened under her headlights, cloaked in heavy shadows. Somewhere, sunrise had arrived, but the heavy clouds hid it. "Never alone. Lord, please help me find her, so she won't be alone anymore."

She drove slowly, stopping at any point along the road that reminded her of her dream. Kathryn walked through muddy fields and slid on shale-covered slopes, scratching her hands on branches when she snatched at them to save her balance. Scratches, wet sleeves, and muddy boots were all she had to show for her efforts by 9 a.m.

Bea was wet and had mud three inches up her belly fur. After the second stop, Kathryn gave up on wiping her off with a towel before letting her into the truck. She spread an old, ragged blanket on the seat and told the big dog to sit still.

Nothing, so far. No signs of hurried passage across fields and through brambles and bushes. No footprints. No shreds of clothes or bits of golden hair caught on branches. Could the rain have been fierce enough to wash it all away in the mud? Kathryn was halfway up the mountain and a little too close to the forbidden area. She didn't relish the idea of meeting up with more rangers. The Arc Foundation did its work best when avoiding explanations and scrutiny from officials. If there were something to hide in these mountains, she would get no friendly reaction from the authorities if she had to explain why she was here. She couldn't give them the type of the answer they would want, without taking hours to explain the foundation, Vincent's mysterious connections, and her semi-prophetic guidance visions and dreams. She didn't need to end up in jail. Or held for psychiatric evaluation.

"Okay, Lord." Kathryn put her foot on the brake as another likely crossing place for the fugitive appeared around a bend in the mountain road. "I thought I knew what I was doing. If my ideas didn't come from You, could You tell me what I'm doing wrong?"

A wry smile touched her lips for a moment as she heard Sophie's voice in her memory. The newest daughter of Quarry Hall was a delight, and not just because she provided vital, long prayed-for Internet wizardry. She combined common sense with sharp humor, and loved to attack a topic from multiple angles and viewpoints. Some of the most entertaining and exhausting evenings Kathryn had known in years were when most of the daughters of Quarry Hall were home at the same time, and talked until all hours. Sophie's favorite topic was on the multitude of ways God spoke to His people, and how to discern if someone was legitimate, if they had been fooled by enemy powers and forces, or if they were scam artists—or psychotic—and if they should be pitied or feared.

"Just because you didn't hear God speaking to you today isn't His fault," Sophie had said several times. "Why don't you try turning down your stereo for a change?" Then she would point out that the stereo could also be the television, homework, problems at work, hectic schedules, and on and on.

Kathryn looked for oncoming traffic from ahead of her and behind, then slowed to look out over the clumps of trees on a long slope heading down the mountain. Just ahead of her truck wheels, where the berm widened to offer barely enough room to pull over, something glistened in the puddle in the middle of the road. Glass fragments, perhaps. Maybe from a broken headlight. She rolled down the window and listened to the soft soughing of the wind during this lull in the storm, the trickle of water coming down the slope on her left, the chirping of a few birds somewhere in the trees behind her to the right.

"Wait a minute." She tapped her brakes to slow more as she stared at the sparkle in the road again. A twinge of something she couldn't put a mental finger on told her there was something *off* about that glistening. Maybe the angle of the light? The intensity of the light?

Bea whined and took her jacket sleeve in her teeth, tugging once and then letting go. She turned around in the seat and pressed her nose against the window.

"You could have gone the last time we stopped."

Kathryn tapped the gas to move up, and pulled over onto the berm, leaving enough room between the guardrail and the passenger door to let Bea out. She parked, jammed the keys into her pocket, and hurried to get out and open the passenger door. No way was she going to let her companion walk all over her seat with her muddy paws.

The Akita nearly leaped over her shoulder when she opened the door. Kathryn let out a laughing gasp of exasperation and turned to watch Bea hit the guardrail with her front paws and keep going, vaulting with enviable grace. A moment later, she darted toward the closest clump of wildflowers, then circled it twice, sniffing and pawing at the ground.

"Idiot mutt." She straightened the blanket the dog had been sitting on and turned to look at the slope again. That shiver of recognition washed over her. This angle gave her a different view of the slope above her... *if* that was the slope the missing woman had come down.

Could this be the place? She had been wrong four times already. Even discounting the difference in light, the lack of rain, this was the closest match yet.

Kathryn turned to study the area and watch Bea. She was an exceptionally good dog and didn't need to be on a leash. Kathryn only carried her leash to mollify people who thought such a big dog had to be dangerous. Of course, Bea *was* dangerous; she had been trained as a bodyguard. Or in the words of Su-Ma, a creep-o-meter. Right now, though, with all the tension on the mountain, she didn't need a ranger to drive by and cite her, record her presence, maybe even drive her out of the area because she didn't keep her dog on a leash.

Bea slithered down the wet slope of grass, with muddy slashes where the force of rainwater had sliced away at the grass. Her nose to the ground, she wove from side to side about a foot in either direction. Then froze.

Kathryn held her breath, waiting for her to move. Bea raised her head and looked straight toward a clump of trees surrounded by low, tangled bushes. She took two steps toward the trees, then turned to look up the slope, straight to Kathryn. Her lips pulled back from her fangs in a silent growl.

Bea only reacted that way to guns and blood.

If there had been someone holding a gun, hiding in the trees, they would have shot at the dog by now. That left blood. Kathryn reached into the truck and pulled out her backpack.

Thank You, Lord. Please don't let us be too late.

She nearly fell twice, the soft, slippery mud and waterlogged grass threatening to give way under her feet. Kathryn imagined the woman coming down this slope in the dark, in a storm, running from danger. Her shoulders hunched as she imagined what kind of damage a fall could do. Especially with a few trees in the way to break her tumble in an abrupt, bone-jarring fashion.

The young woman was half-hidden by bushes, her features obscured by mud and bits of storm debris, twigs and leaves and bark. Her blond hair was still wet, tangled and matted with mud and blood that remained glistening red because of the damp. She lay half on her side, one leg drawn up, one arm flung out. A wide, darkening bruise that glistened with half-clotted blood showed where she had hit at least one tree with her forehead before she stopped.

She wore a green sweater, brown loafers and blue jeans, just like in Kathryn's dream. She was blond and looked somewhere between twenty-five and thirty years old.

Kathryn hunkered down and studied the unconscious woman. She breathed, visibly. How long she had been lying there, unconscious and bleeding, Kathryn couldn't begin to guess. Between the rain and mud, and the damp hindering wounds from clotting, it was hard to estimate. Everything was too wet to have any sure indicator. She hoped Dr. West was sure of his oath, as an ally of the Arc Foundation. He was going to get his trial by fire soon.

Gingerly, Kathryn reached out and stroked the unconscious woman's cheek, giving her a little warning before she lifted one eyelid. Just in case the victim was in a daze and not entirely unconscious. Kathryn knew enough to test for concussion by looking at the size of the pupils. Of course, that meant she would have to turn the wounded woman over to see her other eye. That might not be wise, if there was any damage to her spinal cord, or if she had broken bones. How much longer could Kathryn leave her there, waiting for her to wake and assess her injuries for herself?

A moan escaped the woman, as if in answer to the unspoken question. Her eyes fluttered, and Kathryn sat back to wait.

Another moan and the stranger started to push herself over onto her back. A gasp of pain, her face wrinkled, she pressed one muddy hand to the back of her head, then her forehead. Her eyes stopped fluttering and widened as she looked at Kathryn. Then she looked around the shady clump of trees.

"What—what am I doing here?" She pushed against the ground to sit upright and sank wrist deep in mud and muck.

"Getting muddy, mostly." Kathryn handed her a handful of leaves to wipe her hands.

She did so, her lips curling back in distaste. When she finished, she wiped the remainder of the mud and the damp from the leaves on her pant legs. It didn't make any difference in the condition of her clothes.

"This is disgusting. Help me out of here."

"Can you walk?" Kathryn held out a hand.

"I think so." The blond leaned forward and pivoted to get up onto her knees. The movement visibly hurt. She paled and swayed as she pressed both fists to her temples.

"Let's take it slow and easy for a little bit, okay?" She helped the woman sit back against a tree trunk, perched out of the worst of the mud on the tree's tangled roots. "Let me check you out some before you try anything else. Thirsty?"

After thinking a moment, she nodded, and winced at the movement.

"Hold on." Kathryn dropped her backpack into the bushes to keep it clean. Dry was impossible.

She tugged the first aid kit from the larger zipper compartment and retrieved the bottle of aspirin. That and a cup of still-warm coffee went down the subject's throat with minimal fuss. Kathryn watched her warily for the first minute or two, ready for signs of it coming back up.

Chapter Four

"Let me look in your eyes." Kathryn checked, and the pupils looked pretty much the same size. She said a quick, silent prayer that her guesses were accurate.

She checked the blond's arms and legs in silence, wiping away mud to reveal scratches but nothing broken or torn. Her sweater was a mess, snagged in spots, torn in others, with mud smashed into the outside and oozing through to stain the lacy, short-sleeve shirt underneath. Her jeans were torn in four places, none bad enough to be un-wearable. They could probably pass as a fashion statement. By some miracle, the stranger had retained her loafers. Kathryn was glad to note that. She had spare clothes this damsel in distress could use, but no spare shoes.

"Okay, it seems to be mostly mud and bruises," Kathryn said, pouring a second cup of coffee for her. "A good washing and clean clothes will take care of most of your problems. Head hurt still?"

"Yes." She pressed one hand to her forehead and muffled a whimper as she brought away smears of mud and blood on her palm. "Dizzy, mostly."

"There's a doctor in town. We'll go there once you're cleaned up." She stood and held out a hand to help her to her feet. "What's your name?"

Gray-blue eyes went wide. The pouty lips opened in a silent 'o' and the stranger sat still with her hand half-extended to meet Kathryn's. Fear. Anger. Confusion flickered through her eyes the longest.

"Figures," Kathryn whispered. She reached out a hand and gently touched the stranger's bruised forehead with two fingers. "You probably don't know what you're doing out here, do you?"

She had already labeled her subject "Jane Doe," but Kathryn refused to say it aloud. She had always hated the callousness of the label. She hated labels of any kind, especially the ones used to put people "in their places," or give others control over them.

"Wait a minute." The slightly dazed look vanished, replaced by fear mixed with a petulance Kathryn had only seen on the toddlers in the church nursery. "*You* don't know who I am?"

"I wasn't told that much. Par for the course." She caught Jane Doe's hand and half-dragged her to her feet.

"How did you know to come get me?" She let Kathryn get her walking. Bea emerged from the shadows and followed them, head down and tail up. Kathryn spared a moment to wonder what she detected, what trail she followed now.

"I was told to come help someone here who was in trouble. That's about all."

Please, Lord, help me get around this one. She's confused enough without thinking she's been picked up by a fanatic.

Fanatics, in Kathryn's lexicon, were people who preached one type of action and belief system, rabidly devoted to it, trying to do other people's thinking for them. Then they turned around and acted totally opposite to their words whenever it was convenient for them. When brought to task for it, they twisted Scripture to prove they had been in the right all along. She didn't need to get lumped up with those self-righteous lunatics. Not when she needed Jane Doe's trust to get them both to safety.

"That's crazy."

"I was told to look for someone in this area, matching your description, and to help with whatever was needed. Right now, that's getting you off this mountain, cleaned up, bandaged, and to a doctor."

"But—"

"Now's not the time. Think about this, though: somebody was shot last night and a house burned down, and you were obviously hurt when you ran from somebody." Kathryn kept Jane Doe walking. She was grateful the stranger only protested with her mouth and not her body. She was in no mood to carry anyone right now.

"Shot?" Her voice cracked.

"Any of that sound familiar?" Kathryn swallowed a sigh when the woman just shook her head, immediately wincing and losing a few degrees of color. She didn't learn very fast. "Most important thing right now is to get you to a doctor and check out your head. It's a given you're in trouble. We just have to figure out what side of the law you're on."

"Side of the law?"

They reached the truck. Kathryn helped Jane Doe climb over the guardrail and opened the truck door for her so she could sit on the step.

Giving the other woman something to think about could keep her quiet and pliable. Kathryn allowed herself to hope that simply taking her to Dr. West in Millersburg would count as getting her out of danger. He might have some idea or clue who she was and could take custody of her from there.

Not that she didn't want an excuse to drop in on Finn.

"I don't know what side of the law anybody is on around here. This is all new territory for me," Kathryn said.

"Who told you to come get me?" Jane Doe said. "Maybe we should go to them."

"Won't work. I know just as much as my contact knows about your situation. As for taking you to him..." She grinned, despite the seriousness of the situation. "Heck if I know where he is."

"But—" She let out a groaning sigh. "This doesn't make any sense."

"It will later." Kathryn felt a flicker of guilt for playing mysterious to this confused woman who needed her help. "It always does. I have some extra clothes you can wear, and water to wash all that mud off. Why don't you concentrate on getting cleaned up, okay?"

"That won't solve any problems."

"No, but it'll avoid more. If anybody sees you looking like this, we're going to get buried under a load of questions we don't want to answer." Kathryn tugged her duffel bag out from the compartment behind the seat. It was a matter of moments to pull out her spare jeans, a flannel shirt and spare socks.

"We?" The other woman went perfectly still. Then a smile brightened her face.

"Yeah, *we*." She gave her the clothes, then scurried around to the back of the truck. In the storage box were two gallon-size plastic jugs of water and a few rags.

She gave one to Jane Doe and quickly searched for a good place where she could change. With their luck, a caravan of cars would come around the curve in the road the moment she started peeling off her muddy, torn clothes.

A car did come, but it only held two people and didn't even pause at the sight of Kathryn's truck pulled over against the guardrail. It took the curve wide and kept going, up the side of the mountain. Jane Doe had plenty of cover in a thick clump of bushes off the side of the road, four feet behind the truck. Kathryn perched on the guardrail and threw sticks for Bea to catch while she waited for her to clea up.

Bea brought a stick back to Kathryn and paused, looking past her. Kathryn turned to see Jane Doe coming back to the truck. She held the empty water jug in one hand, her filthy clothes wrapped in her wash rag and towel in the other.

"Feel better?" Kathryn turned, swinging her legs over the guardrail and hurried to take jug and dirty clothes.

"A little," her new companion said without even an attempt at a smile.

Kathryn bit back a comment that she would have felt like a new person with all that mud washed off and dry, clean clothes on. That smack on Jane Doe's forehead must have been a bad one.

"Next step." She gestured for the woman to sit down on the doorstep again so she could clean up her forehead.

Washing had opened the wound, and blood seeped into the hair plastered across her face before trickling down her hairline. Kathryn spread analgesic antiseptic cream on the bruised cut and taped a thick white bandage in place. Her touch was gentle but Jane Doe winced and gasped and flinched several times during the procedure. Kathryn had to bite her lip to keep from snapping at her. If her charge had simply held still it would have taken half the time.

"All aboard for Millersburg," she said when she had put the first aid kit away.

She stored the dirty clothes and towel in a net bag fastened to the side of the truck in back, put away the water jug and closed the storage box. When she came around to the driver's side, she found Bea sitting on the folded blanket on the passenger seat and Jane Doe standing in the doorway, staring at her, lips pressed into a thin line. Kathryn thought she saw only fear, but she couldn't be sure.

"Get in the back, you greedy furball," she said, and swatted Bea's rear end.

The Akita snorted and clambered between the seats to sit in the compartment with Kathryn's backpack, duffel bag, sleeping bag and cooler. There was more than enough room. Kathryn had often slept back there with her when the weather was rotten. She balled up the ragged blanket and threw it after her. Bea settled down with her head peeking between the seats, nose resting on the side of Kathryn's seat.

Jane Doe climbed in slowly and perched on the edge of the seat. She braced herself with her fingertips against the dashboard and glanced sideways at Bea.

"He doesn't seem to like me," she said, her voice flat. Fear or petulance, Kathryn couldn't tell.

"Shut the door, would you?" She waited until Jane Doe had complied. "Bea doesn't *like* anybody right when she meets them. Her job is to protect me. My job is to help you." She smiled, but the other woman didn't relax. "Give her some time to get used to you. Then you'll be friends."

Jane Doe gave her a doubtful look, then eyeballed Bea again. This was going to be a long assignment — no matter how short a time it took to complete.

Lord, are You teaching me patience again?

Kathryn bit back a snort of laughter. Who had warned her never to pray for patience? A Sunday school teacher, she was sure. A man, somewhere in her distant memory, had warned his students never to ask God to give them patience. The only way to gain patience was to endure trials and testing.

God, give me the strength to endure and a kind spirit to help Jane, Kathryn prayed silently as she turned the key in the ignition.

She glanced in her rearview mirror before starting to maneuver the truck to turn around on the road. Her gaze caught on the green baseball cap hanging from the hook in the back. Finn had given her that baseball cap after his team had won the interdepartmental championships, in memory of the two solid weeks they had been able to spend together when they were both between assignments. She had held onto it and was absurdly grateful when he didn't demand it back after the last semi-argument. How long ago had that been, anyway? She couldn't seem to look back far enough to calculate the time. Everything that had happened since learning she was dying of the same genetic time bomb killing her uncle seemed like decades ago, instead of just a few years.

"Here. This ought to help." She snagged the cap from the hook and handed it to Jane Doe.

The next moment, she regretted the gesture, even though it made sense to cover up that bandage and try to change her new charge's appearance. How petty could she be, even if it was Finn's hat and precious to her because of all the memories it held?

Jane Doe looked at it for a few seconds, then turned it around in her hands several times. Just when Kathryn was ready to snap at her and tell her to just put the silly thing on and consider it later, she bowed her head and slid the cap into place. Kathryn tugged on the bill, bringing it down so the shadow covered the lower half of the bandage.

"Well, one problem taken care of. That hat covers a multitude of sins." She put the truck into gear and turned the wheel hard, to prepare to pull out onto the road. "Now for the bigger one." She looked in both directions, several times, checking for oncoming traffic.

"I don't understand." Jane Doe slid back in the seat and held onto the door handle as the truck bucked a little, protesting the tight turn.

"Until you know who you are... I think we'll just assume you're in danger from both sides of the law."

"But that—"

"Just trust me, okay?" Kathryn took a deep breath, consciously fighting down the snapping tone creeping into her voice. "I have more experience with this sort of thing than I care to remember. We've changed how you look, so now you need a name."

"But I don't *remember* it," she nearly wailed.

"I'm not going to spend the rest of this trip calling you Jane Doe. And that's final." Kathryn turned her glare into a teasing smile and waited.

To her amazement, her companion managed a weak smile and a nod.

"It's going to be okay," she continued. "I'll stay with you until everything is settled."

"But why?"

"Because I'd want someone to do it for me, if I was in your shoes." She finished making the turn. Sighing, Kathryn settled back in her seat and prepared for the winding trip down the mountain. She rolled down her window and welcomed the blast of cool air in her face.

Bea shifted in the compartment behind the seat and wedged her head between the side of the truck and Kathryn's arm, to stick her nose out the window.

~~~~~

The sound of the truck's engine coming down the mountain road caught the attention of two men picking their way through a patch of forest on the inside curve of the road. Porter and Carson were a team; both built like quarterbacks, dressed like lumberjacks, Porter in green and Carson in blue. They could have been brothers, both solidly built, tall, with short-cropped dark hair, brown eyes, and square jaws. Porter had gray in his hair and Carson always chewed spearmint gum, constantly refreshing it so the cool smell floated in a cloud around him. Otherwise, according to their co-workers, they were interchangeable.

Carson stepped closer to the road to get a look at the truck while Porter stayed squatting, examining an oblong mud puddle in the forest loam that could have been a footprint. A dark blue pickup truck came slowly around the corner. Carson reached the edge of the tree shadows in time to look straight into the passenger side window. He got a good, five-second-long look at the profile of the woman in the passenger's seat.

~~~~~

Jane Doe frowned, her lips drooping in a pout, and turned to Kathryn.

"I remember something."

"That's good." Kathryn glanced at her companion and her smile halted half-formed. Something about the woman's expression and the tone of her voice struck her odd, but she couldn't identify how.

"My name is Regina," she said with a lowered tone and a touch of what Kathryn thought was reluctance.

Wouldn't someone who remembered her name after even a few hours of amnesia be glad?

Regina—judging by the silence, that was all the name she had right now—was likely a spoiled brat. Not that Kathryn wanted to slap a label on her, but she knew the signs. The young woman in her charge was one of those people who punished everyone whenever she was unhappy, as if the world existed simply to make her life better. Someone had to pay for her misery.

Kathryn had too much experience with snots. Starting with the face she saw in the mirror every day. No matter how long ago the character renovation had come, it would never be long enough ago to suit her.

"It's a start," Kathryn said, forcing her smile to stay on her face.

Movement in the corner of her eye jerked her attention off the road and Regina. She glanced in the rearview mirror, trying to identify what she saw. Something moved among the trees. A deer, perhaps? Kathryn thought she saw something metallic green, but it could have been a trick of the light.

"Well, Regina," she said, as the road curved again and put the patch of trees behind them, "everything's going to be all right."

~~~~~

Millersburg approaching noontime had only doubled the traffic Kathryn noticed coming through in the early morning hours. She counted four trucks or SUVs or Jeeps to every car. Nearly every truck had a gun rack or a fishing pole rack. Most trucks had a dog sitting in the back. Bea never let out a sound in challenge, or pressed harder against her shoulder to indicate she wanted to get out. Kathryn was proud of her companion.

The commercial section of the town was easier to estimate now that the rain had stopped and she could see beyond the reach of headlights and the few light poles. It looked to be four blocks long and three wide, extending up the mountainside where the slope wasn't so steep. Kathryn debated the chances of finding a phone booth with a phone book to look up Dr. West's address. Look for a library? She couldn't get internet to do a web search. Regina had been quiet during most of the ride down the mountain, but Kathryn hadn't missed the frowns cast her way. Her companion visibly doubted her ability to take them to safety. If she made any move that showed uncertainty, Kathryn suspected she would get one of two reactions. Either Regina would throw a fit right there in the middle of town and gain them the wrong sort of attention. Or, she would ditch Kathryn the first chance she got; probably too close to the center of the danger zone. That could get them both in trouble.

Kathryn drove slowly down the first side street at the edge of the commercial district and prayed Dr. West's sign and office were easily visible. How many doctors did a small town like this need, anyway? If campers, hunters and day-hikers had severe injuries, she supposed the rangers would take them to the nearest large hospital. Dr. West, unless he had associates in his office, was there just to serve the people of Millersburg.

The place reminded her of Mayberry, but not quite as populous as Mt. Airy, its real-life inspiration. Maybe a third of the commercial buildings she passed were constructed of the same gray sandstone and granite, with the pillars and arches popular at the turn of the previous century. Now she could see the sheriff's office connected to the town hall. The building took up the entire block. She counted ten two-story buildings that weren't commercial, and most of those were of brick and looked like houses that had been converted into stores and offices.

At the far end of the street sat a section of newer stores, single-story, all square lines and windows that took up two-thirds of the front wall,
~~~~~

with identical faded forest green awnings and recessed doorways. Newer, meaning they were probably built in the fifties. The pack of little boys on BMX bikes and backpacks could have come from the fifties, all dressed alike in striped jerseys, blue jeans, and hi-tops. Kathryn smiled to see them dashing down the street, yelling to each other. She wondered if they were heading home to lunch, or back to school. Then her gaze drifted to the storefront they had passed.

Two trucks filled with burlap sacks and assorted small farming equipment passed between her and the storefront. Kathryn slowed to a stop as she came even with it and waited for the trucks to pass. No one came up behind her. Everyone was likely already at home for lunch or back to work or school.

Navy blue letters edged in gold splashed across the top of the storefront window, advertising Dr. Jeff West, GP. His office hours in smaller gold and blue letters were in the lower right hand corner of the window. Kathryn grinned and acknowledged her momentary fear that the office would be closed on a Friday. In a small town like this, who wouldn't start their weekend early?

She saw a black car pull out of a slot five spaces down from the doctor's office, in front of a drugstore with a huge mortar and pestle painted in the front window. There were plenty of empty spaces directly in front, which meant the doctor had no visitors right then. Kathryn preferred to throw little distractions in the way of any casual watchers. No one would remark on a stranger going into a drugstore, but they would wonder about two strangers walking into the doctor's office.

"Are we there yet?" Regina said, rousing from her slumped posture of the last half hour, staring with glazed eyes out the side window.

"Here." Kathryn nudged Bea with her shoulder and the Akita moved backwards, taking her nose from the open window.

She rolled up the window and reached into the back compartment for her backpack. Regina watched her, frown changing to confusion when Kathryn dumped out the thermos and first aid kit and put her cell phone and wallet in the front pouch.

"What are you going to tell him?" Regina stared at the wide plate glass window of the drugstore, filled with Styrofoam coolers and folding chairs, posterboard advertisements for groceries and the lunch special for the day—tuna salad sandwich and bean soup.

"The truth."

Chapter Five

"But—" Regina shook her head and looked again at the store window in front of them. "This doesn't look like a doctor's office." She lost the sulkiness when she turned to stare at Kathryn, her eyes begging some explanation.

"It isn't."

"He'll just cause trouble if you tell him someone was shooting at me." Her tone wasn't as argumentative as it had been.

"You remember that much?"

"Isn't that what your friend told you?"

"Yeah." Kathryn took a deep breath to still the sudden leap in her pulse. What had she expected? All the answers dumped in her lap, along with Regina's returned memory?

She leaned forward, reaching across her passenger to tug open the glove compartment. A sigh escaped her when Regina jerked backward, eyes widening.

"One more thing before we go inside," Kathryn said. She wondered what had brought that reaction. Had someone hit Regina recently? Or was it just a general nervousness brought on by injuries and amnesia?

Kathryn brought a full packet of fish hooks from under the pile of maps, flashlight, notebook and discarded fast food napkins in the glove compartment. The cellophane wrapping was torn, but she hadn't removed any of the new hooks from the cardboard. She hadn't needed them since she replenished her supply three months ago.

She fought a mischievous grin when Regina stared, a puzzled expression replacing her pout. She wove the small hook, just the right size to slide around her thumb, into the underside of her blue plaid jacket collar. The clean silver glimmered in the sunlight glancing in through the truck window. Kathryn turned her collar back down into place and smoothed it.

"Okay, now we're set." She opened the door and gestured for Regina to do the same. Kathryn gestured for Bea to stay still, hit the locks, and closed the door. It amused her a little that her companion never said one word, though her curiosity had to be itching at her.

One mud-spattered red truck passed, carrying three men dressed for hunting, and three dogs leashed into the back bed. No one and nothing else moved on the street as they walked the few yards down to Dr. West's office. Kathryn tried to calculate if that was normal for Millersburg at this time of day or if something unusual was going on. And if it had anything to do with Regina.

Seen through the big picture window, the doctor's office had a waiting room six feet deep, stretching across the full width of the unit. Green vinyl upholstered chairs with chrome arms filled the end walls and across the wall facing the window. The door into the next room broke the monotony of chairs, blue paint and Norman Rockwell prints. It was white-painted wood with no window. Three plastic crates filled with toys and one filled with magazines sat in the middle of the room. From the neatness of their contents, Kathryn guessed no one had been in to see the doctor yet this morning.

A battered tan metal desk sat in one corner with a white princess phone, clipboard, paper, and pens. Kathryn wondered about the clipboard. Then she decided Dr. West had such slow traffic through his office, he didn't need a secretary; the clipboard was for patients to sign in.

Five copper cowbells jangled on the front door as she pushed it open. She winced and tried to step through quickly to cut down the clatter. A glance at the desk and clipboard showed no one had come in today, though it was nearly noon. Kathryn liked that. A quiet, healthy town with few injuries was a nice place to stop for help.

Regina sat in a chair. The wheezing of air escaping the cushion was loud in the waiting room. Kathryn looked at the white door and listened for the sound of approaching feet.

Nothing.

"Hello?" she called.

A muffled voice responded from the back of the office. Kathryn couldn't make out the words. She heard a distant, soft thump, then the squeaking of rubber soles on linoleum.

"Sorry," a man said as the door swung silently open. "I was in the back making lunch."

Dr. Jeff West—if he was the doctor—was a young man, maybe five years out of residency at the most. His curly brown hair hung long in the back, but was clipped short around his face; likely in deference to the old-fashioned element in town, Kathryn thought. He wore jeans, dark enough to be new, and neatly pressed, a green plaid shirt and a bulky, baggy white sweater with more pockets down its front than a sweater had a right to own. Kathryn grinned as she noted the notepad in one pocket, tongue depressors in another, pen in yet another, stethoscope peering out of the pocket below the pen, a pocket for bandage strips, and even one for a candy bar. There was one enormous pocket at the hem that didn't look like it held anything. Kathryn wondered what he saved it for.

"Can I help you ladies?" His chocolate brown eyes reflected his smile.

It couldn't have been forced, even though they had interrupted his lunch.

An enormous lunch. Kathryn wondered how he could hold his sandwich in one hand. It almost rivaled the sandwiches Dagwood used to make in the Sunday comics.

"My friend hurt her head pretty bad," Kathryn said after a barely perceptible pause. She gestured at Regina.

"Just your head?" Dr. West's smile flattened a little and the gleam died from his eyes. He sat down on the chair next to Regina and gently slid the baseball cap off her head, revealing the bandage. Some blood had seeped through in spots. He started to lift the other hand to touch the bandage, then paused and looked at the crammed sandwich in his hand as if he had forgotten it was there. With a sigh, he slid it into the largest pocket.

Kathryn bit her lip against a grin. So that was what that pocket was for. She hoped Dr. West was as prepared for their appearance as he seemed prepared for everything else.

"Let's get you into the back and check you out." He stood, took hold of Regina's hand and tugged her gently to her feet. She swayed a little as she stood, and that turned his flattened smile into a frown. "What happened to you?" He looked from her to Kathryn.

"Is Dr. Luke here?" Kathryn said to forestall answering that question for a few seconds. The sooner she impressed on him the seriousness of the situation, identified herself, and made sure he was Dr. West, a friend of the Arc Foundation, the better. "I was told to ask for him." She tugged back on her collar, revealing the fishhook.

Sometimes she laughed at the cloak-and-dagger measures Vincent had instituted, but this wasn't one of those times. The simple presence of the hook could convey to Dr. West the possible dangers of their situation in a few seconds and save her many words.

"No, there's no—" Then his gaze caught on the hook. His eyes widened. He glanced at Kathryn's solemn face, then back to the fishhook. He swallowed hard, once, then a lopsided smile twisted his mouth. "Dr. Luke isn't here. I'm his associate. Not quite up to Theophilous, but I'm getting there."

"Kathryn." She held out her hand.

"Jeff West." His grip was strong, though it did tremble a tiny bit. "Jennifer mentioned a Kathryn. Among all her new sisters."

"This is Regina." Kathryn caught the tiny glance he cast at her, the question in his eyes. "Just Regina."

He nodded and hurried to open the door, holding it so they could pass through first. The rest of the office seemed to be a series of examination rooms created by curtains on tracks in the ceiling, with tables and chairs, and a series of glass-front white storage cabinets down one wall. Kathryn expected the place to look cold, white, and drearily sterile, like so many clinics she had seen. The floor had a mishmash of different colored tiles and the walls were painted with rainbows and comical animals, all walking away from a stylized Noah's ark. At the very back of the office, she could make out a tiny table and chairs, sink and stainless steel refrigerator.

"I'll be with you in a minute. Have to make a phone call." Kathryn let her backpack slide down to hang in the crook of her elbow.

"Help yourself." He gestured toward the phone on the desk in the corner.

"Thanks, but..." She pulled her phone from her backpack. Kathryn suspected she might have to take him up on his offer if the surrounding mountains interfered with the phone's reception.

"Okay." He raised one eyebrow, glanced once more between Kathryn and Regina, and led the injured woman through the door.

Kathryn waited until the door swung closed. She settled down at the desk facing the street. A few people walked past, but no one seemed to look inside. To be safe, she slid the chair back into the minimal shadows along the wall. She punched numbers into her phone and waited. Kathryn held her breath, waiting for the particularly loud hiss of static that meant she would have to use Dr. West's phone and not her own. She doubted anyone could tap his phone this soon, or that anyone would even think to spy on the doctor. Unless Regina was far more important or valuable or dangerous than Vincent's friend had indicated. Still, it paid to be careful and use her own line.

A few flickers of static crackled in her ear as Kathryn waited for the connection to go through. She scooted around in her chair a little, trying to improve the reception. It was a silly imagining, but anything helped.

The phone on the other end finally rang. Kathryn released a breath she hadn't realized she had been holding. Grinning a little at her own nervousness she slouched in the seat and waited.

"This is Finnegan Roberts," a man's voice said on the other end. Even and detached in tone, it reflected nothing of the curly mop of black hair cut just on the long side of regulation length, the sparkling brown eyes and wide shoulders of a weekend quarterback. She missed the mischief in his eyes, and the way he lectured her when he was worried.

"Oh, phooey," Kathryn muttered.

"You know the routine," the voice continued. "Tell me where you are and your emergency. I'll get back to you when my current emergency is over."

As he went on to list various numbers where he could be reached, or other people to contact if this was a priority call, Kathryn closed her eyes and imagined Finn's office.

The chair behind the desk was empty, since he was out of the office and had left his cell phone behind, as usual when he had a desk assignment. Floor-to-ceiling shelving at either end of the desk left precisely eighteen inches between his two two-drawer filing cabinets and the shelves. All the shelves would be a cascading spill of paperwork in various stages of filing and processing, intermixed with books; mostly scientific research books, a few novels, regulation handbooks and his football and baseball trophies. The curtains on the window that stretched from waist height to the ceiling and wall to wall were probably still not mended. They hung off half the track and were held closed with four huge safety pins, tucked up on the left where his beat-up coffee maker sat. Someday, Kathryn hoped Finn would get new curtains and be free of those horrid paisley prints, so faded she couldn't tell what their original colors had been.

The closet door on the right side of his office would be halfway open and the connecting door on the left side would be locked and the way blocked with boxes of files and books from his latest research project. His computer and phone would be half-buried under paperwork and fast food containers. The menu varied from week to week, but on Friday afternoons Finn always had pizza. He was probably downstairs right that moment, paying the delivery boy, who was never allowed into the building past the lobby.

Finn insisted the policy of never letting unauthorized personnel past the security checkpoint was specifically to give the office moochers a chance to see what everyone ordered in for lunch or dinner.

Thinking about Finn and his sloppy, comfortable office wouldn't help her any, unless being homesick for the comfortable friendship of years ago was an improvement. Kathryn took a deep breath and waited for the operator's voice to list her options. Before the woman could finish saying "to leave a message, press three now," she pressed the button and waited for the two-second beep.

"Finn, this is Kathryn." She let her gaze drift back to the traffic — two cars and a lady with a stroller and Irish Setter — passing by the window. "I need a favor. One of *those* favors. I'm helping someone who's been beat up pretty bad, running from people hunting for her, doesn't know anything but her first name. My contact says someone shot at her, but couldn't tell me much more. He's not going to contact me until he has more data and knows what's going on. I can't trust the local authorities until we know more. Be my ace? Help? You still owe me a couple dozen, remember."

She tried to put a teasing note in her voice. It was no use trying to tell Finn she was fine and he shouldn't worry; only tone of voice would convince him. If she sounded like she was half-teasing, he wouldn't jump through the phone at her the next time she called him, demanding to know what trouble she had gotten herself involved in yet again. Honestly, just because she had broken her leg last year in a situation that should have been blandly, boringly routine, that didn't mean her life was in danger every time she went on the road for the Arc Foundation.

"I'll meet you at the usual place," she continued, "tomorrow afternoon, if this thing doesn't get straightened out before that. Okay? I'll check in again tomorrow morning, let you know my schedule. Talk at you later."

She cut the connection and snapped the phone closed. Her hand trembled. Kathryn stared at it a few seconds until it finally occurred to her to put down the phone before she dropped it.

"Don't be stupid," she muttered. "Finn's going to get the message in a few minutes, anyway. You're not alone. It won't kill you not to hear him yell at you to be careful, will it?" Kathryn rubbed at her face with both hands and looked around the still-deserted waiting room. "Okay, I've done what I can think of. Everything else is going to be improv from here on out." A groan escaped her as she pushed herself to her feet and scooped up phone and backpack. "I *hate* improv."

Closing her eyes, she pressed both hands against the wall and prayed hard and fast, so she almost wasn't conscious of the words racing through her mind and soul. Sometimes the prayers that seemed to be mostly, *Please, God, help, I'm in Your hands, use me for Your purpose,* covered every situation. Amazingly, they always made her feel a little better, instantly.

She tugged the door open and stepped into the back of Dr. West's office. Curtains rattled, startling her so she fumbled the phone. Kathryn jammed it into her backpack as Regina stepped out from a curtained changing room, dressed in a sleeveless, loose, pale blue cotton gown. She gave Kathryn a trembling, thin-lipped smile and walked over to the examination table where Dr. West waited. He gestured at a chair against the wall where Kathryn could keep watch but not be in the way.

While he examined Regina and put salve and bandages on her various small cuts, Kathryn recited what little she knew of the situation. The bare bones of her phone call from Vincent last night, her search, Regina's condition when she had found her. Regina confirmed what she said. Kathryn didn't voice her speculations or discuss the details of her dream. This was Dr. West's first contact with anyone from the Arc Foundation since Jennifer had recruited him and he had been vetted, but he was informed on procedures and what not to say in front of strangers. Jennifer would have educated him, and Vincent would have come out with her to finish the job.

Kathryn didn't want Regina to know all the ins and outs of the foundation and the growing network of people dedicated to help whoever fell through the cracks. Not now, so early into the assignment, with so many questions waiting to be answered.

"You did a good job," Dr. West said, when he unwrapped Regina's forehead wound and peeled off the antiseptic-soaked gauze pad. He gently pressed against the far edges of the bruise. "Sorry about that," he murmured in a detached tone when Regina hissed and pulled away from his touch.

More blood seeped in bright red pinpricks along the length of the gash, breaking through dried, closing spots. He picked up a swab sitting in a shallow tray and dabbed at the darkly bruised area.

"Oh, that's..." Regina smiled and blinked rapidly a few times. Her eyes were bright with repressed tears. "What is that? It was cold, then I didn't feel anything."

"Antiseptic and a topical anesthetic." He winked at her and dabbed again. "You did a good job," he continued, glancing over his shoulder at Kathryn. "It needs stitches, but you got it cleansed of all debris and got her a good start on the road to recovery. There won't even be much of a scar."

"A scar?" Regina's voice cracked.

"It won't even be visible unless you're into really dark tans. As a doctor, I don't recommend that." He patted her shoulder.

"As soon as I'm safe, I'm calling a plastic surgeon."

"If that's what you want." He stepped around behind her and gently helped her lie down on the examination table. He cast a questioning frown at Kathryn over Regina's head.

Kathryn shrugged. She had an idea what he was asking; some explanation for the princess attitude, maybe. What could she tell him? She supposed getting hurt and waking up in the mud with amnesia would put a lot of people off balance. Still, Regina seemed to focus on the wrong priorities.

Regina screwed her eyes shut and clenched her fists as Dr. West put five neat, tiny stitches into her forehead. Kathryn watched, trying for clinical detachment, but her imagination kept getting in the way. Dr. West had put that anesthetic on the cut, so why did Regina seem to be so uncomfortable?

Then it was over. Regina demanded and got two amber-colored pills for her pain before she went back into the curtained alcove to change back into her borrowed clothes. Kathryn sauntered over to the examination table and sat down, so she and Dr. West could talk in lowered voices.

"So, how is she really?"

"Besides the obvious?" He glanced at the curtained alcove. "Her attitude affects her recovery more than anything."

"Uh huh." Kathryn knew that answer could be interpreted any number of ways.

"I wouldn't blame her amnesia totally on her injuries. Emotional trauma is better at damaging memory than physical blows." He gathered up the debris from tending Regina's injuries; bloody gauze and wrappers from the bandage strips, cotton full of antiseptic and salve, snipped ends of the sutures.

"She's scared. Someone was pretty rough on her, even discounting her injuries when she fell." She frowned and shook her head. "If those injuries came from falling."

"There's that. We won't really know until Vincent and his friend come through with hard facts, or she gets her memory back and can give us some answers."

"Not us. Me." She smiled at the way his mouth dropped open in dismay. "We have to get moving. Whoever was shooting at her could still be in the area."

"You'd be safe with me. I live on the edge of town and I'm good friends with the sheriff."

"That would be great ordinarily, but... Vincent said not to trust the locals. There was high security at the place that burned last night, and other people shot. They're thinking an inside job. Local people who helped them get in. If not the sheriff, what about the people under him?"

"They're good men, all of them." Dr. West frowned and his eyes took on a distant look as he considered her words. "I've heard a few odd rumors about whatever happened last night on the mountain. Of course, there have been odd rumors for a couple years about whoever is holed up at that place, so that doesn't help with figuring out the truth. I have to agree. Get her out of town and get help from higher up." He broke into a grin. "Much higher."

"Always do." Kathryn slid down off the table. "Thanks. For everything."

"My pleasure." He dumped the garbage in a lidded can he opened by stepping on a lever at the floor. He glanced again at the curtain hiding Regina. "You know, after Jennifer recruited me and Vincent finished my training... well, I've been sure, living out here on the edge of the sticks, I'd never get called on for anything like this."

"Exciting?" She couldn't help grinning. She found herself wishing he'd say no.

Chapter Six

"It's not quite what I expected." Dr. West walked over to the sink and peeled off his examination gloves. She followed. "Of course, no one wanted to build up my expectations. Just to be ready to give a cup of cold water when asked."

"You did that. Sometimes it's big, sometimes it's small."

"What brought you into the group?"

"Born into it." She leaned against the long counter and watched him wash his hands. "And born again into it."

"Cryptic." Dr. West glanced at her, his smile fading as their gazes met. "You don't have to answer if—"

"Poor little rich girl. I probably would have messed up my life, left to myself, but throw in the really shady connections… Jennifer told you about our founder?" She waited until he nodded. "He's my uncle. He kept us safe, made sure no one found out we were connected to him, but… the darkness in this world can't be fooled. When Uncle Harrison turned his life around and got right with God, that made us targets, just to harm him. The darkness knew what sort of weapon for the Kingdom he could be."

"Get you into trouble to destroy his testimony?"

"Not exactly that. I was more a spoiled, useless brat. Wasted time and resources and…" She sighed, shrugging as if the action could free her of the emotional weight settling on her shoulders. It probably had been a mistake thinking of Finn, much less contacting him. What had prompted her to turn to him, when Vincent and his friend were probably all she needed? "I didn't do anything, when you think about it," she continued after a few moments of trying not to fall into Dr. West's big, sympathetic, chocolate eyes. "But there were things I *could have done,* and I didn't. Sins of omission are just as bad as the sins you commit."

Kathryn smiled a little, hearing the echo of her tenth grade Sunday school teacher's voice in those words. Sometimes she still felt amazed and grateful she remembered anything from those wasted high school years. Her mother had dragged her from one church and religious organization to another, trying to find answers and peace and absolution. Kathryn had learned to tune everything out as a survival mechanism. What was the teacher's name? Mrs. Robinson? She probably hadn't meant those words the way Kathryn applied them to her life, but they were still true.

"That's not how they recruited me," Dr. West murmured. He watched her and reached blindly for the towel hanging on the rack on the side of the refrigerator.

"Everyone has different gifts and different reasons. How'd they tap you?"

"My roommate from med school got in trouble. He came to me for help. I was the only one he trusted, even after all the downright nasty things he said about my faith..." He shrugged and tried to smile, despite the memory of pain in his eyes. "The only thing to do was go to the authorities, even knowing my friend's life would be ruined. I stalled for a while and tried to help him myself, in secret. And I did a lot of praying."

"We all do."

"Then I ran into Jennifer when I was about ready to give up. We knew each other a long time ago, when we were military brats. She came in from the other angle, when my friend's family got pulled into it and his baby sister was threatened."

"Jennifer has a radar for helping children in trouble."

"Thank God for that. Meeting her, seeing her in action, hearing about the Arc Foundation... opened a whole new dimension on the concept of a cup of cold water." He knuckled his eyes and coughed. He opened his mouth to speak and Kathryn was sure he was going to ask more questions. The curtain rattled on its tracks as Regina came out.

"Ready to go?" Kathryn said, turning to her. She almost grinned at the slight frown her companion wore, the way Regina looked back and forth between them. How much had she heard, despite their efforts at keeping their voices down, and what kind of questions had their conversation raised?

"I'm starving." Regina's voice had a touch of sulkiness that made Kathryn sigh. After only a short time, she had enough pieces to put together a picture of Regina she didn't really like. She much preferred her charge afraid, thinking beyond her own wants and needs.

"That's the surest sign of recovery I've ever known," Dr. West said with a chuckle. "I don't have much in the 'fridge, but you're welcome to join me."

His grin froze and his eyes widened. His hand dug into the enormous pocket where he had deposited his sandwich more than an hour before. His face took on a mournful, hound dog look as he regarded the slightly smashed bread, with mustard seeping through and the lettuce wilted, the meat sliding out one side and the tomato dripping and trying to slide out the other.

Regina giggled. Kathryn liked the sound. Her un-self-conscious smile made her into a totally different person.

"Thanks," Kathryn said.

It would have been pleasant to stay and eat with Dr. West, but she thought of shadowy figures with guns searching the mountainside, looking for Regina. How many could be among the park rangers? How soon would someone remark on seeing her searching the mountainside, or just her truck and license plate? Logic said the next step, if she found what everyone else was looking for, would be to visit a doctor.

"Thanks, but the sooner we get out of here, the better for all of us."

Dr. West nodded. Regina pouted. Kathryn much preferred a confused Regina as companion.

What is wrong with me, lately? I'm almost as much a snot as she is.

A chill crawled up her back. Bad humor was sometimes a warning sign of an approaching bad spell. Kathryn took a few deep breaths and concentrated on her knees and elbows, the base of her neck, the taste in her mouth, trying to gauge her physical condition. After wandering a rainy mountainside, slogging through mud, who wouldn't be a little weary and achy? She hoped what she felt was just normal strain and chill. Once she got back in her truck and could sit down, turn the heater on and dry out, she would be fine.

Please, Lord, let me be fine.

~~~~~

Jeff West stood in the door of his office, one foot on the sidewalk, watching Kathryn's truck go down the street. He waved, and a grin touched his face when he saw her hand raise in farewell, and then a moment later gently elbow her big, dark, furry dog's head out of the open window. He liked dogs, had gotten along fairly well with Jennifer's big Dalmatian, Puck, but he was glad Kathryn had left that one in her truck.

Well, that wasn't half as bad as I feared. He grinned, admitting to all the visions he had entertained of his first job for the foundation. Demands for help he couldn't give. Impossible situations. Gunfire. Secrets he had to keep from the local authorities.

That thought turned his smile to a frown. If Sheriff Tom Green directly asked him about the two young women who visited his office, he would have to tell him something. He owed him as much truth as was safe to tell. The man was his friend as well as the law for this little town. Jeff hoped he wouldn't ask.

But that led him to new thoughts. Someone had been chasing and shooting at Regina. If that was really her name. Despite what little Kathryn had told him, it wasn't much of a leap of logic to connect the injured woman with all the wild rumors of fires and gunfire and chases up and down the mountainside all last night. Sooner or later, the sheriff or one of his underlings would come to him to learn if anyone had come for treatment of injuries. The best move right now was to close up the office and go home. If his door was closed, the lights were off, and he wasn't available, strangers just might believe him when he said he hadn't seen
~~~~~

anyone. No one in Millersburg would think it odd for him to close up for the afternoon. If anyone really needed him, everybody knew his home number for emergencies.

Nodding, still frowning, he stepped back inside the office. Two tugs on the faded blue blinds dropped them into place across the big storefront window. He turned the *open* sign around in the door so it read *closed*, and hurried through the door into the back of the office. A flicker of movement caught his attention as he closed the door, but it was only a dark green 4X4 pulling into a parking space across the street.

Deadbolt slid quietly into place, locking the door. He picked up his abused sandwich and tossed it into the garbage can by the sink. Two tugs and he peeled off his sweater. It had been a gag gift, handmade, from his Aunt Patrice, but was more useful than either of them ever anticipated. He grinned, thinking of Kathryn's reaction when he put the sandwich in the bottom pocket, and hung it on the peg by the back door. He snatched up his keys and backpack and reached for the doorknob. One downward swipe of his hands turned off the lights. Five seconds later, he was outside, the door locked and he was free of the office for the afternoon. Jeff thought maybe he would just go fishing. He would bring a good book and pick up one of those monster submarine sandwiches Barney's Kitchen made. He grinned and nodded, liking his idea better as it grew. Kathryn had done him a favor, actually. Barney's subs were a far sight better than the sandwich he had made. Fishing and reading were better for him than spending the day alone in his office, waiting for stubbed toes and upset stomachs.

His green, primer-spotted Mustang waited in the shade of the few trees tucked between the steep slope of hill and the far side of the land-of-a-thousand-lakes parking lot. Thanks to the storms, today he wouldn't have to roll down all the windows and turn on the vent fan full blast for ten minutes before the temperature inside dropped from furnace to bearable. One of these days, he would have to see about getting a new car. Or maybe a truck. He liked the looks of Kathryn's truck.

Footsteps in the muddy gravel of the parking lot made him glance over his shoulder. A husky-looking man approached him from the driveway between the stores. The intensity of the stranger's gaze and the flat line of his mouth sent a shiver up Jeff's back. He didn't believe in premonitions, but he did believe in gut reactions. After seeing Jennifer and Puck in action, and getting a somber, slightly frightening indoctrination from Vincent, he believed in divine intervention. His guardian angel had just dropped an ice cube down his back.

"Something I can do for you?" he said, stopping and turning to face the stranger.

A dark green, mud-spattered 4X4 pulled down the alley driveway into the parking lot and stopped, and another man, dressed like the first, got out of the driver's seat. They both looked like hunters. The only things they lacked were rifles. Going by his experience working at an inner city clinic, Jeff judged they were more the handgun type, used to suit jackets over holsters in shoulder harnesses.

"You live around here?" the man in blue said. He attempted a smile. Jeff nodded. "Can you tell me when the doctor'll be back, or where I can find him?"

"Is someone hurt?" Jeff looked over the truck again, the mud spattered on its doors and wheel wells and the streaks of drying mud on the boots and pants of both men. They could have just come into town to find help, he reasoned. It happened all the time.

The ice cube down his back returned, and he changed his assessment. If they were here because of the ruckus on the mountainside, which higher-level authorities were rumored to be trying to hush, they were part of the problem rather than the solution.

"Why would you ask that?" the man in brown asked as he crossed the parking lot to join them.

"This is an outfitter's town. Hikers, campers, hunters. People who come to me on a day like this are hurt, not sick." Jeff offered a grin, more to encourage himself than disarm them. "Even the kids don't pretend to be sick on a day like this because it's Friday. They don't want to lose their weekend."

"You're Dr. West, then?" the first asked. Neither man smiled in response to his humor.

"I suppose I am. Do you mind telling me what you want?"

"We're with federal security, Doctor. Could you answer a few questions for us?"

"That depends." Jeff took a deep breath and decided to take the initiative. How they answered would determine his answers. "Does this have anything to do with that ruckus on the mountain last night?"

"What ruckus?"

Okay, so we're going to play that kind of game. God, please help me say the right things.

Jeff fought to keep his smile in place, but from the tightness in his face muscles, he knew it wasn't a nice smile. Suppose these men *were* with federal security? Kathryn had said she couldn't trust any authorities in the area. If she couldn't trust Tom Green, whom he knew, why should he trust someone who claimed to be with the government, whom he didn't know even with two inches of paperwork to prove his identity? He decided not to tell them anything until he had real, irrefutable proof they were on the right side of the law.

"This is a very small town," he said slowly, letting his smile fade. "It's hard to keep much of anything a secret, especially with so many rangers scurrying around in the middle of the night. The sheriff and all his men have been going since before dawn. Everybody knows something was burned down, past the old abandoned ski lodge, last night. What are you looking for?"

Both men looked at each other, silent communication passing between them. They didn't like something he had said. If this were a movie, this was where they would either flash their badges at him, pull a gun, or knock him out with gas or a good thump to the head, and take him prisoner. Or they could just walk away. What were his chances of that?

The one in brown opened his mouth to speak. The one in blue took a step closer to Jeff and raised a hand, stopping his partner from speaking.

"Are you the only doctor around here?" the one in blue asked. His question visibly surprised his partner.

"Yeah."

"How long have you been around here? Do you know the man who was here ahead of you?" He licked his lips, glanced at his partner, then to Jeff's amazement, colored a little. "Maybe he trained you?"

"Carson—" the other man began. He scowled when his partner signaled him to silence again.

Jeff didn't know if he should run while the two men glared at each other, one demanding answers with his gaze, the other pleading for patience or support. He had the awful feeling he was supposed to be responding to some secret code that he had never learned.

"Can't believe I'm messing this up—never thought I'd need it." Carson glanced at Jeff, then his partner again. He dug in his pocket and pulled out his cell phone, glanced at it, shrugged, then flipped it open.

"Want to use my phone inside?" Jeff offered. He didn't have to lean forward to see there were no bars whatsoever on the phone's display screen.

"Not secure." He glanced at the other man, eyes narrowed, and Jeff got that unpleasant shiver again at the suspicion that Carson didn't trust his partner.

~~~~~

Kathryn stopped at a little mom-and-pop burger shack just outside of town, before they got onto the highway and headed north. She bought burgers and pint cups of fruit salad for Regina and herself, and four uncooked hamburgers for Bea. Regina cast disgusted looks over her shoulder at Bea while she ate. Kathryn couldn't see what was so upsetting about the way her bodyguard-companion ate. Bea did it quickly, neatly, and quietly. She didn't whine and beg for more, though she knew Bea could have taken twice as many slabs of ground, pressed beef.

At the first rest stop, twenty minutes down the highway, they
~~~~~

stopped. Bea ran and did her business, working off her light lunch and being cramped into the back of the truck for so long. Kathryn filled her water jugs at the old-fashioned pump. Since they had the place to themselves, she rinsed out Regina's muddy, torn clothes under the stream of icy water. They would never be the same again, but if she had the chance that evening, she could mend the jeans and close up some of the unraveling spots in the sweater to give Regina more clothes to wear.

Regina sat in the truck cab and napped. She refused Kathryn's advice to get exercise while she could. Kathryn didn't know if her companion was tired and dizzy from the pain pills Dr. West had given her, or if this was another phase of her sulking. It was tempting to play catch with Bea for a few minutes just to irritate Regina, but she resisted. Any danger Regina faced was real. If necessary, Kathryn would stand between her and that danger. That was part of the job.

She had never considered the chance that the person she would be called on to help someday, maybe risking her life, would turn out to be a spoiled brat. Regina's injuries and amnesia and very real fear could just be exacerbating and exaggerating a character flaw, but Kathryn doubted it.

Fifteen minutes after they pulled off the highway, they were back in the truck and out into the flow of traffic. Regina's clean, wet clothes hung in a net bag in the back of the truck. Bea settled down so her head stuck out between the seats and rested on the map box/console. She didn't touch either of them, but Regina scooted over closer to the door. Kathryn bit her lip to fight a grin.

"Why do you call her Bea?" Regina said after half an hour of silence. She had tried to curl up against the door and nap again, but the jouncing of the rough, crumbling concrete under the truck's wheels made that impossible.

"Short for Beatrice. The divine guide."

Regina gave her a blank look, which was somehow worse than a confused look. Kathryn swallowed a sigh.

"Did you ever read Dante?" She waited for some response. A flicker of something that she couldn't quite call comprehension. "You know, 'The Divine Comedy'?"

"Oh. Yeah."

From the flatness of her tone, Kathryn suspected Regina had been forced to read the classics, or someone had forced her to listen when they were read aloud.

"Bea is my guard and guide," she continued. "Just like Beatrice kept Dante out of trouble during his tour of the many levels of Hell — that's not saying that Hell is on Earth, or anywhere I go is like Hell, but, well, you get the general idea?"

Bea let out a soft *woof* and nudged Kathryn's elbow with her nose.

She chuckled and twisted her arm around to scratch the top of the big Akita's head for a few seconds.

"I'm well-acquainted with Hell on Earth, thanks very much," Regina muttered. She edged closer to the door and ignored Bea.

Wimp. Kathryn swallowed a sigh. *This is a test, right, God? What am I supposed to say? What's wrong with her?*

She cast another look at Regina. The white bandages peeping out from under the baseball cap and the sleeves of her borrowed jacket sent a stab of guilt and pity through Kathryn. If anyone had reason to be afraid of everything and totally unsettled, it was Regina.

~~~~~

Jeff West loved his log cabin home. It had everything he had ever wanted, even before he went to medical school with lofty dreams of curing cancer — or at least the common cold. Situated on the edge of town, near the foot of the mountain, surrounded by trees, with a branch of the river running along the property line in back and his own dock and boat for fishing. He couldn't think of a better way to finish out a day at the office, whether it had been stressful or boring. He loved to sit on the deck in back and listen to the rippling of the river against the piling stones long into dusk, then settle into his front room and read a chapter or two from one of the books in his library. At last count, he owned nearly fifteen hundred.

Today as he drove down the sparsely populated street, he welcomed the sight of his dark green front door even more. Kathryn's visit and his first chance to help someone from the Arc Foundation had been exciting, even if it wasn't what he had imagined. His short talk in the parking lot with Carson and Porter had been downright disturbing. Taking the leap of faith to be honest with them had taken more effort than he had anticipated. After all, what if his gut instinct was wrong, and Carson knew the right words to say, the right attitude to effect, to fool him? What if he had put Kathryn into more danger by his effort to help her?
~~~~~

Chapter Seven

Jeff wanted nothing more than to settle down on the edge of the dock, dangle his feet in the water, and let his thoughts flow with the river while he figured out what everything really meant. Oh, yeah—and pray hard between every other sentence. That was a necessity. Maybe he hadn't been praying enough, and that was why he had such a hard time with today's trials and tests?

Relaxing and going into mental neutral gear had to wait another ten minutes, though. Today was trash day and his two dark green, heavy-duty plastic trash barrels lay on their sides halfway into the street. At least this week they weren't completely in the street, or even pushed up against the hedge across the street. For some reason, the town's sanitation team couldn't manage to put the barrels back upright after they were emptied. Sighing, a tired smile on his face, Jeff drove around the barrels and up into the driveway. He got out with the engine running and unlocked the garage door, then pulled his car in. When he turned the engine off, he heard another engine.

The sound came from the street. He stepped out of the garage and stopped short at the sight of the glossy, maroon rental car sitting across the end of his driveway. He couldn't see more than the outlines of two people through the tinted windows. The hairs prickled on the back of his neck, followed by a spark of anger. No way was he going to let more strangers intimidate him in his own driveway.

Ignoring the occupants of the car, he walked down to the edge of the driveway and snatched up the handles of the two trash barrels. He almost hoped to find the strangers had run over or dented the barrels, so he could have reason to shoo them off his property without the obligation of being sociable. Friendliness was a requirement for living in Millersburg, after all.

The car doors opened while he put the barrels back into the garage. Jeff was half-tempted to close the garage door from the inside and force these people to ring the doorbell. He was just too tired to play that kind of petty, mental game. Forcing his shoulders straight and flat, he turned and stepped out of the garage.

They were a man and woman, both dressed in dark business suits, with severe hair. The woman was taller, strawberry blond with stylish, tinted glasses that made her light brown eyes look bigger. The frames reflected the color of her hair, and that irritated Jeff for some reason.

The man stayed two steps behind the woman. He carried a briefcase. His stance was that of a guarding, mud-brown bulldog, and his physique matched. He didn't belong in that suit, Jeff decided. Did those bulges under his coat come from muscles or guns?

What was wrong with him, that he looked for guns everywhere? It was ironic, he knew, because the Arc Foundation didn't believe in guns.

"Dr. West?" the woman said. She stayed at the end of the driveway and looked up the slight slope at him. Something about her stance told him she expected him to come down the driveway to her.

"That's me." He leaned back against the guide track for the garage door.

"I'm Agent Cooper. This is Agent Edwards." She flashed open a slim brown case.

Something winked gold, like a badge. He was too far away to tell. For all he knew, it was a trick to get him to come closer to her, either within range of attack or just to intimidate him. Well, news flash: Jeff West wasn't in the mood for intimidation. Not after the day he had had.

"We don't have time to waste being sociable, Doctor. A young woman's life is in danger. We need to know if you've seen her lately, or if any strangers have come through town in the last few days."

"This whole town is a camper's way-station, Agent Cooper. Three-quarters of the population, any day of the week, is a stranger."

Cooper studied him a moment, then nodded to her companion. He held up the briefcase flat for her and she pressed the buttons to release the top. From inside, she took out a color, eight-by-ten photo and held it out to him. When Jeff hesitated, she took a few steps up the driveway toward him. If she could compromise, so could he. They met halfway and he took the photo from her.

It showed Regina seated on a tall stool with lab equipment behind her; racks of test tubes, a chart of the elements, sketches of molecular models. With her hair pulled back in a severe style, she looked ten years older. She wore an icy blue business suit under her long white lab coat and she looked at the camera with a slightly bored, slightly uncomfortable expression. Jeff imagined she didn't like cameras and she wanted to get back to work.

Would someone out to get her, hurt her, have an expensive, posed photo like that? He suspected there were some logic holes in that bit of reasoning, but his head threatened to burst into a full-blown headache. These people seemed to go with the general image of Regina he had picked up, both from the young woman's attitude this morning and the photo. He definitely could see them as the type of people who would be assigned to work with her, industrial liaisons or bodyguards. Or maybe they were babysitters, to keep the snooty young woman under control. She was probably one of those geniuses who couldn't socialize without a diagram to guide them.

He was tired. Too tired to keep analyzing and trying to out-think people who might just be professional liars. Jeff thought a quick prayer for guidance, took a deep breath, and dove in.

"I treated her for a head wound late morning today," he said, handing the photo back to Cooper.

"How bad a head wound?" Edwards asked. His voice had a hard quality to it with rough edges, as if he didn't bother speaking much.

"No concussion or physical disorientation. A little memory... trouble. Some minor cuts and bruises. Somebody was pretty rough on her." He kept his voice and face in that detached, clinical style taught in medical school. Supposedly, patients expected it; the unemotional tone reassured them. He had never accepted that style or the reasoning behind it, but now he was glad he had picked it up anyway.

"Where is she now?" Cooper asked.

"I have no idea." That, at least, was the truth. "She left my office under her own power, after assuring me she had someone waiting for her."

"Was she with anyone?" Edwards asked. "Did anyone bring her to you?"

What was wrong with these people? Didn't they hear what he said? Or did they know already he was lying and planning to tell more lies?

"With?" Jeff scratched his chin and glanced over their shoulders to the house across the street. No one moving about. No friendly neighbors to conveniently step outside and get involved in his life. Why did they always stick their noses in when he didn't want them around, and then ignore him when he did want some witnesses? "I don't think she was with anybody. She walked in under her own power."

"Let me get this straight, Doctor," Cooper said. Her cold tone made it hard for him to keep his bland expression and not recoil a few steps. "A girl comes in, beat up and with no memory —"

"I didn't say she had no memory," he hurried to point out. "I said she had memory trouble. I asked her the standard questions anyone with half a conscience asks when someone in her condition shows up, and she stumbled in answering, or didn't have answers."

"Granted. But still, you just let her walk out the door when you were finished with her, no questions asked?"

"I asked plenty of questions, Agent Cooper." Jeff jammed his hands in his pockets, in case they started shaking.

He didn't like the way these two stared at him, as if they could read the truth written on his face. Didn't they hear what he had just said? Or maybe they had talked with Carson and Porter, didn't like his answers, and came at him from a new angle to get more information — which he didn't have or wasn't willing to give?

"She didn't have any answers. I offered to take her to the sheriff and she declined. When I insisted, she said she had already talked to him. When I asked why a deputy hadn't brought her over, she said she didn't need help. Then I got an emergency call and when I turned around she walked out the door. I couldn't chase her when I had a frantic mother on the phone, now could I?"

"How did she pay for the treatment?" Edwards asked.

Jeff longed to tell them the price had been paid a long time ago, but he doubted they would understand the reference and spiritual ramifications. Kathryn's words about not being able to trust local authorities rang in his head. Even if these people were legitimate, he had no reason to trust their words or intentions. Why hadn't he moved close enough to really examine Cooper's badge? He wished he had lied from the start. If these people were indeed legitimate associates of Regina's, he might just have some pity for the young woman.

"Pay?" He shook his head and wished Kathryn had given him some kind of story to use when this situation arose. She was the old pro at this game, after all. "She had cash on her. A couple of twenties in her pocket. I don't charge much just to look into people's eyes and put iodine on cuts, and she had plenty of money."

"Plenty of money," Cooper murmured. She turned her head slightly to meet her partner's gaze.

Jeff knew in that moment, these people had been near to Regina some time before her fall and they knew she didn't have any money. Maybe they knew the extent of her injuries, too, and knew he had been lying.

"You didn't check her wallet for identification?" Edwards asked.

"She didn't have one. Just the bills tucked in her pocket. She said all her possessions were with the sheriff, and someone had given her new clothes because hers were muddy and torn."

"That didn't seem odd to you?"

"Why should it? The sheriff is a good man. I trust his judgment. It isn't like somebody is going to be mugged in Millersburg. Especially if they're walking right out of the sheriff's office and down the street to mine." He shrugged and tried to look nonchalant.

"Did she say anything when she left? Any indication where she was going?" Cooper said.

"Well, I really think you should check with the sheriff. That's where she started from, and she said he had all her things. That's where I'd certainly go if I needed help."

The two agents might have been trying for a bland, unreadable expression, but Jeff could see the slight frowns, the wrinkling of doubt around their eyes. They wanted to grill him, but he hadn't given them any reason to press further. Or had he?

"Thank you, Doctor," Cooper said after a few seconds of silence that felt like years. "You've been very helpful."

Despite the softness of her words, he knew she was being sarcastic. He felt an implied threat. What was Regina involved in, and what kind of trouble was riding around with Kathryn at that moment? He tried not to sag in relief when Cooper nodded to Edwards and the two agents headed down the short driveway to their car.

"We'll get back to you if we have any more questions," Cooper continued. She gave him a flat little smile and nodded farewell. Neither agent looked back at him as they got into their car, started the engine and drove away.

Jeff watched them go, not moving until the car had vanished around the corner. His legs wobbled as he stepped up to the garage to close the overhead door. By the time he got his keys out to unlock the front door and went inside, they were full-on shaking.

Instead of his usual routine of hurrying up the stairs to the loft to change his clothes, he dropped into the saggy comfortable old couch facing the fireplace. For a few seconds he sat there, staring at the pile of kindling waiting for the next fire. The crammed bookshelves lining the walls didn't give him the usual sense of security.

He had to do something, but what? Jeff mentally reviewed his conversation with the two agents.

The sheriff. He had mentioned the sheriff often enough they would be fools if they didn't go to him next.

Or had they gone to him, and the sheriff had said nothing about Regina? Was that why he sensed their doubt? Did they just think he was a fool for believing Regina's story and letting her get away so easily?

He pulled out his phone. Maybe driving back into town to the sheriff's office would be more secure. For all he knew, his line was being tapped or bugged or whatever it was called, right that moment, but what if those two agents were waiting for him to make an uncharacteristic move?

"Lord, please… I wasn't made to think like a super-spy," he muttered as he dialed. "Keep them both safe. Help me figure out what to say. Please don't let Tom be part of all this."

Jerry Willis, a deputy answered the phone. Jeff asked for Sheriff Green.

"Tom, anything strange going on in town today?" he asked before the sheriff could get past greeting him.

"Anything strange?" the sheriff repeated in his rumbling voice. "What are you asking for?"

"What do you mean, what am I asking for?" Jeff put a chuckle in his voice. "I'm the doctor. If there's anything strange going on here, I usually get called in, one way or another."

"Uh huh. Anything you think I should know?"

"Nope, nothing to report." This was not going well. "Just wondering."

"You've never 'just wondered' about anything, Jeff. You want to spill it, or do I have to bring you in for questioning?"

"Don't you take that tone with me, Tom Green," he said, forcing a chuckle. "I took that arrow out of your backside when your son decided he wanted to be Robin Hood. I know things about you the rest of the town—"

"Jeff!" The tone held pleading, humor, and a demand for information.

He knew then, Cooper and Edwards hadn't been to see the sheriff yet. That struck him as odd. If he were looking for someone, he would have gone to the sheriff first and then started questioning people in town.

"Okay, here's what I have. Early afternoon, two men in a truck approached me and said they were federal security, looking for a missing girl. Then maybe ten minutes ago, a man and a woman in business suits, real icebergs, big city attitudes, came to my house with the same story."

"What'd you tell them?"

"What could I tell them? I don't know anything. It just made me curious, you know?"

"Me, too."

"Yeah, you and half the town. Want to tell me what was going on up near Ski and Mill roads last night?"

"Sorry, wish I could, but I got my orders from high up to keep it as quiet as I can," the sheriff said, using that flat tone Jeff had learned meant he was frustrated and getting angry.

"No, huh? If anything does happen, you'll let me know, won't you?"

"You bet. If anything does, you'll probably be in the middle of it, patching up someone."

That told Jeff a few things. Maybe that was what the sheriff intended. They exchanged a few pleasantries before he hung up.

"This isn't what I thought it would be when I signed up, Lord," he whispered. He slouched forward and rested his head in his hands, his elbows on his knees. "Now what do I do? Please, let them be safe. They're barely more than kids. They're in more trouble than they know." He wanted to warn Kathryn, but he knew what kind of unholy havoc the mountains played on cell phone reception. He might be able to leave her a message, but would she ever get it? That was why everyone in town used landlines instead of cell phones and had cable if they wanted to watch more than the two static-filled channels that seeped between the mountains. How could he get hold of her?

His gaze strayed back to the telephone. He couldn't call Kathryn, but he could get a message to someone who could contact her. He dialed again, and while the phone rang three times, he realized that though he had never needed to call that particular number, it came to his memory without hesitation.

Usually, the sound of Jennifer Deverall's voice lifted his spirits, but hearing her outgoing voicemail message made them drop.

"Jennifer, this is Jeff West in Millersburg," he said, trying for his school-trained, distant voice. "Kathryn was here this afternoon. She brought an injured woman to me for help. Vincent told her not to trust the local authorities until he has further information for her. Two groups claiming to be government are now hunting them, and I think I messed up by admitting anything at all. I should have lied completely, because somebody is lying."

He stopped. What else could he say? Anything he could think to add would only make him sound even more incoherent than he felt already.

"I don't know if I'm making things worse or helping, but you should know. I guess I should have called the foundation directly. I'll call them next, but you should know, get the prayer chain going or something. Call Vincent? It sounded like he was close enough to get to her or meet her or something. Kathryn knows the situation isn't good, but I think it just got ratcheted up a few notches. Somebody should tell her."

He decided in that moment he hated answering machines and voicemail and any kind of technology that made glorious promises and then failed to follow through. He swallowed hard, tried to think of something else to say, then finally said goodbye and hung up.

After several long moments on his knees, battling to pray and come up with a more verbally coherent report, he reached for his Bible on the dusty coffee table. He flipped it open to the back, where he had written the contact phone numbers for various people at the Arc Foundation.

~~~~~

Lisa McCain tapped three times with just the tips of her fingernails on the connecting door between her room in Harper's office suite and the central "throne" room. Harper himself had designated it as such in one of his rare moments of whimsy. Without waiting for a reply, she nudged the door open just enough to slide through the gap and proceeded to the horseshoe-shaped desk at the far end of the long room. Harper glanced up once from the four built-in screens in the surface of the desk directly in front of him. The blue-tooth earpiece gave off a steady red pinpoint flash as he listened, tapped at the different touch-screens, and ignored the ten news channels displayed on the wall screens behind his desk.

She stayed five paces away from the desk, her hands folded neatly at
~~~~~

her waist, holding a folded sheet of paper, and focused on the edge of the desk directly in front of her. Not that she wasn't interested in whatever Harper was working on, because eventually she would be given responsibility for finishing whatever he had started, or doing more research. However, there were some times when it just didn't pay to be curious around Cameron Harper.

Now was one of those times.

Especially when she had such unsatisfactory information to pass on to him. She maintained a neutral expression and silently cursed the cowards who made her their intermediary instead of sending their reports directly to their employer, to show up on one of those screens he played like a virtuoso.

"No one ever learns, do they, McCain?" Harper said, after the red dot stopped flashing on his earpiece.

"Disappointing news is still better than no news at all," she said, and unclasped her hands to unfold the paper. "Whether they can do something with what little they found out remains to be seen." She waited a moment for him to indicate what he wanted.

Harper sat back, not far enough to actually rest against the chair's high, stiff leather cushion. Both hands continued working the screens in front of him. He nodded to her.

"Dr. Malvern has found help and is getting off the mountain. The locals are smart enough to be suspicious and they're putting the pieces together despite the four different agencies sticking their noses in and confusing the issues. A local doctor seems to be the only one who has actually seen and spoken to her. Either he is lying about the extent of her injuries and what she told him, or she lied to him. Someone is helping her, but there is no information available other than the possible color and make of the truck she might have been riding in. I have a network search going right now looking for what few traffic cameras and satellites might have been focused on that area in the last thirty-six hours. Maybe we'll catch a break," she offered with a shrug, but knew better than to smile.

"Those idiots might catch a break," Harper said, his hands pausing a moment. "Do you think we should talk to the doctor?"

Chapter Eight

Lisa knew that wasn't really a question. Harper never asked anyone's opinion. Those who translated questions as subtly delivered orders rose quickly in his organization, while those who mistakenly believed he cared about their opinions were lucky if they didn't go anywhere.

"We might be able to find out something just from what he doesn't know. Searching his office waste basket might reveal how badly Dr. Malvern is hurt."

Harper's left eyebrow quirked up, along with the left corner of his mouth. Lisa nodded to him and strode out of the office, her heart beating just a little faster than her brisk, hurrying-but-not-hurrying pace. She raced through her mental list of the people in the area whom she could pull off the search for Regina Malvern, to take a side trip and investigate Dr. West. She hoped the man was an elderly, genial uncle-type who was easily fooled by damsels in distress. People who lied to Cameron Harper, even those who didn't know they were lying to him, paid for it.

~~~~~

Regina dozed for half an hour, then woke and stared out the side window for nearly ten minutes before she dropped back to sleep. Kathryn worried a little about that. Was it a natural reaction to all she had gone through, or was it dangerous? Dr. West said she had no concussion, but there could still be some damage from her tumble down the mountainside and smashing her head against something, couldn't there?

Still, Regina's silence was easier to take when she was asleep rather than pouting out the window.

Kathryn concentrated on the road and what she would say to Finn when she saw him. If he called her back. If he could reach her while she was still in the mountains. She speculated on how soon he would insist on taking Regina off her hands. This whole situation smacked of federal trouble, agency work rather than Kathryn's usual assignments of providing advice and emotional support and finding experts to handle situations. The closest she had come to this type of trouble in months was when she helped ferry a fugitive, battered mother and her frightened children from a compromised shelter to a safe house.

The psychotic father had caught up with them at a highway rest stop in the early morning hours. He slashed the tires of her truck before he went after the four of them in the rustic little bathroom facilities. Bea came
~~~~~

back from running through the woods and went into defense mode, knocking the man down before he got within ten feet of the doorway. She had stayed sitting on the man, growling and taking nips at his shirt, and kept him immobile until the closest authorities arrived. Kathryn had prayed vigorously, often out loud to drown out the man's curses, until the police handcuffed him and put him into a cruiser. She had said several prayers of gratitude and protection for whoever was involved in creating cell phones.

Still, that didn't mean she welcomed danger and a chance to prove yet again that her guardian angel was on duty. She hoped her niggling irritation with Regina was the worst problem she would face for the rest of this trip.

Finn won't like this at all, she thought. Just the idea of telling him what Vincent had said and what she had witnessed made her sigh. And a moment later, grin. Finn would scold her about unreasonable risks and shake her a little. Then he would get that crack in his voice and hold her close a long time. As long as she cared to let him. Then he would kiss her, and if she wasn't careful Finn would side-step up to his favorite topic: taking care of her in a permanent arrangement.

Problem: Finn never outright asked her to marry him. He always hinted and teased and tested her by posing hypothetical questions. Sometimes it was fun to stymie him and make him keep circling and hinting. Sometimes she wondered what his reaction would be if she beat him to the punch and asked him to marry her. Sometimes she swore if he didn't have the guts to ask her outright, just five simple words, then she should walk away, or at the very least ratchet back their relationship to good friends. Stop the kisses, at the very least, because kisses meant something special to her. She suspected kisses meant a lot to Finn, too, but that was the problem, so much was speculation and guessing.

She loved Finn. She really did. The idea of spending the next fifty years with him and having a baby or two was a nice, warm, summer-hazy dream. She hadn't indulged very often in such dreams even before she fell ill, too busy having fun in this exciting new life offered by the Arc Foundation. Too busy feeling like she was finally doing something worthwhile. Too busy paying in gratitude and sacrifice for the new life she had found, partially through Finn's influence and constant prayers. She certainly didn't permit dreams like those now, when she had no idea if she would live to see fifty or die within a month.

Sometimes, Kathryn thought she had forgotten how to dream that way. Finn was a good Christian man, and that was important. He knew about her past because he was the one who had prayed and nagged and challenged her back onto the straight and narrow.

But Finn was FBI. There was no guarantee that his stationary assignment would remain so. He might be sent back tomorrow to the life that had consumed him since college, moving and investigating and rescuing people. He could be gone for weeks at a time on assignments, working on jobs and situations he couldn't tell her about even after the danger passed.

Kathryn knew she could deal with that kind of a relationship, simply because she had done so already, but could Finn? If he knew the full extent of her illness, that her up and down spells of good and bad health would grow to be mostly bad, he would insist she get off the road, stay at home, conserve her energy.

Better not to go anywhere near the inevitable argument.

Even worse, she feared Finn would change his assignment, get off the road, refuse adventure and risk so he could be near her. He wasn't made for a desk job, any more than she was made to help Elizabeth with the foundation's administrative work. She wouldn't do that to him.

Kathryn knew one thing for certain: she wouldn't sit down until she was so badly off she had to lie down. There was still so much work to do, people to help, miles to travel, burdens to carry, and sorrows to face. When she had an assignment, something to occupy her thoughts and keep her moving, something to do and someone to help, Kathryn was fine. The empty times with nothing to do but think were when her fears and speculations crowded in on her and even Bea was no company or comfort.

Her phone chirped, muffled inside her backpack and underneath Bea. Kathryn jerked. She reached around behind her seat, keeping one hand on the wheel. Bea didn't move fast enough to get off her backpack. She hooked her fingers through her collar and tugged. The dog whined a little, licked her fingers, and scooted to the other side of the compartment.

"Yeah?" Kathryn said almost before she had flipped open the phone.

There was no place to pull over, and no one ahead of or behind her for at least half a mile. She watched the highway ahead as Su-Ma passed along Dr. West's message about the two groups searching for Regina. Kathryn smiled a little in mixed amusement and pity. He had found out rather abruptly that trouble always came with excitement. The noble sentiment of "a cup of cold water" sometimes had a price tag of bruised knuckles, worry, and a feeling of helplessness.

"So, what are you thinking? Any change in strategy?" Su-Ma asked after a few moments of quiet broken only by the hum of her tires and the soft rumble of her engine.

"I'm taking her to Finn. Smartest move is to go to the Feds I know I can trust. Planned on it before I heard this." Kathryn saw a widening of the berm, a bulge in the guardrail indicating a place to pull over. She did so. "Any news from Vincent?"

"He hasn't contacted us yet. Jennifer said she couldn't get through, which tells me he's kind of busy."

"Figures. It's the old Chinese curse, huh?"

"Word is out on the prayer chain."

Regina moaned and snorted, signaling she was waking from her nap. Kathryn fought a grin. How could someone who carried herself like an upper-crust lady sound like a dockworker when she woke?

"Thanks for the warning," she said. "Gotta go."

"Godspeed." The connection broke.

"What's that?" Regina grumbled as she turned from her curled up position facing the window. She frowned as Kathryn flipped the phone closed and reached behind to put it back into the pouch of her backpack.

"Checking in with headquarters." She looked back down the highway, saw no one coming, and pulled out again.

"Called them for help?"

Was that a sneer she saw on Regina's sleep-creased face, or just a yawn trying to break through? Kathryn fought a ripple of dislike for her and sent up a mini-prayer for forgiveness. She didn't need attitude problems making an already unpleasant situation worse.

"They called to warn me. We have two sets of Feds on our trail." She glanced at her companion. Regina stared at her, mouth dropping open, and real fear in those big, shadowed eyes. "If they really are agents. Could be a lie to get information. Do you remember anything else?"

"No." The word came out a little too quickly for Kathryn's taste. Regina hunched her shoulders and wrapped her arms around herself. She looked cold and alone.

"It's okay. Dr. West wouldn't betray us. Tomorrow, we'll be with friends who can protect you until you remember what's going on."

"What kind of friends?"

"The less you know, the better." Kathryn meant it to be teasing, to cheer up Regina.

Her companion's frown made her immediately regret those words. Such a remark certainly didn't help Regina relax, but there was something about her that brought out the nasty, critical side in Kathryn.

"Why are you doing this?" Regina nearly snarled. The sudden change in tone startled Kathryn enough she hesitated.

"Doing what?" she hedged. At the back of her mind, she could hear Elizabeth gently scolding her for her smart-aleck responses.

"Driving around the country, just diving into people's lives. You think you're Sir Lancelot?"

"Hardly." Kathryn coughed, choking back a giggle that would just make Regina angrier. "I'm trying to be a sheep instead of a goat."

"What?" Her voice rose, threatening to crack an octave above high-C.

"The goats are the ones who see people in need and turn away because they're strangers. The sheep are the ones who see needs and see people they love in that need." Kathryn shook her head, glad to concentrate on the road so she couldn't see Regina's face. "I was hungry and you fed me, I was thirsty and you gave me something to drink, I was naked and you clothed me, I was sick and in prison and you visited me. Everything's connected. What goes around comes around."

"Oh. Like those Eastern religion things, like karma and all that." Regina sounded relieved to discover that explanation.

"Hardly. More like, every road eventually leads to Jerusalem."

Echoes of rainy evenings at home discussing apologetics and literature and philosophy, with a healthy dose of faerie tales and mythology mixed in. Kathryn missed Quarry Hall and her cozy room and knowing several of her adopted sisters were right down the hall, offering advice and comfort one day, needing it the next in a warm, comfortable give-and-take.

"Oh... Is there any music to listen to?" Regina grabbed at the radio knob and twisted it hard, skipping through stations so quickly Kathryn couldn't recognize one snatch of song from another.

Not the right time, she decided. Regina was in a bad mood already, and she obviously didn't want to understand what Kathryn had already made an awkward attempt at explaining.

Static and ear-cracking blasts alternated for the next two miles until Regina retreated to her former hunched, sulking position against the door. Kathryn bit her lip against a grin and tried her hand at the radio. She turned the knob slowly, listening to each song or radio announcer's voice until she could determine if she wanted to hear it or not.

Then she heard the opening pulses of Aaron Jeoffrey's *I Go to the Rock.* This station either liked golden oldies or she had caught a signal coming through a time warp. By the second go-through of the chorus, Kathryn was tapping on the steering wheel and singing along under her breath. She ignored Regina's sulks and went into full-voice sing-along when the music shifted to a double-play of Wayne Watson. Again, songs from albums more than twenty years old. Not that she had anything to complain about. If they decided to do a marathon of Petra, Reba Rambo, Dallas Holm, and the Imperials, with a heavy dose of Rich Mullins, she would be in her glory.

Or maybe not. Kathryn felt a throbbing in her temples, and told herself it was an echo of the music and not a warning sign. She couldn't afford to stop and rest. Not now.

The question, however, was if she could afford *not* to rest.

~~~~~

Jeff West rarely went out on his rowboat to fish. It was too much work. He far preferred the myth that perching on his dock with his slouch
~~~~~

hat pulled over his eyes, sprawled in an Adirondack chair that had seen better days, his fishing pole tied to the leg of the chair, was the way to fish. Today, though… he couldn't reason away the ominous sensation that seemed to gather under the overhanging trees around the back of his cabin. He felt like something watched him. He either had to retreat to his cabin or go out on the water. Staying on the dock was too exposed. Maybe it was stubbornness, but he refused to retreat inside. Especially when the sun was so glorious in contrast to yesterday's storms.

The water ran high and the normally lazy current had changed to echo his sentiments about getting away from the cabin. He arranged the cushions in the prow of the boat, checked to make sure his tiny outboard engine was up to pushing him against the heavier current when he wanted to head home, tossed out the totally inadequate anchor to provide drag, and let the current tug him down the center of the river at a lazy crawl.

He dozed and pretended to bait a hook and pay attention to his rod and reel. There was something relaxing about the slight rocking of the boat. Too bad he hadn't brought some cookies, or a book to read. Well, now was as good a time as any to catch up on his prayers.

~~~~~

"I don't suppose you're up to driving?" Kathryn said as the sign for a rest area loomed closer.

"No contacts."

Regina didn't look at her as she responded, her cheek against the window, more like she was talking to the side mirror of the truck. Something made Kathryn think Regina didn't really need glasses for driving. Her answer meant she didn't want to. Maybe she didn't have a license? A moment later, a yawn cracked her jaws. She admitted defeat to the headachy drowsiness that had had her blinking and rubbing her eyes and worrying about swerving off the road for the last ten miles.

Naturally, the moment she turned onto the ramp from the highway to rest area on a higher elevation, her drowsy feelings fled. Kathryn knew better than to believe she had gotten her second wind. Last night's interrupted sleep and the strain of searching in the darkness and wet had caught up with her. If she didn't get at least an hour's nap, they wouldn't get much farther down the highway.

Then an aching sensation washed through the backs of her legs, like the residue from a charley horse or a major cramp. Definitely, she needed to get out of a sitting position and stretch out before things built up into a cascade effect that could paralyze them for the rest of the day. Especially since Regina wouldn't or couldn't drive.

"Why are we stopping?" Regina sat up and looked pale.

"I need to rest my eyes for a little bit. Going cross-eyed isn't good for staying on the road." No need to tell her that her rescuer could eventually
~~~~~

fall to pieces.

"But we need to get entirely out of the state before—" She stopped, eyes wide and suddenly brimming with tears, then pressed her fists against her temples. "My head."

"I get the feeling Dr. West was right about the emotional trauma. You certainly don't want to remember something."

"Why would you say that?" She curled up again in the seat, turning her back partially to Kathryn. "Who would want to go through life not remembering anything?"

"People in pain." Kathryn considered her passenger for a few seconds. Why did she find it increasingly harder to feel sorry for her? She reached out and patted Regina's shoulder. "It's okay. Don't force yourself. I'm going to spread my sleeping bag out and prop my feet up. We're perfectly safe with Bea standing guard. How about I take her outside with me, and you can recline the seat and get some real sleep, relax, enjoy a little privacy for a while, okay?"

"O—okay." Regina nodded and rubbed her eyes with her fists.

Kathryn made sure to take her purse with her keys and phone when she climbed out and held the door open for Bea. She wouldn't put it past Regina to lock her out of the truck and then fall dead asleep and not hear when she tried to get back in.

The rest stop had a hand pump and Kathryn washed her face in the iron-tasting, icy water before spreading out the tarp and her sleeping bag under the shelter of a massive pine. The ground was thickly carpeted with dead needles and smelled faintly spicy. She prayed as she stretched out on her back and smiled, her whole body suddenly aching with exhaustion, as weariness pulled her eyelids closed.

"Remind me to try—" Yawn. "Try the phone," she murmured, feeling Bea stretch out alongside her. She started praying through the list of concerns and suspicions in her mind, but everything disintegrated into dizzy gray swirls when she got to Vincent and his mysterious instructions. That was all she knew for more than two hours.

~~~~~

Somewhere in his drowsy musing about ways he could have made his retreat a little more comfortable, Jeff West caught the sporadic rumble of wheels on wood and steel. He didn't open his eyes. After a while the sound changed, so it grew nearer and then passed overhead. He figured he had finally drifted under the Cutter Street bridge. That put him about two miles down the river from his cabin. Two miles of winding river was only a little over a mile by road. Not that the roads anywhere around Millersburg could claim to be straight for more than one hundred yards at a time. He opened his eyes to check his watch.

The wail of a siren made him jerk upright, so hard the boat rocked
~~~~~

and he grabbed at the sides, half-afraid he would go overboard. The flashing of lights in the corner of his eye had him turning, in time to see the town's one fire truck come tearing down Cutter Street toward the bridge. It crossed to his side of the river and turned right, following the street that haphazardly followed the jogs and curves of the river.

His street.

Jeff held his breath, sending up a silent prayer for whoever needed emergency help right now, and waited for the fire truck to turn left where Water Street made a T intersection with River Road.

It didn't turn.

He scrambled to the other end of the boat and lowered the totally inadequate little outboard into the water, muttering, "Please, please, come on, please," as he pressed the switches and prepped the engine. He barely remembered to pull up his anchor. His hands shook but he grinned like an idiot as the engine caught with the first tug of the pull cord. In five seconds he turned too sharp and headed the boat back under the bridge. If anybody on his street was injured, they would come looking for him pretty soon. Maybe someone was looking for him right this moment.

The breeze picked up as he came out from under the bridge and puttered toward the only major bend in the river. He didn't notice the smell of smoke at first, distracted by his mental checklist of the conditions of his neighbors' homes, the weekend projects someone probably got an early start on this afternoon, and the possible home repair injuries that might be involved. Something bad enough to call out the rescue squad. At least Millersburg had a team of paramedics, even if they didn't have a separate truck for them. Other towns hereabouts had to call for help from neighboring communities or even the county.

Jeff flinched as the stench of smoke seemed to go straight up his nose, making him choke. He blinked and looked around as the prow came around the near-hairpin bend in the river, and saw the distant pillar of smoke arching up out over the water. Someone's house was burning. He twisted the throttle on the outboard for more speed and gritted his teeth when the recalcitrant little engine sputtered and whined and threatened for just a moment to die. The whine turned into a growl and the splashing of water against the prow seemed to rise a little higher. He couldn't tell if he was actually going faster. Why had he let himself drift so far?

Chapter Nine

The fire truck came to a stop, lights still flashing, barely visible in the distance where the trees thinned between the road and the river. The plots of land and the yards around the houses were smaller. He had joked with his neighbors that they settled here for the river, not for lawns to mow and flowers to tend. If the land didn't climb up high enough toward the road to keep a house above the yearly flood levels, the house usually sat on stilts of some kind. No one believed in cellars or basements, and that was fine. Most of his neighbors were either retirees or single, no need to accommodate children at play.

From the right he caught movement and turned to look and jerked the guide rod of the outboard. He had come too close to the other bank, where it jutted out, making the river narrow at this point. Fishermen liked to come to this spot where the land was flat and the water was shallow, where they could wade out nearly halfway across to the opposite bank without going more than knee-deep if they wanted.

"Doc!" A flicker of movement drew his attention back to the right bank, when he needed to concentrate on the left bank and figure out which of his neighbors was in trouble.

Jeff scowled, not quite understanding for a moment as the dark green 4X4 barreled down the slope that wasn't made for vehicles. Who was that idiot leaning out the window, shouting at him?

"Dr. West, stop!" the driver shouted, and his partner leaned out of the window, waving both arms, gesturing to him.

He turned his back on them, and belatedly recognized the two men who claimed to be federal agents when they questioned him behind his office. That sensation of ice down his back returned, and he didn't like it. Hunching his shoulders, he headed for the left side of the river, and nearly hit that chunk of rock that usually rose a good foot above the water. Thanks to all the rain, it was submerged, almost invisible, lying just under the surface, ready to rip the bottom out of a boat.

Shaking, he jerked hard on the outboard and nearly capsized the boat. The little engine sputtered and he had to throttle it back down to keep it alive.

"Dr. West!" Carson ran down to the furthest tip of the fishing flatland and waved his arms hard to stop himself when he nearly ran into the water. "Doctor, you're in danger!"

No joke. Tell me another one. Sighing, he wiped the sudden coating of sweat off his forehead and turned the boat to head over to the middle of the river.

Carson gestured down toward the thickening plume of smoke and the fire truck. With the softer rumble of the outboard no longer filling his ears, Jeff could hear shouts and the faint crackling of flames.

"Your house is on fire," Carson said. "You better come with us."

For two seconds, Jeff considered turning the boat completely around and heading down the river, letting the current push him along. He knew even with the outboard and the current combined, he wouldn't be able to outrun those two men in their 4X4, with their concealed weapons.

What if they weren't here to protect him? What if they set his house on fire? What would they do if he refused to cooperate?

"Okay, Lord, I'm trusting You to get me out of this," Jeff whispered as he turned the boat with shaky hands and headed in toward where Carson waited for him.

~~~~~

By the time sunset splashed scarlet, gold, and purple across the sky to the left of the highway, Kathryn needed to stop for an hour or two, stretch the aches out of her legs, and fill the aching void that used to be her stomach. Regina had munched her way through everything she had brought from the motel, along with the emergency stash of crackers and fruit bars. She also found and downed both bottles of sports drink, grumbling occasionally about the warmth and taste. It was time to refill supplies, any way they could.

Roadside signs for a truck stop emerged from the lengthening shadows. Kathryn grinned as she scanned the listing of services; gas, mini-mart, Laundromat, diner, trailer park. Everything she could want and more. Half a mile later, she pulled onto the off-ramp and up the shallow slope to where the truck stop glowed in the encroaching dusk amid a sea of gravel and dusty ruts.

From the edge of the parking lot she heard the thumping music coming from the one-floor, stucco, flat-roofed diner. She smelled the juicy aroma of hamburgers interwoven with cinnamon-sweet, fresh apple pie. This was no greasy spoon, despite the slightly grimy outer shell. Kathryn glanced at Regina as she drove up to the gas pumps. She grinned when her companion sat up straight and sniffed the air and lost some of her sulky, drooping look.

Regina kept quiet and pout-free while Kathryn filled the gas tank, checked the oil and the air pressure in her tires, and washed a layer of bugs from her windshield. She followed along behind Kathryn through the little mini-mart. If she didn't offer to help carry the shopping basket, Kathryn consoled herself that at least Regina didn't make demands of
~~~~~

what to buy. She stocked up on healthy snack foods; cereal bars, fruit bars, crackers, plastic jugs of fruit juice and even a bag of decently priced apples. Kathryn bought a bag of chunk ice and dumped it immediately into the mini-cooler in the back compartment. It crowded Bea, but they could now drive longer without stopping for meals.

Her last purchase was two high-grade cans of dog food, which she immediately opened onto the giant Frisbee she kept under her seat for that purpose. Bea devoured it, curled up in the bed of the truck. Kathryn filled her two-gallon blue bucket with water from the nearby trailer park service area and brought it back for her. Leaving Bea loose, no leash or chain to hold her to the truck, was probably against the rules of the truck stop. Bea wouldn't run away, and if anyone attacked or harassed or tried to steal her, Kathryn wanted her companion able to get away or defend herself. She had seen too many times where an animal kept chained up had been killed by that very chain, used by the attacking human to trip up or choke or beat the animal. Bea would stay in the truck or perch on the hood until she came for her.

"It's about time," Regina muttered, when Kathryn gave Bea one final pat and left her to finish her meal.

Kathryn kept her mouth shut. She also lengthened her stride as she crossed the gravel parking lot to the diner, so Regina had to scurry to keep up with her. There were over twenty vehicles, mostly trucks and Jeeps, parked in the lot. Too many witnesses for Regina to make a scene. Kathryn was fairly sure her companion knew that.

When they stepped through the tinted glass door into the diner, Kathryn thought they had walked through a time warp. The place could have been snatched straight out of the fifties. Pink tiled floor. Maroon vinyl booths along the walls. A gigantic jukebox against the far wall between the bathroom doors. Music selection boxes in each booth. Pictures of Elvis and Buddy Holly over the cash register. The music that thumped through the air made her think of *Happy Days*, though she could hardly make out the words. The dishes on the tables were the heavy white, institutional kind, made for lots of abuse and to last through three lifetimes. The waitresses wore pink uniform shirts and pants, covered with long, white bib aprons. All they lacked were the bouffant hairdos for a true time warp.

Nine-tenths of the customers were men. Kathryn realized that after only two seconds of observation. She nearly grabbed Regina's arm to drag her back outside. On the off chance someone came in looking specifically for them, it wouldn't be hard to find them among all the men. This was Friday night, so where were the dating couples? Too early in the evening for them to come in?

"Hi there." A graying, gum-snapping waitress stepped from behind the cash register. She grinned and snatched up two plastic-coated menu boards and gestured for them to follow her. No inquiry as to smoking or non-smoking preferences.

Kathryn didn't mind that a moment later, when she saw the booth the waitress chose for them. It sat behind a half-wall, directly across from the doors for the bathrooms, with the doorless phone booth opposite them. When they were seated, no one would be able to see them because the wall rose more than a foot higher than the seat backs. The proximity of the jukebox meant lots of traffic going past the booth at all times, providing camouflage and distraction. Kathryn could look out from the booth at the people coming in the door, but no one could see her without some effort.

"Paranoid," she muttered, then grinned at the waitress and nodded her thanks.

Regina studied the menu with an avid glint in her eyes that would have made someone think she hadn't eaten in days. Kathryn sat back on her side of the booth and really studied her companion. Regina wasn't model slim, but she wasn't the bulky pudge her constant eating throughout the afternoon should have made her. That meant she was either one of those people who binged and then worked it off with rowing and stepping machines, or she was one of those disgusting people with a hyperactive metabolism, who could eat anything and everything and never gained an ounce.

One more reason to get rid of her as soon as possible. Kathryn smothered a giggle with the back of her hand and ducked her head behind her menu. Regina never noticed.

~~~~~

In the parking lot, a dark green 4X4, speckled with smashed bugs on the grill and windshield, still spattered with long streaks of dried, flaking mud, drove slowly up and down the rows of trucks and Jeeps. The shadows grew longer across the parking lot as the 4X4 made its inspection tour, until shadows merged with nightfall. After that, a heavy-duty flashlight in the hand of the passenger illuminated each truck. Every blue truck was treated to a further inspection of the license plate and the interior.

At the far end of the lot, next to a partially dried mud puddle in the gravel, Bea sat up and looked over the gate at the back of Kathryn's truck. Her ears twitched from time to time, tracking the progress of the 4X4 as it drew closer. Otherwise, she was a dark, granite-colored statue in the gentle breeze flowing through the parking lot.

Porter drove past four trucks and a fifties-style convertible and started to turn before Carson aimed the flashlight on Kathryn's truck.

"Hold it," Carson said, his voice rising a little. The truck's tires slid a
~~~~~

few inches in the gravel when it braked.

Bea held still, unblinking as the flashlight beam of light slid down to the license plate.

The passenger door opened and Carson got out, his boots crunching on the gravel. The flashlight beam went up, almost glancing over Bea to illuminate along the side of the truck and into the side window to the cab. Then the beam angled back down, directly into the Akita's eyes. They flared red in the bright light for half a second.

Carson froze, one foot two inches off the ground, caught in the act of taking another step. His free hand hovered above the side of the truck, about to rest on the gate, less than a foot from Bea's muzzle.

"Hey, Tom?" he said, voice slightly strained.

"Yeah?" Porter said. "What's up?"

"What kind of dog you think this is?"

"Dog?" The driver's side door opened and Porter stepped around the front of the 4X4. His mouth dropped open, breaking up the dark bristle of a three-day growth of beard. "Nobody said anything about a dog."

"I know. What kind of dog you think this is?" Carson repeated.

"The big, dangerous, protective kind." The other man muttered a curse and stepped backward to climb back into the vehicle.

"I think so too." He flashed a lopsided grin at Bea and retreated slowly.

"You'd better not say it," Porter said, as his partner climbed back into the truck.

"Say what?" Carson grinned and turned off the flashlight. He locked the door and studied Bea, who hadn't moved a muscle other than to blink.

"That you told me so."

"Advice is to just follow them, make sure nobody else is following them, and wait for orders from higher up before we make contact." He continued watching Bea. "Get the feeling, whoever's helping her, they aren't helpless?"

"You're a real comedian, Andy," Porter grumbled. "Only one question now."

"Who distracts the dog and who gets to put a tracker on the truck before the other guy gets bit?"

"Got it in one."

"Of course, there's the off chance we've got the wrong truck," Carson offered, his gaze focused on Bea.

"You're the one who got the license plate and saw Regina in the passenger seat."

"Well... dog-zilla has already seen me, probably got my scent. Guess it's my job to play decoy."

Porter allowed a half-smile, put the truck back into gear, and drove around to the far side of the parking lot. It was a matter of moments for him to get out and start the long trudge around the perimeter of the lot, around puddles and unsteady footing on gravel that tried to sink into mud with every third step. Carson got into the driver's seat and came back to park across the back of two trucks, three spaces down from where Kathryn's truck sat. He got out, taking no care to be quiet, and let the door slam. Bea's head turned to follow his progress as he approached the truck, but stayed on the other side of the lane.

"Hey, buddy, how's it going? They trust you to stay here all by your lonesome? Don't see a chain on that collar you're wearing. Wouldn't be very nice of me to report your owner for violating animal control..." Carson trailed off when Bea's ears pricked up and she got up on her feet, to press against the tailgate and point her nose at him, sniffing loudly. "Hurry it up, would you? He's not tied down."

After a few seconds, when Porter didn't respond and he didn't hear any footsteps, he reached into his jacket pocket.

"You hungry? Anybody feed you yet? Or are they making you stand guard while they're inside feeding their faces?" He pulled out a beef stick and tore the thick plastic packaging open. "Want some? Yeah, like I really want to get my hand within a thousand feet of those teeth."

His hand trembled for a moment as he tore the stick in half and laid one half on his open palm. Carson concentrated on Bea, mesmerized by her eyes. He knew better than to look for Porter and provide the big dog a clue that something was going on behind her back.

"You want it?" He grinned as Bea's ears twitched and she stretched her head out further toward him. "Smells good, huh? Is it better to keep you in the truck, or get you to leave it? Easier for you to chase me, once you're down on the ground." He stretched out his hand as far as he could reach, and stopped four feet away from the truck.

Bea tipped her head to one side and regarded him for several seconds, then abruptly sat down. The truck creaked a little in reaction to the movement.

"Aren't you hungry? Come on, buddy, it tastes great." Carson took a step closer. Bea's ears twitched again, but she looked away, toward the truck stop. He turned to look, half-convinced the owner of the truck and the dog was coming back. No one moved, no sounds, no more vehicles coming into the half-full lot. "Huh. Something wrong with a dog that doesn't want a treat."

"Dog's got good taste is all," Porter said, coming out from between two trucks six spaces further down the row. "That stuff can't be good for you."

"Done?"

"Two, far enough apart, if one is found we've got a chance of the other staying in place." Porter stepped around the 4X4 and climbed into the driver's seat. He waited, watching Bea, until Carson backed up and resumed the passenger seat. "Hungry?"

"Only way we'll get close enough to spot them and make sure we got the right truck."

"I hate it when you get that smug tone in your voice." A few seconds later, Porter let loose a chuckle. He stepped on the gas and drove around to the far side of the parking lot, choosing a space kitty-corner from Kathryn's truck.

~~~~~

Regina wanted the works; chili cheese fries; double burger with cheese, pickles, lettuce and tomato, mustard and mayonnaise; chocolate milk; corn on the cob and baked beans; large caramel sundae. Kathryn thought about how all that food would make her sleepy, if she could even get it all into her stomach. If her companion was drowsy and silent during the remainder of their ride, Kathryn decided the price of their meal wouldn't be too high.

Maybe we should just keep going until we get to Finn, Kathryn mused.

A moment later, she pushed that tempting thought aside. She needed rest. Her nap that afternoon had only bought her a little time. Perhaps an even bigger motivation to hole up for the night: if she demanded too much from Regina, the spoiled brat might transform into a full-fledged screaming witch. After that warning from Dr. West, Kathryn didn't want to attract any more attention than necessary.

"Where are the bathrooms?" Regina said, finally turning from her desultory study of the music selection box in their booth.

Kathryn jerked her thumb over her shoulder toward the bathroom doors and bit back a question about her companion's blindness. She sat with her back to the bathrooms, jukebox, and phone so she could watch the door. How could Regina not see what was in front of her?

You're teaching me patience and kindness again, huh, Lord? Now isn't a good time.

~~~~~

In the bathroom, Regina took her time washing her hands. Her gaze traveled over her reflection in the plate glass mirror.

The bathroom was empty but for her. The two empty stalls had creaky doors of Pepto-pink painted plywood on brass hinges shaped like flowers. The tile floor was a darker pink. The air hung heavy with cherry disinfectant. The single sink was a heavy-duty white bowl on a skinny pedestal, fitted with shiny, heavy brass faucet and knobs, sitting under a wide window with grimy hinges at the top. The sill was clean but the frame looked like it had never been touched, much less opened.

Regina wiped at her eyes with the dry backs of her hands, brushing away tears brought on by the sight of her bruises. Gingerly, she lifted the baseball cap. A sigh escaped her at the condition of her hair, matted to her scalp. She squeezed her eyes tight shut, stopping more tears. When she opened them again, she leaned forward and brushed one finger over the bandage across her forehead.

"What do you think you're doing?" a man said in her memory. It was a thin, hard voice, cracking with age. *"Do I have to take you by the hand and show you how to do everything, even after all this time?"*

Regina stared as the room dissolved into memory around her. For five long, painful, breathless seconds she stood in a laboratory. An old man towered over her, eyes bright with angry fire, his mouth a thin line of disgust.

Her father. It hurt to recognize him as her father. She felt sick with remembered embarrassment and self-disgust and a desperate longing to run and hide. Somewhere. Anywhere.

She wore a long, too-big lab coat over her simple, blue sleeveless dress. Her father never let her wear pants until she was out of college. Never jeans in the lab, always suit pants. Appearances were everything.

Her hair, she remembered, was short. Cut just above her collar. Her father had scolded and fumed about that impulsive move for weeks. Young ladies, he always maintained, wore their hair long. Hoydens and whores and perverts cut their hair short and tried to look like boys.

On the counter at her elbow lay a tumbled mess of test tubes and chemical containers and a tangle of flexible tubing and stands and beakers lying on their sides, spilling their multi-colored liquid and powder contents.

She had been setting up a distilling apparatus. Her father had come in and snarled that she was doing it wrong. Startled, she had jumped, knocked over a foot-tall tube and everything else had gone over like dominoes.

Chapter Ten

"You're supposed to be a genius — why don't you act like one?" His voice echoed sharply through Regina's memory. *"I don't know why I waste my time with you. I don't know what possessed me to take you on as my assistant."*

"Neither do I," she told her reflection. She blinked quickly against the pressure and burning of more tears. "You're dead, old man," she said, voice dropping to a whisper. The idea of him being dead made a hollow space in her mind. "You can't hurt me anymore. Nothing can hurt me. I'm getting away. Far away."

Regina glanced over her shoulder at the door leading into the diner. Kathryn would come looking for her in another moment if she didn't hurry. Kathryn had promised she would see her through to the end of this and take her to someone who could help her. Regina didn't know why she trusted this young woman who appeared out of nowhere and gave help without demanding payment in advance. No one did anything without some kind of profit coming back to them, so what was Kathryn's angle?

"You're useless," her father said in her memory.

"Just shut up," she snapped, and turned to reach for the doorknob.

The cacophony of the diner hit her in the face like a slap as she stepped out of the bathroom. Regina paused a moment to regain her bearings. She saw the waitress come through the gap in the front counter, her arms loaded with plates. How did the woman carry so much and keep it balanced? She counted six platters, loaded with burgers and fries, ribs and fried chicken and cups with side dishes.

Regina's stomach pinched. She stayed still, staring at the waitress, willing her to bring at least two of those loaded plates to the booth where Kathryn waited with her back to the bathrooms, facing the diner crowd. The waitress stopped at the first booth in the row and slid four platters in front of four chunky, weary-looking truckers all dressed in coveralls and matching ball caps. Then the woman walked to her booth. Regina smiled as the waitress put platters down on the table where Kathryn sat.

Her attention wandered to the other occupants of the diner for a moment. Regina breathed shallowly, imagining the air smelled of truck exhaust, grease, grime, and sweat. Why were all truckers fat and bearded, with greasy foreheads and bloodshot eyes? Why did they all have to wear jeans and sweatshirts under flannel shirts, and those oil-stained boots?

Except those two men at the counter. Regina studied them as she took a step toward the booth. The two men at the counter looked like hunters with their sturdy clothes and hiking boots, all flannel shirts and khaki.

One turned in response to something the other said and she saw his face clearly.

Regina froze with her hand reaching for the edge of the booth. For two eternal seconds, she was in a dark room with a thunderstorm raging outside, crouched in a corner, listening to gunfire and herself shrieking. Everything was dark. The power had died in the storm, or it had been cut, or someone had turned it off.

Then the door had slammed open, rebounding against the wall. The man at the counter, who smiled now at something his companion said, had burst through the door. For a fraction of a second, he had been illuminated by a streak of lightning and she saw his features in full detail. Carson, someone had called him.

Shaking, unable to breathe, Regina slid into the booth. She swallowed hard and fought to stay in her seat. Kathryn just sat there with her hands over her eyes, hunched over her plate like someone was going to snatch it from under her nose. Anger warred with the breathless, paralyzed feeling.

~~~~

Kathryn schooled her expression into neutral as she raised her head. Typical for Regina, she had returned to the table in time to interrupt her dinner prayer. She was conscious of the irony of her irritation welling up on the heels of praying for some help in handling her companion.

Then Kathryn saw Regina's extraordinary pallor, her wide-eyed stare, and her silence. She waited a few seconds, just to be sure.

"Something wrong?" she asked, just loud enough to be heard through the roaring laughter in the next booth.

"We have to get out of here."

Kathryn waited. There had to be more to the story. Besides, the aroma of her sandwich nailed her to the booth. She wasn't going to abandon hot food without good reason.

"Two men at the counter—by the door," Regina finally said, after a visible struggle to catch her breath. "I... remember them. I don't know where or what, but it—They had guns."

"Okay." Kathryn knew better than to lean out of the booth and stare at the occupants of the counter. She cast sidelong glances through the flow of people moving to and from jukebox and bathrooms and their booths.

Two men with their elbows on the counter. Husky build. Dark-haired. Both laughing with the waitress who took their orders. Jackets lying on the empty stools on either side of them. No bulges in their shirts to indicate guns. Unless the guns were hidden in their coats?

"They didn't see you?" she asked after a barely discernable pause.

"You think I'd be sitting here if they had?" Regina squeaked. "What
~~~~

are we going to do? I thought you said we were safe."

"We are until you make a scene." Kathryn congratulated herself on not snapping.

"Make a scene?" Her face started to change from terrified pale to furious crimson. Regina leaned back and took a deep breath.

"You've been griping all afternoon," she said, and put her hand down hard on Regina's hand still lying on the table. That made her companion pause. "Why don't you shut up and give me a chance to think, all right?" she asked in a level, reasonable voice. She even managed a flat little smile.

Regina nodded and pulled her hands back, resting them in her lap. She sat perfectly still and watched Kathryn, who leaned a little sideways in the booth to get a better view of the two men at the counter. The traffic past the booth and the higher sides of their seats made a perfect hiding place, as Kathryn had hoped. It also made studying the men difficult.

Chances were good these were one of the two sets of supposed government agents Dr. West had encountered. Or maybe they were back-ups, situated along the road to watch for Regina.

When the enemy sat by the only exit, Kathryn had found that climbing out windows was an acceptable solution. Nobody climbed out windows nowadays. The movies and television taught people to be aggressive and fight when a hasty, hidden retreat was the intelligent move, less time-consuming, costly, and painful.

Kathryn knew she could handle the bathroom window. She had checked it out before sitting down to order. But could Regina? If they needed extra time to maneuver her out the window, the chances of getting caught increased. Besides, the scent of the cherry air freshener had started a throbbing behind Kathryn's eyes. She did not want to go back in there, but what choice did they have?

Problem: Leaving with their plates full *might* attract attention and somebody *might* say something those two hunters at the counter *might* overhear. Besides, she was starving, and she wasn't about to leave without either eating this food or paying for it. She had learned the hard way, long ago, the ends never justified the means.

Lord, You know what I need before I ask, she prayed silently. Kathryn glanced at Regina, who had gone back to terrified, pale, and silent. *We need help. Help me trust You while we wait for the answer.*

Taking a deep breath, she gave Regina a smile and picked up her sandwich. Her companion stared at her through two bites.

"What are we going to do?" she snarl-whined.

"We're going to eat supper." Kathryn took another bite to muffle the smart-alecky remark she was tempted to make.

"But—"

"Look," she said through her mouthful. She swallowed quickly.

"They'd be looking all around the diner if they thought you were here. They're concentrating on their dinner. I think they just stopped to eat, like us. Coincidence. An accident."

"Yeah, and when they shoot us that'll be an accident, too."

"You need energy to heal and I'm not wasting a hot meal. The last thing we want to do is attract attention, right?"

"I guess." Regina's hands strayed to her plate. Kathryn almost smiled at that, convinced the smell of the hot food and hunger made her reasonable faster than anything she could say to her.

"If we leave without eating or paying, that'll get attention, right?" She waited until Regina nodded. "Trust me. Something'll happen."

"That's what I'm afraid of," her companion muttered, just before she took a big bite of her hamburger.

Kathryn smothered a chuckle. "Trust me. I'm the expert here, remember?" She took another bite, then reached for her drink.

Regina's eyes half-lidded in temporary contentment as she chewed and swallowed. Kathryn could have sworn she saw a slight curve of a smile on those usually pouty lips.

What do you know? This might not be so bad after all.

~~~~~

In the parking lot, a rumbling, low-slung motorcycle cruised down the lanes, searching for a parking spot. The driver was a dark figure in a black leather jacket, jeans, studded boots and dark blue helmet, barely concealing the wide shoulders and long, narrow legs and hips of a natural athlete. The bike slid down the rows of trucks to the end and stopped gently in front of Kathryn's truck. The engine died. The driver slid his helmet off, revealing iron black curls and short beard and sapphire eyes. He grinned at the dog half-asleep in the bed of the truck and let out a piercing whistle; three short blasts, one two steps up and long, then one more two steps down. Then he leaped off his bike and ran toward the dog.

Bea leaped over the tailgate and down from the truck. She met the biker halfway, knocking the man to the ground. They skidded a few inches. The driver wrapped his arms around Bea's middle and laughed.

~~~~~

Kathryn was halfway through her salad and toying with the idea of ordering ice cream. She couldn't decide if she really wanted ice cream, if she wanted to irritate Regina, or she was just playing for time. She caught movement at the door of the diner. She tilted her head to the side to see past an elderly couple dressed in pink and turquoise square dancing outfits. The man coming through the door looked around the diner as he unzipped his hip-length, black leather jacket. He paused at the cash register, putting the two men who frightened Regina between him and Kathryn's booth.

Her heart went into triple speed for a few seconds and Kathryn grinned. Every time she saw an answer to a particularly urgent prayer, she still felt that breathless, ready-to-fly feeling.

I don't care what Michael is doing in this part of the country, God. Thanks.

Then the square dancers finished paying their bill and left and the aisle down that side of the diner was miraculously clear. Michael looked straight at her. He grinned and he took a step to go around the counter. Kathryn held up her hand, stopping him. She pressed one finger to her lips and sat back in the booth. Michael nodded understanding and settled down in the only vacant stool at the counter, one away from the two supposed government agents.

"Okay." Kathryn turned to Regina, who was scraping the little ceramic cup to get the last of the sauce from her baked beans. "I think I know what to do now. Did you see that window over the sink when you used the bathroom?"

"But it's so high. I'd break my neck climbing down on the other side."

"I know. I thought of that. Just trust me. We got this far, didn't we?"

"Wherever here is."

Kathryn grinned crookedly and told herself to be grateful Regina didn't whine and pout when she voiced her worries. They were making progress. She simply had to make sure Regina had a full stomach at all times, to put her into a good mood and make her easier to handle.

She tugged the placemat from under her plate, checked it for spill marks, then turned it over. A few seconds of rummaging unearthed a pen from the front pocket of her backpack. Kathryn scribbled a hasty message on the backside of the placemat, then looked for Michael. They made eye contact, she tapped the placemat, he nodded, then looked away again. Kathryn quickly folded the placemat into a paper boat.

"Okay, into the bathroom," she said and stood, picking up her backpack. She glanced over her shoulder in time to see Michael look in her direction again. He nodded and winked.

Regina followed without asking any questions. A creeping sensation went up Kathryn's back as she slipped through the bathroom door. Was that what it felt like to have somebody watching, maybe with a gun pointed at her? She hoped not. She hoped it was just nerves. She glanced back as the door slowly swung closed and caught a glimpse of Michael snatching the paper boat off the table. He shoved it into his pocket and continued toward the jukebox.

Kathryn took a few seconds to study the situation from solid ground before she climbed up onto the pedestal sink. She hoped those creaking noises came from somewhere else in the diner, and not from the pedestal as it prepared to snap under her weight. She breathed through her mouth and imagined she could taste the synthetic ingredients in the cherry air freshener. It was a worthwhile trade-off, she decided, when her headache from the smell didn't return with full force, jabbing spikes into her eyes. She braced her feet on either side of the sink and got to work on the window latch.

Through the walls, the opening bars of a Charlie Daniels song pounded and wailed. Kathryn paused and grinned. Leave it to Michael to find his favorite song in a diner in the middle of unfamiliar territory.

"Okay, let's get the show on the road," she muttered, and pulled up hard on the window latch.

It didn't want to move. Kathryn banged up on it with the heel of her hand. Still no progress. She pressed her hands on the window frame, putting as much of her weight into it as she could without losing her balance. Something creaked and groaned deep inside the frame. The metal felt almost slick, soft with layers of paint. Kathryn wondered how long it had been since anyone opened the window. She would have long ago, if she had to put up with that cloying cherry thickening the air every day.

The smell caught in her throat and started a sick throbbing at the back of her head. She ignored it to focus on the task at hand.

I am not getting sick now, of all times. Please, Lord? As long as it doesn't turn into sparks in my eyes, I'll be just fine.

Another yank upward on the latch, hard enough to bruise her fingers. It moved. Kathryn pounded twice on each corner, hard enough to make the glass rattle. She coughed and blinked furiously to clear her eyes when the pounding jarred loose the dust and accumulated grime of months, maybe years. It was almost amusing that the rest of the bathroom was so gleaming spotless, and this one window was a haven for crud.

The third corner yielded to her fist. The fourth corner gave, opening a quarter inch. Kathryn pressed hard on the latch and the window finally swung open with a loud creak and bang. For five heartbeats she stood still, half-expecting someone to come racing into the bathroom, demanding to know what all the noise was for.

The raucous strains of Michael's song still thudded through the walls. Kathryn grinned and figured no one would be able to hear much of anything for a little while after that song ended. She turned around and carefully jumped down from the sink.

"Okay, up you go," she said, gesturing for Regina to climb up in her place.

"But—" Regina looked at the sink, then at Kathryn, then back at the sink. She lifted one foot a few inches, then put it down again.

Kathryn swallowed a surge of frustration. How could Regina give up already? She wasn't fat. There had to be enough physical coordination in her body, if not athletic skill, to let her climb up onto the sink and heave herself over the windowsill. There had to be, or they might as well spend the rest of the evening in the bathroom.

Then Kathryn saw the realization of their situation and their options finally coming clear in Regina's eyes. Dignity went out the window. She bit her lip and braced her hands on the edge of the sink. Kathryn bent, making her interlaced fingers into a cradle to give Regina a leg up. In moments, the blond stood awkwardly on the edge of the sink and her frown of doubt eased, meaning she saw what Kathryn had seen before she jumped down: two dumpsters with peeling blue paint and rust spots poised under the bathroom window; a nearly deserted gravel parking lot worn down to half mud, a few puddles close to the bathroom windows, and the L-shaped back side of the building.

Hopefully by this time, she saw Michael sauntering around the corner, ready to help her climb down, as directed in the paper boat note.

Michael had to be there, Kathryn decided. Regina stared at something with that hesitant look on her face again; eyes wide, mouth slightly open.

"Hey, it's all right," Michael said, a touch of laughter in his rich tenor voice. His hands appeared from the bottom edge of the window. "I'm part of the Calvary."

Kathryn almost told him not to waste his time. Regina would only be confused and offended by their secret language with all its double and hidden meanings.

"Don't you mean Cavalry?" Regina blurted.

"Whatever."

"Are you sightseeing or something?" Kathryn said. She glanced over her shoulder. Someone could burst through that door at any moment.

"Better get you out of there." Michael's boots scuffled loudly in the gravel, sounding like he moved closer.

"Okay, let's go." She wedged herself between the sink and the wall and reached up to brace and support Regina.

She nodded and feebly hoisted herself up onto the windowsill. Kathryn pushed on her knees, then her feet. Michael grabbed her hands and supported her weight as she slid out of the window.

They overbalanced and fell. Regina let out a breathless little yelp but made no other sound. Kathryn climbed up and looked out, to find them sitting in the gravel only a few inches from the deepest puddle.

"You okay?" she asked, more toward Michael than Regina. He had to be prodded to tell people he had bullets in his gut, while Regina seemed prone to complain about hangnails.

Michael nodded and grinned and clambered to his feet. Regina let him pull her upright.

"Let's see you climb down, now," Regina said.

"Why should I?" Kathryn tried to flatten her grin, and knew she failed miserably. The back of her head throbbed and her knees suddenly ached, as if in rebuke for her attitude. "They're not looking for me."

She tugged the window closed before Regina could retort. In five seconds flat, she was down and sliding through the bathroom door.

At their booth, she wrapped up the remains of their food in the big, thick paper napkins the diner used. The warm, slightly damp packages went into the second outside pouch of her backpack. Kathryn gave Regina's half-eaten sundae a mournful look, then pulled out her wallet and slung her backpack over her shoulder. Half the food in her backpack was Regina's dinner. She wondered what it meant when people ate their dessert halfway through their meal. That reflection prompted Kathryn to give a generous tip to their waitress, to make up for their quick exit.

Neither of the men sitting by the cash register looked up as Kathryn approached. They were totally engrossed in a road map spread on the counter between their plates. She resisted the temptation to look and try to figure out which highway system they were studying. If she could discern where they were going to look next, then she could take a different route.

"Something wrong, honey?" the waitress who tended the register asked. She was the oldest of the women working the diner; stick thin under her faded pink uniform, with silver roots in her strawberry blond hair. She cracked her gum and grinned hopefully.

The two men looked up and looked Kathryn over, head to foot, twice. She caught their glances from the corner of her eye and fought not to react. Let them think she didn't notice them. As quickly as they looked her over, they looked away. She thought a silent prayer of thanks she hadn't been born blond.

"Everything's great. We plowed through dinner like we hadn't eaten in days." Kathryn felt the gazes of both men turned full force on her again. "Could I have our check?"

Chapter Eleven

"Sure. Just a sec." The woman turned away and flagged down the waitress who had served Kathryn and Regina. In moments she had the totals rung up on the register. "How'd you like everything?" she asked as she pounded on the keys.

"Perfect." Kathryn rubbed her stomach and groaned, as if she had eaten too much. That prompted a chuckle from the woman.

"You ate awful fast."

"Yeah, well, I'm on a tight schedule. If I don't get home by noon tomorrow, my mother will have the state police out looking for me."

"She sounds just like my mother."

Kathryn laughed with the woman. She still had a mother? That created an odd picture in her mind.

"Where's your friend?" the waitress asked as she handed Kathryn her change.

"Bathroom." Kathryn glanced toward the bathroom, hoping it looked natural. She took a good, measuring look at the two men sitting at the counter. One continued studying her, the other turned to look at the bathroom door.

"Is she okay? She looked kind of done in, when the two of you got here."

"She's been kind of sick."

"Does she need help?" The waitress glanced toward the bathroom, concern creasing her face.

"Not that kind of help. From the way she ate, she's definitely recovered. She's just washing up. She'll be out in a minute or two. When she comes out, tell her I'm pulling the car around, would you?"

"Sure, honey. You two take care. Highway can be pretty dangerous once it gets dark."

"Thanks, we will." Kathryn nodded good-bye and headed for the door.

~~~~~

Carson and Porter exchanged significant looks. They had been partners long enough, there were times they didn't need to speak to know what the other was thinking.

Porter waited until the door had closed behind Kathryn and she had vanished from sight in the long diner window. He looked back toward the
~~~~~

bathroom door and nodded.

"Bingo," he said softly.

"We're only supposed to watch them. Don't scare them," Carson warned.

"Don't scare them? What about us? What about that dog sitting on her truck?"

Carson shook his head, grinning, and punched his partner in the shoulder.

~~~~~

In the parking lot, far from the sparse lights, Regina watched Michael wrestle with Bea. He had his arm around the dog's thick neck. Kathryn trotted up to the little scene and paused a second. She didn't know whether to join the tussle or just wrap her arms around Michael in thanksgiving.

"About time you got here," Michael said. He shoved Bea away and stood, opening his arms wide. Kathryn laughed and hugged him, hard.

"Perfect timing, like always. I thought you were still in Alaska, scoping out that training camp for your boss. You didn't get a call from Vincent, or somebody had a vision or something, did they?"

"Nope. Finished up last week and decided to take a little vacation on the way home."

"You're about 600 miles east and south of home base. What'd you do, take the wrong highway home?"

"Vacation." He winked. "No dreams, no voices from on high or burning bushes. Just wandering, clearing my head. Didn't know anything was coming down until I saw your truck and the monster there. Dumb luck, I guess."

"Yeah, right. And the sky will be green tomorrow."

"Always wanted to be Irish," he returned with a nauseatingly fake brogue.

"Whatever the blame, thanks." She stepped back and glanced at Regina. The blond watched them with confusion wrinkling her face.

Michael shrugged, eyes sparkling with mischief. "Any news to spread? Data to dig?"

"How about the name of the nearest hotel?" Kathryn decided in that moment, if those two men were going to keep hunting, she was smart to go to ground for the night. Better to head off an imminent spell before it attacked her. A hot shower, clean clothes, a comfortable bed and eight solid hours of sleep made the best prescription yet.

A good night's sleep might help Regina, too.

"Boring."

"Some of us are mere mortals. We need our sleep." She jabbed Michael in the ribs. He doubled over with a false *woof* of lost breath.
~~~~~

"Okay, okay, I give up. Three exits from here is the only hotel worth mentioning. Everything between here and there isn't even good enough for the roaches."

"Can you wait until then, Regina?"

"I think so," the blond said. Her voice sounded faint. In the shadows, it was hard to really see details, but she did look more pale than usual.

"Maybe seeing those men stirred some memories." Kathryn winced at a throb of guilt. Regina was still recovering from her injuries. Of course she was going to be cranky and self-absorbed.

"Maybe," she said, nodding slowly. "I don't like what I'm remembering."

Her eyes glazed momentarily. She wrapped her arms around herself, shivering, and staggered sideways a step. Michael and Kathryn sprang to her side to support her.

"Regina?" Kathryn whispered. She slid an arm around her shoulders.

"He got shot," Regina said in halting words. "There's all this blood, and I can hear the gunshot echoing forever and... I'm holding a gun. But I can't shoot!"

"It's okay." She wrapped both arms around Regina and held her until the shivers stopped. She met Michael's gaze over Regina's shoulder.

"My head—"

"It's been a long day. Dr. West gave me some pills for you. They'll help you sleep. The sooner you get to bed, the better."

For both of us, she added silently.

~~~~~

Porter nudged Carson and gestured for his partner to look at the woman running the cash register. She frowned, staring down the aisle past six booths to the jukebox and bathroom doors. Two gangly girls in strategically ripped jeans and halter tops leaned over the jukebox, but they didn't look like they were causing trouble, other than attracting the attention of nearly every man in the place.

"Something wrong?" Porter asked the woman.

"That girl has been in there more than twenty minutes now." She lifted her wrist, displaying her black sports watch for emphasis. "You know, I thought there was something wrong when those two came in."

"How do you mean—wrong?" Carson asked, voice soft.

"She looked like somebody's been using her for a punching bag. I know the signs, no matter how well they covered it up. I wonder if her friend is helping her get away from somebody."

"Could be," Porter said, tone neutral. He and Carson traded glances.

"Maybe you should go check on her," Carson prompted after a few seconds of silence.

The muted sounds of people talking, laughing and eating barely
~~~~~

filtered up from the back of the now two-thirds empty diner.

"Maybe I should." The woman studied the bathroom door a few moments more, then nodded and scurried out from behind the cash register. On her way, she gestured for another waitress to tend the register.

"Let's get going," Carson said. "I have a bad feeling about—" He stopped when the replacement waitress jiggled up to the register and grinned vacantly at them. "Check please."

"Something wrong?" She took the wilted green order slip and started ringing up their bill.

"No, everything's fine," Porter said. "We just have a tight schedule, that's all."

The first waitress scurried back out of the bathroom. From her puzzled frown, neither man had to guess what she would say.

"Now that's the oddest thing," she said, stepping into her place at the register. The younger waitress moved aside in an obviously well-practiced maneuver. "I know her friend said she was in the bathroom, and I know nobody has come out yet, but there's nobody in there. And that window has been painted over a half-dozen times, so it isn't like she could have just pushed it open and climbed out."

"Wouldn't be too sure about that," Carson muttered. He and Porter exchanged crooked, exasperated grins.

Porter hurried outside while Carson finished paying the bill. He hurried, jamming his change into his pocket and losing two quarters and four pennies along the way. He slammed his shoulder into the heavy door as he went out and felt nothing.

When he joined his partner in the parking lot, Porter stood in the middle of the empty spot where the blue pickup with the big dog in the back used to sit.

"Are you sure we should only watch them?" Porter asked, an almost plaintive note in his voice.

"How did they know?" Carson muttered.

"Obviously, somebody's helping them." He ducked when his partner glared at him and clenched his fists. Carson didn't hit him, only clenched and unclenched his fists a few times and stared at the tire marks in the mud and gravel.

"Okay," he mused aloud, "they think they've lost us. Regina is hurt. They have to stop to rest."

"Whoever's helping Regina, she's good. Maybe a pro. Do you know anything about her?"

"Not *yet.*" Carson stepped back, his gaze on the motorcycle tire marks next to the truck tire marks, and a place where something big had scuffled in the dirt. He shook his head, imagining that big, furry dog attacking someone. Wouldn't they have heard the ruckus, even inside the diner with that loud music blasting? "Come on." He stalked off toward their truck. Porter had to run to catch up.

~~~~~

"Does that happen all the time?" Regina said through a mouthful of cold fries.

The backpack and its cooling contents sat on the seat between them. Kathryn and Regina reached into the napkin-wrapped bundles and ate whatever they picked up. Bea sat in the back, her head between the seats, eyeing the food.

"What?" Kathryn took her gaze off the road long enough to reach into the napkin holding the last of her sandwich. Fortunately, eating helped calm the slightly seasick feeling the cherry air freshener had given her.

She grinned at the red and white blurs of light from Michael's motorcycle in the darkness far ahead. The lights wove back and forth across both lanes of the nearly deserted highway, then whipped to the right and down the exit ramp at the last possible moment. She tugged and pushed on her headlights bar, dimming, then brightening in her own farewell signal.

"Miracles appearing out of nowhere," Regina said after swallowing.

"Sometimes just waking up in the morning is a miracle." She didn't have to look to see her companion glaring at her in the shadows of the truck cab. She could feel the irritation pulsing through the air.

Silence, while Regina's glare burned into her side. Then the sound of paper being jammed on top of cellophane wrappers in the trash bag hanging from the lighter knob.

"Who *are* you people?" Regina half-growled, half-wailed.

Kathryn glanced at her watch, the numbers faintly visible in the dashboard lights. "Nine hours and — well, make it a little over nine hours. You must be recovering pretty well if you're asking *that* question." She reached into the mess of napkins and picked up the last spear of pickle. She slowly crunched it, thinking about her next words. How to answer Regina's questions so she stopped asking them, without giving her answers she would either despise or misunderstand?

"Okay," Kathryn said after taking a deep breath. "We're the walking wounded, I guess. One way or another, we all got into trouble and someone helped us out. Our troubles changed our lives. We all have debts to repay, or we're just so thankful... We pass on the help we received."

"That is just about the weirdest—"

"Either I'm helping you or tricking you," she snapped, "taking you into worse trouble than you just left. You choose."

"I don't even know what I was doing on that mountain. How am I supposed to figure it out?"

The sharpness faded again from Regina's voice. Fear took over from
~~~~~

the defensive offensiveness that seemed to dominate her words and actions. Kathryn felt another stab of guilt and pity, reminded yet again of Regina's battered condition and her amnesia.

"Finish your dinner. We'll be at the hotel Michael recommended in another half hour. You can take a long hot shower and get a good night's sleep. Things'll look better in the morning."

"You think so?"

"I know so. I'm the expert here, remember?" She glanced over at her companion, delighted to find Regina attempting a smile. Maybe there was some hope there, for them both.

One thing she knew for sure. She wasn't going to call Vincent and check in until Regina was busy elsewhere and couldn't overhear what she said to him. Kathryn needed some answers. Maybe if she had some information to give Regina to help her get her memory back, her whiny passenger might be easier to get along with.

After Vincent filled in some data holes in her assignment, she would call Finn. Whatever had gone down on the mountain, Vincent's mysterious government agency friends weren't in any condition to take custody of Regina. For all Kathryn knew, Vincent's friend wanted her kept out of the hands of some of his co-workers. The sooner she got Finn involved and got Regina into more capable hands and started untangling her story, the better for them all.

~~~~~

Carson studied the map, circling all the exits and alternate routes the dark blue truck could take, carrying Regina Malvern, that big, dangerous-looking dog and its mysterious owner far away. Porter drove, zipping down the highway with the speedometer just on the underside of a ticket. Propped up on the console between them, a tablet held a stylized map of the highway and intersecting roads and rivers, and a blinking red light showed the truck several miles ahead of them.

"This is Porter," the other man said, attracting his partner's attention. He was on his phone, checking in with their superiors again. "We found them. For a short time."

"If it really was them," Carson muttered. His partner didn't hear or react.

"We got a GPS on them, but with the luck they've been having, I wouldn't depend on it long-term. We're going to need some back-up." He paused, nodding, driving with one tight-clenched hand on the steering wheel.

The highway ahead and behind them was empty and dark, not even any lights along the roadside at this point.

"Yes, sir," Porter continued after a few seconds. "We'll stay on them until they stop, then find a place for the night and check in." He frowned.
~~~~~

"Confirmed. Make no contact, just keep watching." His frown deepened as he glared at the highway ahead. When he hung up, Carson snagged the phone from the cup holder almost before he finished putting it down. "Who are you calling?"

"The less you know, the better."

"You know, I'm getting a little tired of all this secrecy. I thought we were partners."

"We are," Carson said, pausing with the phone turned on and glowing green, "but the less you know, the better. Once you're in... You can't just quit." He stared at the gearshift between them. "It's impossible to quit." He took a deep breath and raised his eyes to meet Porter's gaze, and managed to smile, grimly. "I'm using up a lot of those favors owed to me."

"That's what you said last night. Your mysterious friends haven't done us any good yet. If anything, we're going to get our heads handed to us, when the upper brass find out we broke protocol."

"At least *they* don't have Regina Malvern."

"Yeah, but who does?"

~~~~~

Kathryn had seen too many hotels like this in the last few years. From the outside, it was clean and neat and kept in decent repair. The bushes lining the sidewalk and providing a buffer between the hotel and the streets were somewhat shaggy, but that was no real indicator. The pavement of the parking lot felt a little rough, but it hadn't been neglected into gravel, mud and ruts. The hotel was three stories tall with the hallway windows on each floor brightly lit, golden in the darkness. It had a pool with underwater lights glowing blue-green-white, rippling in the slight nighttime breeze. If this place could keep its pool going, it was still respectable and safe. It probably served as the gathering spot for the town's children in the summer, so it had to be safe.

Kathryn parked her truck in a dark arm of the parking lot, at the corner of the L where the shadows of the building weren't overcome by the tall pole lights. The taller trees that shielded the parking lot would block sight of her truck from two sides. When she told Regina to stay in the truck, her passenger turned to look at Bea and started to open her mouth to protest. Kathryn slid out of the truck and gestured for Bea, silencing Regina before she could finish taking a breath in preparation. The Akita jumped out and started off across the parking lot for the nearest tall tree.

"I'll only be a minute." Kathryn gestured for Bea to get into the back of the truck. She waited until the dog sniffed a few trees, marked half of them, and dashed back across the crumbling pavement to leap into the bed of the truck.

She studied the town as she took the long way around from the
~~~~~

parking lot to the lobby. There wasn't much to see except street lights, changing stoplights, dark shadows of two-story houses, and a brighter glow a mile or two away where the business section of town was just shutting down for the night. Kathryn's strongest impression of the town was quiet, a slow pace, and small. If she could have ordered a place for her and Regina to hide overnight, waiting for their hunters to pass by, it would have been very close to this bit of nowhere just a few miles off the highway.

The lobby seemed unchanged since the seventies. Thinning shag carpeting in fading orange, brown, and gold matched the low-slung couches in a zigzag print. The walls were paneled in scarred, dark wood; mirrored tiles alternated with dark brown cork squares on one end wall. She remembered the same decor in the youth room at church, many years ago. At least that style of decoration had been changed a few times since.

The half-full rack of tourist brochures, the enormous cabinet-style television set with the volume turned down, and the row of full newspaper racks all fit the picture of a hotel slowly sliding toward obscurity and closure. The perfect place to hide for a night.

Kathryn signed in for herself. She didn't volunteer the information that she had a companion and a dog, and the drowsy, sour-faced woman at the counter didn't ask. Her conscience twinged a little, but she couldn't afford to draw attention to herself. If those two men managed to follow them directly from the diner, they were less likely to check out a dark-haired woman traveling alone, when their quarry was a blond.

The clerk typed Kathryn's registration into the computer, waited for a soft beep, then pushed the cardkey across the scarred golden countertop toward her. Kathryn thanked her, got little more than a grunt in response, and turned to leave. As she touched the door to the parking lot, a heavy-set man stepped through the door behind the counter, shrugging into a faded royal blue blazer that matched the one worn by the on-duty clerk.

He smiled at her. She managed a half-smile. That was all the exchange they ever made when shifts changed. He picked up his nametag from a shelf under the counter and pinned it on the breast pocket of his jacket. It read simply "Greg." Running his thick fingers through his graying sandy hair, he checked his appearance in the darkened screen of the computer monitor. He checked the level of paper in the printer, then went through his supply of pens and a stash of crushed bags of cookies and pretzels rejected from the snack machines on each floor. When the women clerk headed for the employee entrance to leave, he stepped into the back office where he had dropped his backpack.

Chapter Twelve

In the hotel room, Regina stepped through the door and snatched up the TV remote control. Bea slid past her and made a quick circuit of the room, sniffing in the corners before she scrambled up onto the bed next to the window. Kathryn locked the door and set down her backpack and the duffel bag with the few remaining clean clothes she had. She made a mental note to find out if there was a laundry room in the hotel for customers to use. Could she leave Regina alone for however long it would take to wash their clothes?

That question suddenly changed angles in her mind. Not that she didn't think Regina would be safe alone in the room, but she couldn't trust her not to do something that would endanger them. When had her perception of her charge changed from spoiled to brainless? Some time during the long day of driving and complaining, obviously. Maybe the background irritation she felt all day with her passenger was a warning about Regina, and not an imminent bad spell, or a signal she needed a long vacation and time to think and settle things in her head and heart.

After all, Bea didn't like Regina. Not that the big, sensitive Akita disliked her or reacted negatively to her, but she made no effort to make friends. Maybe that was the problem. Something was wrong with Regina, so Bea just watched her, and stayed away.

Kathryn had learned long ago to listen to the inexplicable idea or sense of certainty that popped into her head, with no rational explanation. Vincent teased her that when she hadn't slept often enough for angels to put visions in her mind through dreams, they sat on her shoulders and whispered until she heard something. He wasn't given to flights of whimsy, so Kathryn didn't take his words entirely as teasing. She listened now to the suspicion that she couldn't leave Regina alone.

What if the damsel in distress had brought her troubles on herself, and she didn't have the sense to stay under the radar? What if she tried to make contact with people who would come running and bring a host of troubles in their wake? What if she was such a spoiled brat, she decided now that she had her feet under herself again, and had access to phones and rental cars, she should take off on her own? While Kathryn wouldn't mind being free of Regina, Vincent's call last night and everything she had done today made her responsible. She wouldn't lay down that responsibility, or let it wander away, until she had turned Regina over to someone with the authority and connections to unravel her story and handle her properly. Whatever she was involved in, she wasn't going to vanish into the night. Not on Kathryn's watch.

She needed to take precautions. She slashed her hand down hard and muttered "guard" in Greek. She got Bea's attention, but not Regina's. The Akita's ears pricked up and she trotted over to stand before Kathryn. She clenched her hand into a fist and rested it on the room telephone for five seconds, then walked over to the door and pressed her fist against it for five seconds, each time repeating "no" in Greek. Bea snorted, pressed her nose against the door, then trotted back to the phone and rested her nose on it.

Now, Regina wouldn't be allowed to make a phone call or leave the room while Kathryn was busy elsewhere. She had learned the hard way not to take chances. One of her first jobs for the Arc Foundation had been to take someone cross-country to shelter. She was just learning to listen to what Vincent called her in-born radar about people, and had mistaken her discomfort with the teenager in her charge as nerves over the seriousness of her assignment. The supposed fugitive from an abusive home had turned out to be a prostitute running from one pimp to another waiting for her in the next state. The girl had vanished before Kathryn knew what was going on. She never left anyone alone with the phone now, until her job was finished and the responsibility had passed to someone else.

Here in the quiet, with some time to think, Kathryn found it all too easy to envision Regina making a couple phone calls, getting picked up by a friend, and vanishing, leaving her to face the wrath of whoever had been following them.

Even worse than any possible danger, however, was facing Vincent's disappointment.

"Here's a spare shirt you can sleep in," Kathryn said, pulling out the contents of the duffel bag. "I need a shower, bad. You want to get in first?" She would try calling Vincent again and then Finn, and hope Regina took a long, luxurious shower.

"No, you can," Regina muttered, staring at the flickering image on the TV screen.

Kathryn grinned and shook her head. She wasn't about to protest, if it meant she could get really clean and comfortable immediately. She took her phone into the bathroom, just in case Regina tried to use it. Not that she could make any calls without knowing the password, but Kathryn didn't want to risk a snit fit damaging her phone.

<center>~~~~~</center>

In the lobby, Greg stepped back up to the desk and unloaded his backpack of books, preparing for a long, quiet night of study. Two accounting books; one text and one workbook. A dog-eared collection of

90

short stories, with a sheaf of classroom handouts and questions to answer stuck in the middle. A manual from a correspondence school that guaranteed he could get his bachelor of arts degree by mail, with less cost and time than through conventional methods.

The front door creaked open the same moment Greg cracked the binding of his accounting textbook. He stifled a sigh and looked up with a professional smile to welcome the two rough-dressed, tired-looking men who came through the door.

"You sign in," Porter said. "I'll look around." He stepped into the lounge area of the lobby while Carson continued to the desk.

~~~~~

In the hotel room, Regina continued flipping through the available stations on the TV. She knew better than to expect cable in a deteriorating spot like this, but she still grumbled under her breath when she found nothing but static-streaked local stations. Twice, she glanced sideways at Bea. The dog lay on the other bed, head on her paws, eyes half-closed, watching her.

Regina decided all her problems getting along with Kathryn were because of that dog, always watching her, always getting in the way. Dogs were just animals, acting on instinct, but she had the unsettling feeling Bea knew what she was thinking. The dog was just creepy. Why did Kathryn keep it around?

Finally, she gave up on the TV, turned it off and lay back on the mattress. She sighed. At least the mattress was thick and the bedspread smelled clean. Eyes closing, she gave in to the dizzy weariness that wrapped around her. Blindly, she reached for a pillow. The springs creaked, sounding like a gunshot.

Memory slung her into a forest filled with mud and rain. Lightning slashes lit the ground and the sky and turned to fire surrounding her. Gunfire bloomed in the darkness, whizzing past her head, making her stumble and gasp and choke back screams she couldn't afford to release.

She slammed up against a tree. Falling, she clutched at a branch. It came off in her hand and the wet, sticky warm bark turned cold and hard and became a gun. As she stared at the gun, it exploded in her hand.

Regina tore free of the memory and sat up on the hotel bed, both hands jammed against her mouth to muffle her scream. Gasping, she shifted her fists to her temples, pressing against a pounding pain that threatened to crack her skull into many jagged pieces.

"It's not my fault," she whimpered.

The sound of the running shower filled the silence. Regina glanced over at Bea. The big dog watched her with unblinking eyes. She wished she had that gun now, to shoot the dog and get it out of her way.

"It's not my fault," she repeated, a little louder. "None of it is. It's his
~~~~~

fault."

The question echoed through the back of her mind. *Who is he?* The vague spots, filled and blocked by rain and thunder, fire and gunshots and darkness, made her whole body ache with echoes of memory she didn't want to explore.

Regina stood. She had to do something. Anything. The room was too small. She got up to explore.

The phone caught her attention and she reached for it before she knew what she intended. Bea slid off the bed and put her paws up on the dresser next to her. She nudged her with her big, dark head. Regina let out a little shriek and jumped backward, dropping the phone.

"She didn't say I couldn't make phone calls," she grumbled. She wanted desperately to hit Bea with something, but she doubted a pillow would make an impression.

Call who? Her head ached a little as she tried to remember what moved her. Someone had given her a number to call. She knew it only moments ago, but it was gone now.

"Bet if I called, the people there could give me better answers than she has," Regina muttered. She settled back into her spot on the end of the bed and slumped, staring at the blank TV screen.

Kathryn said she was there to help, but was she really? She didn't like to answer questions, and when she did she said nonsense things. Did she really expect Regina to believe there were people driving around the United States, waiting to help anybody who needed it? That made no sense at all. Nobody did anything for anybody for free.

Whatever she really meant, Kathryn wasn't making any effort to be nice. She chose to eat in filthy dives and made Regina climb out windows into muddy parking lots and now chose this hotel in the middle of nowhere without even any decent cable stations. She even made Regina leave behind half her dessert when they ran from the diner.

That got her thinking. Carefully, watching Bea with tiny sideways glances, Regina sidled over to Kathryn's backpack and searched for her wallet. Crummy hotels like this usually had snack machines somewhere close so people could spend their money on something decent to eat. Regina thought it only justice that since Kathryn made her lose half her ice cream sundae, she could provide money for some candy bars and a few cans of soda to get her through the night.

Bea had settled back into her spot on the bed and watched Regina take money from the wallet without even twitching her ears. The dog started to get up when Regina stepped over to the bathroom door, which was next to the room door. She froze, staring back at the dog, then stepped over to the end of the long dresser where the tray with the ice bucket, glasses, and coffee machine sat.

Watching Bea carefully, Regina sidled over to the bathroom door again. The dog lay back down, still watching her. She shifted the handle of the ice bucket to her left hand and pounded on the bathroom door with the right hand.

"I'm going for ice and pop," she called through the door.

The shower slowed and Kathryn's voice came muffled through the door. Regina didn't know what she said and wasn't about to find out. She reached for the handle of the door into the hall, blocking the movement with her body. It clicked open. Bea slid off the bed. Chuckling, she yanked the door open, darted out and slammed it shut before the dog reached her.

"That'll teach you," she sneered. The sound of Bea's whines and then scratching on the surface came clearly through the door. "Always watching me. Just waiting for a chance to bite. You won't get it, hear me?"

She stuck her tongue out at the door and hurried down the hall. The hotel diagram showed the snack and pop machines in the stairwells.

~~~~~

"Regina?" Kathryn turned off the shower completely and slid back the curtain. "What did you say?" The sound of Bea whining and scratching on the bathroom door sent a chill up her back, contrasting with all the delicious steam that swirled through the room. She wrapped the skimpy towel around herself and yanked the door open.

One glance showed Regina had left the room. Bea nudged her leg with her muzzle and whimpered. Kathryn wilted a little. This, when everything looked like it was finally going right.

"Fine watchdog you are," she muttered.

Bea darted into the bathroom, snagged her discarded jeans in her teeth, and dragged them the few feet to the door. She dropped them at Kathryn's feet and looked expectantly up at her.

"Okay, okay." She would have laughed, but a mixture of dread and disgust with Regina's selfish stupidity smothered the sound in her throat. She toweled herself dry quickly and grimaced at the thought of struggling back into the clothes she had worn all day.

Barefoot, her hair dripping dark spots on her stale t-shirt, she slid the room key into her pocket and stepped out into the hall. Bea wanted to come and she lost a few seconds pushing her back into the room. The last thing Kathryn needed was for the few hotel residents to see her dog and complain to the desk. Besides possibly getting her and Regina thrown out, it would attract too much attention. Kathryn hurried down the hall, trying to guess where Regina had gone. The ice bucket was missing, so she had likely gone for ice. Knowing the way Regina ate, she was probably going for a month's supply of greasy, sugary snacks, too. That meant she needed to check her wallet. She should have taken her backpack into the bathroom, and if Regina's feelings got hurt at this sign that she didn't trust
~~~~~

her, that was just tough.

The pneumatic hinge on the door to the stairwell was broken. It hung half-open, showing Regina standing on the landing inside the stairwell, her arms loaded with cans of cola, bags of chips and several candy bars. The ice bucket was full, sitting at her feet. She seemed frozen, her back to the pop machine, staring down into the stairwell. Kathryn pushed the door open slowly and stepped up behind her.

The sound of slow, heavy footsteps came up the stairwell. Kathryn moved closer to the railing and looked down.

The two men from the diner had just reached the mid-way landing in the stairs and were turning to come up the second flight of stairs to their floor. Kathryn's first thought was to grab Regina and get out of there, but any quick movement would attract attention. Regina would probably scream or drop something, or even resist.

The two men turned and kept climbing, facing them now. The one in the lead raised his head and looked up to the landing. He stopped short and his mouth dropped open when he saw Regina staring at him and his partner. He caught the other man by the sleeve, stopping him. The other man stopped, glanced at him and then up to the landing.

"Who's your friend, Regina?" the first man said, nodding toward Kathryn standing behind her.

"No friend of yours." Kathryn wished she had ignored common sense and brought Bea down the hall with her.

"I really think we should change that. Why don't the four of us go to your room and talk, okay?"

He reached into his coat pocket. Regina whimpered and cast Kathryn one terrified look.

Kathryn grabbed her by the elbow and yanked her around, spinning her toward the door. Regina dropped two cans of cola and one bag of corn chips. Kathryn shoved her through the door and down the hall.

"Hey, wait a minute!" the man yelped.

Kathryn stumbled backward, nearly tripping over the ice bucket. She scooped it up and swung it around, emptying it into the faces of the two men. Then she followed with the bucket itself and both cans of pop. The second man stumbled backward a few steps, ducking out of the way. His partner slipped in the icy water spreading on the linoleum. Kathryn scurried through the door, dragging it closed behind her.

There was no lock on her side of the door, just a panic bar. Gritting her teeth against curses she hadn't used in years, she hung on the bar, keeping the door closed, and turned to look for Regina. The blond stumbled down the hall toward their room, leaving a trail of junk food. Kathryn spotted the fire box bolted to the wall next to the door. It had a hose and a valve for the water. And a fire axe. She yanked the flimsy aluminum door open, nearly cracking the clear plastic pane, and yanked out the fire axe. She jammed it under the door, in the gap between metal panel and floor.

Two seconds later, one of the men reached the door and yanked on the handle. The door didn't move. Through the narrow window, Kathryn stared into his startled eyes. How had her trick worked and jammed the door shut? She wasn't going to hang around to find out how long. She turned and ran.

She didn't slow when she reached Regina, but caught her by the elbow and dragged her into a wobbly run down the hall to the other stairwell. She didn't know how long it would take the two hunters to think of the other stairwell, but she knew she had the time it took them to climb down to the first floor and reach the end of the hall. By then, she and Regina could reach the first floor and flee outside. After that, there were plenty of hiding places in the darkness and overgrown bushes and the rest of the town.

Regina made no protest or resistance in their headlong flight down the stairs and out the door. They stumbled into the half-lit parking lot around the back of the hotel. Kathryn's truck was a dark blob in deeper darkness, less than fifty feet away. She gave it one longing glance and headed in the opposite direction.

"Where are you going?" Regina squeaked. She tried to head for the truck and nearly got yanked off her feet by Kathryn's momentum.

"Anywhere."

"But—" She tried again to move toward the truck.

"I don't have my keys!" Kathryn hissed. She took a firmer hold on Regina's arm and headed off across the parking lot at a trot. She had nothing but the room key, her blue jeans, and a damp t-shirt.

Please, God, You got us this far. Now what?

All they needed to be safe was for Regina to stay hidden in their room until morning, but could she think of that simple tactic without help?

The crumbling asphalt of the parking lot abruptly changed to gravel. Sharp gravel. Kathryn hissed and slowed her pace. Her bare feet hurt.

When they reached the grassy strip between the parking lot and the street, Kathryn paused a few seconds. She strained her ears to listen behind them. Was that the thump of the stairwell door opening? She couldn't be sure, and heard nothing more. She sped up. If Regina didn't like running, that was just tough.

At the first intersection, staying out of the pool of light from the sporadic streetlights, Kathryn turned right, heading into town. She had a vague idea of going to the police, if the situation got that bad. If anything, she could ask to use the phone and try to get hold of Finn or his supervisor. What was his name again? Garretson or something like that. If worse turned to worst, Kathryn could ask Finn to pull some strings and get them shelter under semi-official FBI auspices until he came to get them.

Another intersection, more lights as the street changed from undeveloped to residential. Kathryn turned left. A long parking lot opened up, framed between tall trees that looked like they had been there for generations. She stopped short at the sight of what lay on the far end of the parking lot. Regina stopped, gasping a little and sagged sideways. She jerked, startled, when Kathryn chuckled.

"What?"

In answer, Kathryn pointed. Regina squinted through the darkness at the long, rambling building and the pools of light. She frowned, shrugging.

"It's a church." Kathryn grinned despite being exasperated by her denseness. Then she wondered if Regina even knew what a church was.

"So?"

"You never heard of sanctuary?" She caught hold of Regina's hand and started off around the edge of the parking lot, staying in the shadows of those big, overgrown trees. She kept her eyes on the tall, white steeple, like a ship homing in on a lighthouse at the mouth of the harbor.

"I'm not Catholic."

"Well, at least you remember something. Come on!" When the trees ended, Kathryn took a tight hold on Regina's wrist and half-dragged her around the back of the building. "Doesn't matter anyway, because this doesn't look like a Catholic church."

The church was brick, two stories in some spots and one in others. It looked like it had been added to several times over the generations. Close up, the steeple's paint was peeling, but the grounds looked well-tended; grass clipped short, flowerbeds weeded, hedges trimmed. The parking lot behind the church was gravel, so Kathryn stayed to the grass against the side of the building.

The back door, when she tried it, wouldn't budge. She hadn't really expected it to be unlocked, since there were no cars to be seen, meaning no church activities on this particular Friday night. However, she had been trained over the last few years to expect miracles.

"When God closes a door, look for a window," she muttered. She ignored the dismayed look Regina cast her, which quickly changed to disgust.

Chapter Thirteen

Kathryn tried every window she came to as she walked along the back of the building. Five were locked, with the curtains pulled close over them. At the sixth window, she stopped.

"I could really use some help right now."

"Who are you talking to?" Regina demanded in a stage whisper. The irony that she was finally learning to soften her voice for danger wasn't lost on Kathryn.

"God, of course. It's His house."

"You're crazy!" Her moment of circumspection hadn't lasted long. "I wish you'd never found me."

"Right now, so do I." Kathryn turned and headed for the next window. "Come on, Lord, how about a miracle?" She slid her fingers along the edge of the window, trying to find some place to pry it open. It was the old-fashioned kind with horizontal panes that opened inward.

"We shouldn't be doing this."

"God's house is here for everybody. It's our right to get in where it's safe." Kathryn figured it would take a gymnastics routine to get up onto the narrow brick sill of the window and slide through the opening without standing on and breaking the glass, if she could get the window to open at all. Once she got inside, she could come down the hall and open a door to let Regina in.

"You really are crazy." Regina stepped back, out of the building's line of shadow, straight into a pool of light from the sporadic parking lot lights.

"Better than being dead." Kathryn grabbed her arm and dragged her back into the sheltering shadows. She turned back to the window.

A hand, then an arm appeared in the window. It creaked and slid open, tipping into the building, just as Kathryn expected. Then a face and a whole body emerged from the deeper shadows inside the church.

He was thin, with blond, shaggy hair and sharp cheekbones and deep, sea-green-blue eyes. For a moment, she forgot what she was doing there. A sense of recognition shook her down to her toes, but it fled before she could remember where they had met before.

The man wore a faded blue work shirt and blue jeans, and he held cleaning rags in one hand. He tipped his head to one side and looked back and forth between Kathryn and Regina a few times.

"Something you ladies are looking for?" he asked in a soft baritone voice. His eyes smiled even if his lips didn't.

He was the custodian, Kathryn decided. He had to be. Who else would be dressed like that, working inside the church at night, when nobody else was around?

"We'd really like to get inside," she said. If she could have climbed in through the window, she would have.

"Oh, I can see that." He tipped his head to the other side and studied them another few seconds. "What for?"

"How about you let us in and when we're safe, then we'll tell you, okay?" Kathryn thought she heard the rumbling of a truck's engine coming closer through the darkness. Any moment now, headlight beams would come around behind the church and affix them to the side of the building like butterflies on pins.

"Sounds like you're in trouble."

"That's an understatement," Regina grumbled.

The custodian considered them a few seconds longer. Kathryn tried to hold still. She could almost feel Regina seething, ready to explode and worsen their situation. Then the man nodded and gestured back down toward the door they had first tried. He closed up the window and disappeared into the shadows again. Kathryn grabbed Regina's hand and led her at a trot back to the door.

It hung open when they got there and all was darkness inside. Kathryn hesitated a second. She felt Regina try to pull back.

This is a church. God's going to take care of us, she reminded herself, and put her foot on the threshold.

The custodian appeared out of the darkness with a flashlight in one hand, and held out the other hand, beckoning. He led them through dull, echoing darkness that smelled of oil and metal, down a hall that smelled of that particular biting tang of fresh floor wax and disinfectant, then into a larger room where the echoes bounced off many objects.

Lights came on and revealed they were in the church kitchen. A long folding table with mismatched chairs sat in the middle of the room, with light oak cupboards filling one wall and the sink, stove and refrigerator filling the other. Rag rugs decorated the faded linoleum floor. Kathryn welcomed the softness on her bruised feet as she crossed the room to the table and pulled out a chair to sit down. The custodian winked at her and vanished into the darkness of the hall.

"He's calling the police!" Regina whispered. She scurried over to the table and sank into a chair.

"If he does..." Kathryn shook her head. She was just too tired right now. "If he does, it'll work out. Maybe we're far enough away from Millersburg to be safe."

"How do you know that?"

"I know better than to go wandering the halls in a strange hotel, looking to feed my fat face, when somebody is trying to find me."

Regina gasped and threw herself against the back of her chair. Kathryn braced for the explosion.

The custodian walked back in, carrying a box of grocery store donuts and a pair of beat-up sneakers spattered with five different colors of paint.

"Oh, that's right." Regina's voice turned nasal with sarcasm. "You're the expert. I still don't know why you're involved."

"I told you why. You just can't be bothered to listen."

"God gave us two ears and one mouth," the custodian said and put the donuts and sneakers down on the table. "That means we should listen twice as much as we talk."

"Great." Regina nearly turned away, but she saw the box of donuts. "Another philosopher." She flushed when the custodian chuckled.

"I have work to do," he said. "Make yourselves comfortable. Pastor Small should be here soon to work on his sermon. He'll help you."

"Is there at least a bathroom around here?"

"Around the corner."

Kathryn glared, feeling a little embarrassed, and watched Regina stumble out of the room. The custodian seemed amused by her, but that didn't help.

"Sorry. She's under a lot of pressure," Kathryn offered.

"So are you, little sister." He handed her the shoes. "If you're going to keep defending someone who doesn't appreciate it or deserve it, better not do it barefoot."

Kathryn gaped, caught between amusement and embarrassment. He grinned and left. She tugged the donut box over, yanked it open, snatched up the first donut, and crammed it into her mouth. Slouching, she tried to ignore how her face burned.

She laughed, though she wasn't quite sure why.

~~~~~

Church sanctuaries wreathed in shadows and streaked with moonlight from the high windows were good places for contemplation, for gratitude and regret. For facing her mortality and not minding too much, because the veil between Earth and Heaven felt a little thinner, the doorway to eternity a little closer than usual.

Kathryn liked this place. It was simple, neat, no spirituality lost and tangled in fancy decorations. Two wide rows of twenty padded pews each; brick walls in a mixture of gold and red tones; hardwood floors. They gleamed softly in the moonlight, looking like someone kept them polished and waxed to a high gloss. She thought about the custodian who had let them in, working late into the night to take care of his church. It fit the image of someone who would let two strangers into the church just
~~~~~

because they said they were in trouble. Whatever he was doing, it had to be at the far end of the church from the sanctuary, because she hadn't seen him or heard him at work since he gave her the donuts and shoes and walked away.

Colorful cloth banners decorated the walls, made of a rainbow of felt pieces, illustrating various Scripture verses. Kathryn wondered if Sunday school students had made those banners or if there was a ladies circle dedicated to making them through the years.

The moonlight provided more than enough illumination to see the simple platform at the front of the sanctuary, the ten-foot-tall red oak cross that decorated the brick wall, the upright piano and the podium.

Simple. Clean. Neat. Everything well-tended, with the devotion and pride a church deserved from its family of believers. Kathryn suspected the missions budget was just as large at this church as at the fancy ones with congregations numbering in the thousands. Places like this spent their money on others and not on decorations and special effects. This was the best church of all in which to take refuge.

The pews had thin cushions on them and were deep enough for her to stretch out on her back and try to rest. She needed to rest. The incipient headache kept taking short testing dives into her stomach, threatening nausea. Despite the weary aches in her legs and back, she couldn't make herself lie still.

"Please, Lord," she whispered from her spot in the second row from the front. She leaned forward, resting her head on her crossed arms on the back of the front pew. "Help me trust You. I know You have a plan for getting us out of this mess, but I really don't see what it is. I know You got us this far and I should trust You and stop worrying, but I can't. Bea and everything I need are at the hotel and we're here and I'm going to strangle Regina if she gripes at me one more time."

A tiny snort of laughter escaped her. She didn't know how Regina could stretch out on that pew three rows back and sleep so easily. She didn't miss the irony that Regina, who thought the sanctuary was slightly creepy in the moonlight, who didn't trust the vanished custodian, slept without a hitch. Yet Kathryn, who knew they were truly safe here, could barely make herself sit still.

A moan broke the quiet of the sanctuary. Kathryn stiffened and turned to look at Regina. The other woman moaned a bit louder, twisting a little on the narrow padded seat of the pew.

"No—Dad, don't!" A whimper broke her voice. "Stop it! I didn't—"

Regina jerked upright, almost sliding off the pew. She twisted and blinked rapidly and flailed her arms as she regained her bearings and sense of place. Kathryn got up and hurried to her. Regina settled down the moment she touched her shoulder.

"You okay?"

"Bad dreams." In the moonlight and shadows, Regina looked ten years younger, and ashamed of her cries.

"Maybe you're remembering more?"

"Unfortunately." She looked around the sanctuary, taking it in as if for the first time. She also didn't shrug off Kathryn's comforting touch. "Something horrid happened up there on the mountain. And before..."

"Like what?" Kathryn asked quietly, when Regina's voice just trailed off and it looked like she wouldn't continue.

"A fire." She shuddered. "And people shooting at... my father."

"Your father?" That admission gave Kathryn some hope she had regained more of her memory than she let on. When Regina remembered, they would have answers they needed for their own protection.

"Those men in the hotel knew me. They called me by name."

"Yeah, I noticed that." She waited for more information, but Regina just gnawed her lip and frowned more wrinkles into her face. "You think one of them killed your father?"

"Probably."

"Seeing your father murdered is a good way to lose your memory for a while, just like Dr. West said. Shock, terror, a bunch of psychological mumbo-jumbo." She waited, but Regina didn't react to her attempt at humor. *Par for the course.* "You're under a lot of stress. Especially if someone is trying to catch or kill you, too."

"Duh." She slid down in the pew so her head rested on the hard wooden back and she balanced on her tailbone on the edge of the cushion.

"I love being in places like this, alone," Kathryn offered. She didn't look at Regina. If she felt that confused, she wouldn't want anybody looking at her, either. "Doesn't matter if it's a fancy cathedral or a little chapel in the middle of nowhere. There's a feeling..." She smiled and shook her head.

"Holy ground?" Regina half-whispered. There was no hint of mockery in her voice.

"You've been watching the wrong movies." She offered a grin to show she was teasing, and was amazed when Regina responded with a sickly attempt at a smile. "But I have to admit, places like this still... fill a hunger. If there's such a thing as holy ground, with power to protect or heal, it's a power that *we* give it, you know?"

"I guess."

Kathryn knew she was losing Regina. "How we act, the things we do or don't do, make a place holy or profane."

"Why did Bea let Michael pet her, when she looks like she wants to bite me half the time?"

"Huh?" She swallowed a sigh. *Well, at least I made some kind of start.*

Don't push it. "Well, Bea likes him because Michael is a dog person. He trains guard dogs, when he's not out touring the country on that bike of his." Nothing could make her admit that Bea didn't like Regina because she wasn't a nice person.

"Oh."

Regina sounded so disappointed, Kathryn had to laugh. She tried to muffle the sound so she wouldn't totally alienate her companion.

"What, you were expecting some mystical explanation? I said Bea would like you once she got to know you."

"Something weird is going on here." Regina's voice threatened to turn into a self-pitying wail. "It's not just all the blank spots in my brain. Are you people even human?"

"I'm just as human as you are."

"I really wonder about that. Look at how you found me, and how you get around all our problems. Everything is easy for you."

"Not *easy*." Kathryn felt tempted to tell Regina about a dozen situations where she had done what she thought was right, yet the people she had been helping turned out almost worse off than when she entered their problems. That wasn't the right tactic, if Regina didn't quite trust her even now.

"I've just learned how to look for every tool that comes my way," she continued, trying to make her voice reasonable and calm, even bland, "and use them, and trust God to guide our steps. My friends and I are very human. We make mistakes and we do the best we can, just like everyone else."

"Does that include an explanation for how you got in here?" a rich tenor voice said from the shadowy side aisle.

Kathryn put out a hand to stop Regina from running, or maybe catch her if she fainted. Fortunately, her companion froze up completely.

A man walked up the side aisle and across the front of the sanctuary. He was of medium height with big, gray-blue eyes and silvery hair, dressed in a red plaid shirt, faded jeans, and black hi-tops. He stopped with his back to the podium and surveyed the two young women in the pews. Wrinkles marred his wide, high forehead, but Kathryn didn't think he was dangerous, only concerned. He carried a worn, leather-covered notebook folder and two thick books on top of it, caught in the curve of his arm and pressed against his side. The books had lost their paper dust jackets.

"Your janitor let us in," Kathryn said after a few seconds of silence while the two sides studied each other.

"He did, hmm? What's his name?"

"He didn't give us his name." She mentally kicked herself for not asking. "He showed us into the kitchen and he gave us donuts and these shoes."

She scooted to the edge of the pew and stuck her foot out into the aisle. There was barely enough moonlight to show all the vari-colored paint splotches. The man stared at her foot. She almost started counting, he stayed still for so long.

"He was dressed all in blue and he had long blond hair," she continued. "He said Pastor Small would be in to work on his sermon, and he would help us. Is that you?"

"Yes..." Pastor Small smiled a little. "Why exactly are you two here?"

"Hiding," Regina said, her voice squeaking a little.

"Hiding? Do you think you could tell me why, and from whom?"

He didn't sound angry, or as if he disbelieved them. Kathryn took that as a good sign and decided to change the tone of things for a little bit. She held up the box of donuts. She and Regina had only eaten five between them.

"Do you have any milk to go with these?" she said.

Pastor Small blinked and his smile widened.

They ended up back in the kitchen. Pastor Small made coffee and dug out glasses and napkins and a jug of milk he had bought the night before.

"Don't know why I did that," he admitted while they waited for the coffee to start percolating in the battered aluminum camping-style coffee pot on the gas stove. "The staff won't be back in until Monday. We don't use milk during the break between Sunday school and the service, and I wasn't planning on coming in tonight or tomorrow." He glanced at Kathryn over Regina's head. "Guess the Lord's interested in little things like milk, too, eh?"

She agreed with a smile. Regina seemed not to hear. She didn't react to the idea one way or another.

Then it was time to tell him a much-edited version of their adventures. Kathryn didn't tell him why she had been looking for Regina. She glossed over their escape from the diner. It was difficult not to slip in a few words about Regina's stupidity in leaving the safety of their hotel room.

"That's everything," she said, twenty minutes and two cups of milk later. "He went back to work and we haven't seen him since. We settled down in the sanctuary because it's comfortable."

"In more ways than one, yes?" Pastor Small winked and they shared a smile.

Kathryn sensed he believed every word she had spoken, and that made no sense at all. Without her background in constant small miracles, she doubted she would have believed the story if she worked at this small church and someone else had told it to her.

"How do we get back to the hotel without them catching us?" Regina asked. She had a rim of powdered sugar around her mouth. She didn't bother wiping it away before she took a long drink of her third cup of coffee.

"It just so happens a boy from this church is the night clerk over there. I don't think he'd argue if I went over to sign you out, and brought your truck back here."

"I would," Kathryn muttered.

"The Lord works in mysterious ways," he said with a chuckle. "This particular young man has been turning his life around. He spent a few years in prison and it's been hard coming back to his hometown to straighten out his life. He'd do anything for the people of this church, because we're the only ones who've been supporting him all along."

"Especially you," she guessed. Kathryn decided not to argue with the timing. "Just one more problem. My dog."

"Her killer bear is more like it," Regina said.

"In your room, or in your truck?" Pastor Small asked.

"The room. I locked her in when I went looking for Regina."

"She could have helped us fight off those two creeps," Regina said.

"I was more worried about getting thrown out because Bea was running loose in the halls," Kathryn retorted. "You shouldn't have left the room to begin with."

Regina turned her head away. Kathryn saw the angry red slowly creep up her cheek under the fall of her hair, and down her neck into her collar.

"Well." Pastor Small cleared his throat. "How do I make friends with her?"

Kathryn was stumped. But only for a moment. She was dealing with someone who had gone through seminary, after all. A spark of mischief touched her eyes and voice as she asked if he spoke Greek.

Chapter Fourteen

Fifteen minutes later, Regina and Kathryn stood at the back door of the church, watching Pastor Small set off across the parking lot on foot. Now that the moon hung high overhead, the path across fields and through back yards to the hotel was visible, nearly a straight line. Kathryn thought of the corners turned and streets crossed to get to the church, and she sighed, smiling. Hindsight was always much clearer.

"Crazy," Regina muttered. Then she laughed. "Why does he have to recite the opening lines of *The Odyssey* in Greek? Bea understands Greek?"

"Nope. Well, not the meaning behind the words. We train our dogs using Greek words because in a dangerous situation, chances are good the enemy won't understand what commands we use. As for reciting *The Odyssey*... Pastor Small will be so busy thinking of the right words, he won't have time to be afraid. Or *smell* or *sound* afraid. That's what'll convince Bea he's a friend." Kathryn hoped that fifteen minutes of wearing a navy blue sweater taken from the lost-and-found had put enough of her scent into the fibers. The minister carried it gingerly in one hand, arm stretched out, to avoid impinging his own scent over hers.

~~~~~

Outside the hotel, a dark sedan drove slowly up to the front door. Agent Cooper , sitting in the passenger seat, flinched slightly when she saw and recognized the two men at the front desk. Porter and Carson. The last people she wanted or needed to see. Her eyes narrowed as she studied the two men, trying to decide if their presence here was a good sign or bad. Had they caught the trail of their common quarry, or were they giving up for the night? A faint smile touched the corners of her flat mouth as she sorted through her options until she found several that pleased her. She nodded at Edwards, who was driving, and gestured with a wave of her hand to keep going. He nodded back, put the car into gear, and followed the curve of the driveway around the back of the hotel.

~~~~~

In a room on the second floor, Pastor Small recited the opening passage of *The Odyssey*, as Kathryn had instructed him and held the sweater out at arm's length. So far, so good. The big, bear-like dog—incongruously named Bea, in his opinion—backed up and let him come further into the room. He wasn't sure if the dog's silence was a good sign or not, mostly because she didn't wag her tail. He stumbled over a few words when Bea moved around to settle down with her back to the door, and continued watching him.

"So far, so good, eh?" he murmured, after he put the sweater down and still the dog did nothing. A small huff of laughter escaped when it occurred to him that he had to exercise as much faith in Kathryn, that the sweater would carry enough of her scent to convince Bea he was a friend, as he usually exercised with God and his congregation. "Well, let's get this errand taken care of, and get you back to Kathryn and all of you on your way, shall we?"

Carefully, he searched Kathryn's room, found everything that belonged to her, and put it into her worn duffel bag. There was very little to re-pack. Halfway through, he forgot about Bea's presence and concentrated on what he could guess about Kathryn from her possessions. He stopped and pulled out his wallet and emptied a thin fold of bills into the front pocket of her backpack.

~~~~~

In the back parking lot, Porter slung his bag into the cargo space behind the passenger seat and climbed in. Carson took a moment to glance around the lot once more before he opened the driver's side door of the 4X4. There was no use in them staying any longer at this hotel, since they had lost Regina and her friend. The two of them were probably miles down the road by now. The wise move was to turn on the GPS and follow them. Just follow them. He caught a glimpse of movement, but didn't stop to look at it. He opened the door and climbed into the truck and used his rearview mirror to check out the spot where the movement had appeared.

A dark sedan came around the corner of the building, slowly. Too slowly, in Carson's estimation, to be someone cruising through the parking lot with any good intentions. Especially at that time of night. He nudged Porter and nodded toward the rearview mirror between them. His partner nodded understanding and pulled down the mirror in the sun visor. He twisted the visor as Carson started the engine, put the truck into gear, and surveyed the quiet, nearly empty lot behind them.

Porter nodded when he spotted the car. His tight smile boded trouble and prodded a smile from Carson in return. They took the long way around the hotel to get to the exit and the street that led back to the highway.

Just before they came even with the lobby doors, Porter gave a grunt of satisfaction and put the visor back into place.

"Recognize them?" Carson said.

"You bet."

"Me, too."

"Spotted the girls' truck, too. Wherever they vanished to, they haven't left the hotel."
~~~~~

Carson smiled thinly and grunted acknowledgment. He continued watching the car that followed them. It stopped when he hit the brake momentarily. His smile hardened, and he pulled into a parking space in front of the lobby doors.

"Where?"

"Around the back, almost hidden by some bushes by the air conditioning units and the pool shed." Porter grinned. "Bet if the truck's there, and those two are following us, they don't have the girls, either."

"Think they've left the hotel?"

"If they have, the GPSs I placed aren't worth diddly."

"I just got a bad feeling. If our new shadows saw us before we saw them..." He frowned into the rearview mirror. The sedan hadn't moved, still waiting around the side of the building with about a foot of the nose of the car sticking out.

"We have the equipment to find any bugs they put on us," Porter said, lowering his voice to just above a whisper, "but we need to lose them long enough to remove it, so they don't know we know."

"So what do we do?"

"I get a newspaper, that's what." He jumped out of the truck and took a few running steps to cross the driveway and step up onto the sidewalk. He made a production of searching his pockets for enough change for the newspaper dispenser box.

The sedan pulled into a parking spot four spaces down from where Carson waited in the 4X4. From the corner of his eye, he watched for activity in the car. Porter made a production out of searching the front page of the newspaper as he turned around and headed back to the truck, using the body of the paper to cast his face in shadow as he took a good look at the car. Carson made a note to tease his partner about brushing up on his acting skills, but later, when this was all over and they could relax enough to laugh.

When the 4X4 pulled out into the street, the dark sedan was twenty feet behind it. Carson didn't head for the highway, but into town. He had a few ideas of how to confuse and frustrate the people in the car behind him. He would judge if his truck had been bugged by how well their opponents stayed on their tail. He grinned as the list grew longer. First stop was the closest all-night restaurant, where he and Porter could sit and make phone calls and drink enough coffee to keep them going for the next few days. He doubted a town this small had a twenty-four-hour grocery, but the time it took to drive around and eliminate every store would add to the frustration of the two in the other car. Then of course he had to get gas. He would think of other things to create many stops and take them into traffic where he could lose their unwelcome shadow.

~~~~~
~~~~~

Greg at the front desk did a doubletake when he saw a truck he didn't recognize pull into a parking spot directly in front of the hotel lobby door. In the spill of light, he saw Pastor Small at the wheel, with a big, dark dog sitting in the bed of the truck. He checked the clock, and his puzzlement grew when he saw the late hour. His pastor was one of the last people he expected to see driving around town at this time of night.

"Something I can help you with, Pastor?" he called as the minister stepped into the lobby. They were the only ones in the room.

"I'm helping out two young ladies in a tight spot. Can you tell me if anything... odd happened a while ago?"

"Well." He thought a few seconds, then nodded. "Yeah, some people complained about a ruckus in the stairwell. Somebody was playing around with the fire axe on the second floor and jammed a door closed. Then two guys wanted to see the registration forms."

"You didn't let them, did you?" Pastor Small looked a little worried, with a few vertical wrinkles forming in the space between his eyes and extending up into his forehead.

"Hey, I know better than that. Just because they flash badges at me doesn't mean they're legit. I told them I had to get permission from corporate, or else have one of the locals verify them." Greg shook his head. "They didn't like that, but they didn't argue with me, either. Something weird going on. You're signing out the lady in room 205, aren't you?"

"What makes you say that?"

"She's the only one who hasn't called to find out what's going on. And those two who were nosing around described her pretty close."

"Greg, you ought to be a detective."

"Nah, too much stress." He shuddered faintly.

"Sorry. Wrong choice of words." Pastor Small put out a hand to clasp the other man's arm a moment.

"Just some really powerful memories. Wouldn't it be something if I did become a detective?" He forced a grin. "Hey, is she really in trouble?"

"I think you'd better notify the police." He reached into his pocket for the room key and handed it to Greg. "Can you do something with the computer so it looks like they're still here, in case those men do get permission?"

~~~~~

On the other side of town, Carson checked his rearview mirror. Two Jeeps, a pickup, a station wagon, and a car with the logo for the local police department. No other vehicles in sight. As he watched, the other cars turned down other streets.

"I think we lost them."

"Is that good or bad?" Porter mumbled. He gestured with his chin at the bright lights of a diner on the other side of the intersection ahead of
~~~~~

them.

"Better call it in that those two are involved. Let someone figure out just how much worse things got."

Porter nodded and reached for his cell phone, while Carson pulled into the next shopping strip driveway. As he left a message, the 4X4 pulled behind the stores, into a puddle of light, and parked. Both men got out and took a bag of equipment from the back of the truck to begin the process of sweeping for anything their opponents might have attached to their truck.

~~~~~

Cooper stared at the dark blue pickup that pulled out of the hotel driveway as she and Edwards returned. A gray-haired man drove it, and the truck slid into the darkness out of the parking lot lights before she lowered her gaze to study the license plate. She glanced at Edwards and decided not to ask him if he had caught the license plate. His mood at this stage of the hunt was even worse than hers. She certainly didn't need him reporting her lapse to their superiors. Edwards parked close to the lobby doors but outside the range of any possible security cameras. Cooper got out and stalked into the hotel, carrying a photo of Regina.

The lobby was deserted for the moment. She looked in all directions, didn't see any sign of even basic security, then curled her lip as she took silent, stiff-legged steps up to the front desk. She reached for the bell to ring for service just as the heavy-set clerk came out of the back room, carrying a cup of coffee. He paused and frowned, visibly not pleased to see her. She fought down the urge to make his day worse than hers.

"FBI," Cooper said before he could open his mouth to greet her. She pulled out a slim leather case and flashed a badge at him, expertly flipping it closed so he could get nothing more than a blur of gold metal. "How long have you been on duty?"

The clerk stepped up to the desk and put down his cup.

~~~~~

Regina muttered her farewell and scrambled into the truck. Kathryn stayed leaning against the front of the truck, scratching Bea behind the ears and talking with Pastor Small. She knew her companion wanted to get out of there, but she also knew the minister had questions. He had been patient and helpful and accepted what she told him. She couldn't repay him any other way except with as many answers as she could safely give.

"I really appreciate this," she said. "Not many people these days will help strangers with such a flimsy explanation."

"That isn't reason enough?" Pastor Small laughed and gestured over his shoulder at the white steeple with the gray metal cross on top.

"It should be, but—" She decided not to get into that area.

Sometimes the nastiest, most uncooperative people she had run across in her journeys were people who *claimed* to be Christians. Nine times out of ten, they based their long lists of what a "real" Christian should be on their own opinions and schemes to earn their way into heaven, and never checked what the Bible said.

"What really convinced you? Back when we were talking in the sanctuary, there was a moment when I thought you were going to throw us out or call the police, then you changed your mind."

"Those." He pointed at the shoes the custodian had given her.

"Oh. Sorry." She went to one knee and started to untie the paint-spattered sneakers.

"No, you ought to keep them." Pastor Small bent down and caught hold of her arm, tugging her upright again. "Four years ago, our youth group put together a time capsule as a joke when they renovated their classroom. Those are my shoes. It was quite a mess, with all the painting we did. We had a great time." He winked. "Those shoes should be in a locked metal box three feet underground, sealed in plastic wrap and cement."

"You're kidding." Kathryn felt a chill race up her back, but it was a good chill.

"Plus," he continued with a lopsided smile, "we don't have a custodian right now. The deacons and trustees and the ladies mission groups and other committees take turns with the upkeep and cleaning. The place hasn't looked this good in years..." Pastor Small tried to laugh. "Whoever helped you, he wanted you to be here. Who am I to argue?"

"Good idea," she nearly whispered. "Thanks." She hugged him. The man startled, stiffening for half a second, then hugged her back. He waited, hands jammed into his back pockets, as Kathryn stepped around to the driver's side, opened the door, waited until Bea climbed into the back, then got inside.

"You sure you won't stay and talk to the police?" he asked.

"I'm taking Regina to someone I *know* can protect her," Kathryn said, leaning out the window.

"I'd like to hear how this turns out. Would you mind just—"

"As soon as she's safe, I'll send a friend to explain. Promise."

Kathryn looked in the rearview mirror for the hotel as they rolled down the entrance ramp to the highway. She would remember this particular exit, for good and bad reasons.

As soon as Regina fell into her snuffle-snore rhythm, Kathryn pulled out her cell phone and called Vincent. His phone rang for what seemed forever before going to voicemail, and that made her shiver. What kind of trouble was he in, that he couldn't answer her call? She knew from experience Vincent slept with one eye open, and he would have answered her call in the middle of the first ring. *If* he had been able. Unable or unwilling? Which option was worse?

She called Quarry Hall and left a message, reporting on what had happened, where she was, and gave the address of the church so Pastor Small and his congregation could be investigated thoroughly and discretely. A church that lived what it believed was more rare than she liked to contemplate, and if they needed help that the Arc Foundation could give, then she wanted to know so it could be offered. Kathryn frowned as she put her phone back in the cup holder of the console. It only made sense that no one was manning the switchboard at Quarry Hall, going on midnight, but it still bothered her that she couldn't talk to someone.

"Just tired," she whispered, and flinched as sharp pinpricks stabbed both temples. "Please, Lord..."

She promised herself she would drive at least half an hour before looking for a place to stop. While she could force herself to keep going until she got Regina to Finn, Kathryn knew she would be utterly useless after that effort. The last thing she wanted was to distract Finn from doing his job to bombard her with questions. He might be able to write off the changes in her appearance if she claimed she was tired. A long, hot shower and eight solid hours of sleep could erase a lot of evidence against her. However, if she showed up shaking, gray, dizzy or nauseous from headaches, he wouldn't be so easily persuaded that her condition was nothing to worry about. He was FBI, after all, and valued for his analysis skills even more than his solid right hook and sharpshooter talent.

Besides, he loved her, and he had displayed in dozens of ways an uncanny talent for sensing when something was wrong. He would want to rescue her. They would probably argue. Kathryn dreaded having to tell him that this time, there was nothing he could do, no matter how many strings he pulled on her behalf.

"Please, Lord, give me the strength..."

~~~~~

The big, rattling clock in the tower of the town hall chimed the half-hour, making it 1:30am when Pastor Small finished working on his sermon and left the church. He shook his head as he stepped out the back door and looked up at the moon, and a little shiver went up and down his back. He glanced at the window where Kathryn said she had first seen the man she thought was the custodian, and the shiver grew a little more intense. Oddly enough, it was an entirely pleasant shiver. How many times had he prayed for an opportunity to help, to reach beyond the community where his congregation slowly managed to make a difference? He had never imagined that people in danger would show up on his doorstep. Recalling what Kathryn had told him about the supposed
~~~~~

custodian, his appearance and especially his words, Pastor Small shook his head again. Usually he had his sermon finished by Friday night, and he celebrated with a solitary pizza and a movie, tucked up safe and comfortable in his own home. Tonight, about the same time Kathryn and Regina stepped through the door of the church, he had suddenly decided his sermon wasn't right, and of course the books he needed to check to fix his sermon were in his office.

"Keep them safe, Lord," he murmured as he got into his car.

Greg at the hotel had been a big help. Pastor Small decided he would drop by and fill in the missing pieces of the story, now that Kathryn and Regina were safely far away from town and whoever was trying to catch them.

It was a matter of moments to take two side streets to the back entrance of the hotel. He came around the side to reach the office and nearly hit the brakes when he saw a police car sitting by the door to the front lobby. After a few seconds of thought, he pulled into a parking space opposite the doors and went inside. Whatever had happened, he suspected he was part of it because of Kathryn and the men chasing her and Regina. He said another quick prayer for safety for the two, and wisdom for himself.

The lobby was fine, but the front desk had been trashed, thoroughly. The computer monitor had been yanked out of its slot in the desk, the screen smashed and the plastic housing cracked. The keyboard lay on its face, broken down the middle. Papers lay in drifts of wet, torn, partially burned confetti all over the floor and in a trail leading into the back office. Through the door, he saw filing cabinets turned on their sides, drawers pulled completely out and turned upside down and the contents strewn everywhere. It would take days to put everything back together and know what had been destroyed and what taken.

Greg leaned against the counter, minus his uniform jacket, looking weary and rumpled and too tired for all of this as he talked to two police officers. Pastor Small felt sorry for him. He knew how Greg hated having anything to do with the police, even if he was innocent, after the years he spent in prison. He only knew half the story of what the other man had done in those years away from his hometown, but that half was enough to make any man feel guilty and edgy around authorities.

Chapter Fifteen

"Pastor!" Greg saw him and stepped around the two officers to meet him halfway across the floor. "I was just about to call you. Are you all right?"

"I'm fine." It took a minute for him to understand. Greg obviously thought someone had traced the young women to him and the church. "What happened here?" he asked, trying to remember everything he had told Greg about Kathryn and Regina only a few hours ago.

"Diversion," the woman officer said, "then a snatch-and-grab."

"Somebody knocked over the pop machine out back and I went outside to see what was going on. I even locked both doors." He gestured at the front door of the hotel lobby, as well as the office. "When I came back—" Greg turned and swept his hands across the scene of destruction. "Did the lady you were helping get away all right?"

"Nearly two hours ago."

"Maybe you shouldn't have let her leave," the other officer said. He took off his cap and scratched his balding head. "Whoever trashed this place took all the hand-written registration files and then destroyed the memory in the computer. Greg here says a few people were asking to look at the files right after she left. What we're worried about are the license plate numbers. We don't have any way of recovering that information for ourselves. That girl you helped, who was being chased last night—she could be in a lot of trouble if they know her name or what she was driving, and then track her down through the DMV."

"Well," Pastor Small said half under his breath, "let's hope Kathryn lied about everything when she came in last night."

Greg started to look shocked, then it changed to a grin. The two officers just looked at each other and shrugged.

"Can you contact her?" the woman officer asked.

"No, but she said she'd send word when everything was settled. Why?"

"Just before the office was ransacked, a federal agent stopped by, looking for a missing scientist involved in a murder. We called the clerk who had the earlier evening shift. The description of the woman who checked in last night didn't match the picture the agent showed Greg, but she could have had a companion waiting outside."

"You said murder?"

For two seconds, Pastor Small found himself very willing to believe Regina could have murdered someone. Then he pushed that thought aside and silently scolded himself. The young woman was too selfish and weak, in his opinion, to be a murderer. She was more prone to stomp and scream and run away than fight back or even kill her enemies. He shook his head. Whatever trouble Kathryn was helping Regina solve, it couldn't be murder. He had too much faith in Kathryn. Even if he didn't, the actions of her mysterious helper vouched for her integrity and the value of her mission.

And yet, Regina didn't know why she was running from those men. Kathryn had said so.

"Kathryn didn't strike me as the type," he continued after a tiny pause, "but you said a missing scientist?" He couldn't take the chance on Kathryn getting hurt. "Do you have a picture of her?"

"No, but we can contact the local FBI office and get one," the other officer said. "It shouldn't be too hard. They have to follow procedures, just like us." He grinned, showing two golden teeth.

"What were their names?" the woman said.

"Well, the blond girl is Regina. That's all she told me. She's been through a rough time; bruises, stitches in her forehead, and she doesn't remember a lot. Kathryn is helping her, taking her to someone who can find answers and protect her." He frowned, suddenly caught by a detail he had missed earlier. "Kathryn has a friend in the FBI—that's where they're heading. Why couldn't these agents who came by have stopped at the local office, or even had the local people ask?"

"Who knows with the Feds? Sometimes the in-fighting you hear about... Those two girls could have just come to us instead of hiding in your church," she said. "No offense, Pastor."

"None taken." He had to grin.

"Who's this Kathryn?"

"Good girl. Smart. About five six, long dark brown hair, hazel eyes, late twenties." He went on to describe Regina, and Greg confirmed the description matched the photo the second set of agents had shown him. Pastor Small was relieved no one commented on the fact Kathryn had only registered herself, not Regina or her dog. He felt oddly protective of her, and didn't like any criticism of her actions or choices. "Is there anything else I can help you with?" he asked the officers. "Are you about finished?"

"We're waiting for the manager to show up," the woman officer said, and rolled her eyes. "I've known Sybil Danstead all my life and she never hurries for anyone or anything. Yeah, we're about finished up here. When we get that photo, we'll bring it by the church, okay?"

"Fine."

Saturday

Kathryn finished combing out her wet hair and put the comb away in her duffel bag. Regina had borrowed her brush and hadn't given it back yet — if she hadn't lost it.

"Please, God, I didn't ask You to teach me patience," she said, her voice thick with something that could be equally sigh and chuckle. Kathryn tugged her sleeping tee-shirt into place. It had a tendency to stick to her body just after drying off from her shower.

She hoped she could fall asleep now. The only other option was to haul all their dirty clothes down to the first floor and that convenient little customers-only laundry room. Considering the way Regina was banging around in the bathroom, she would make just as much noise when she finished and settled into bed. Kathryn didn't want to risk falling asleep and being awakened, and probably staying awake after that, so she needed something to do until they were both in their beds and she could turn off the light.

Regina would probably be in the shower for the next half hour, the way she had grumbled about being sticky, sweaty dirty all day. What should she do that she wouldn't be able to do with Regina watching her?

Evening exercises? Bible study? Call Finn? He wouldn't be in his office, but she could leave another message, give him a good estimate of what time she would get to him.

If Regina mocked her for doing her evening bends and stretches, Kathryn decided to challenge her to keep up. Judging from the way she had huffed and puffed and her overall clumsiness climbing out that bathroom window, that response would shut her up.

"Finn, first," she muttered, and got off the end of the bed to retrieve her phone from her backpack. At least now they were far enough from the mountains that the reception had cleared up.

Keeping Regina from knowing about her check-in calls would avoid unwanted questions and panic. Her passenger had questioned her ability to handle the situation often enough. Kathryn didn't want more openings for arguments. She was ready to jump into a doozy as it was.

Settling down on the end of the bed again, Kathryn glanced around the room. This one was a little nicer than the average non-chain hotel. Thicker blankets on the beds, newer carpet, more color to the room beyond the institutional browns, beiges, and blues. The beds had headboards of real wood, not plastic, and the dresser and desk matched the headboards. She planned to take advantage of the complementary tea bags and the little hot pot set up on the vanity bar outside the bathroom in the morning. Splotchy, abstract paintings in blue and green and scarlet hung over each bed and the dresser. Kathryn supposed they could be flowers. The television set looked fairly new.

She punched in the number and caught the phone between her shoulder and ear. Bea snuggled up against her, shoving her head between her arm and side, just begging for a good petting.

Finn's answering machine kicked in. She closed her eyes and sighed and listened all the way through. She used to be able to tease him about knights errant who were never there when someone needed them. After all, Sir Galahad never used an answering service or had call waiting. Right now, however, she was more than grateful to leave a message. With the threat of a headache sending nauseous threads down her throat, she didn't need to dance around subjects better left for later, trying to fill Finn in on the situation before Regina came out of the shower and heard her. Especially since some of her report would not be complimentary.

"Hi, Finn," she said, trying not to sound achy tired. He would worry and scold her. "This is Kathryn again. Aren't you ever in your office? Just an update. We're stopped for the night. Warning—somebody's following us. Might need some firepower and a place to hide when we get to you." Kathryn hesitated a moment. Had she just made a mistake telling him that? Then again, since Vincent knew she was taking Regina to him, he had probably brought Finn up-to-date on the entire situation by now. "We got away, so we're probably okay. Call me if you need any information before we get there. Don't call me if all you're going to do is lecture, okay?"

She laughed, and immediately regretted it, because it sounded lame to her. For half a second she debated saying she looked forward to seeing him. Would he interpret that as panic, or encouragement?

"We'll see you tomorrow afternoon. I'm planning on taking a lazy morning, not leaving the hotel until they kick us out. Bye."

Kathryn was still grinning after she put away her phone and started her evening relaxation exercises. She needed to loosen her muscles for a decent night of sleep.

When Regina finally straggled out of the bathroom, Kathryn was just finishing up. She braced herself for the first snide comment, but nothing came. Regina simply tugged down the covers of her bed and sat down, dressed in Kathryn's spare t-shirt, and started brushing her hair. Kathryn noted with a little amusement that at least Regina hadn't lost her brush.

Regina grabbed the overpriced bag of chips she had bought on their walk from the lobby to the room, and turned on the TV. After ten minutes of flipping through the channels, *Star Trek* was the only halfway decent show on any of the local stations. Kathryn decided it was better to bite her tongue and get some studying done, rather than remind Regina it was past 2a.m., she needed some sleep, and she had been eating all day. She had outgrown her fascination with *Star Trek* years ago, but she still knew every episode of the Classic series by heart. That made it easier to ignore the phaser blasts and concentrate on her study guide.

"How can you read with the TV on?" Regina muttered only ten minutes into the show.

"Practice." Kathryn kept her answer short and her tone of voice abrupt to discourage more questions.

"What are you reading?"

"Hebrews."

"You read Hebrew? Who'd want to?"

"Not Hebrew, the language. Hebrews, a letter to Jewish believers in the Bible."

"The Bible?"

Kathryn didn't have to look at Regina to see her expression. The sneering curve of her lip was evident in the rise in her voice.

"I knew it. You're some kind of religious—"

"Don't say it." Kathryn raised her head and looked across the gap between their beds.

"How can you believe that stuff?"

"Do you believe the owner's manual that comes with your new TV or stereo or computer?"

"Yeah." Regina stopped and blinked, visibly nonplussed by Kathryn's response.

"This is the owner's manual for being Human."

"That's silly!"

Kathryn wasn't sure if she liked Regina's laughter better than her scorn.

"I wouldn't say that if I were you." She sat up and crossed her legs. "This book and what it teaches me are about the only things that keep me from punching your lights out. You're a real snot, you know that? A genuine, USDA-grade spoiled brat."

Regina went white. Her eyes glistened with a threat of tears. She clutched the second pillow on her bed like a teddy bear.

"Then why are you still helping me if you don't like me?" she whimpered.

"I didn't say I didn't like you." Kathryn sighed and rubbed at her eyes. She didn't need that warning throb that hit the base of her skull and temples at the same time. "You're just really irritating. I know you're confused and your head hurts and nothing is going right in your life. Could you try to think about what you're doing and how it affects others? Just a little?"

"Sorry." Regina sniffled a few seconds, then slid off the bed and scrambled into the bathroom.

Kathryn bowed her head and rubbed at her gritty eyes as she tried to pray through her blossoming headache. Somewhere in the distance, she heard Regina blow her nose. It was a loud honking sound, worthy of Harpo Marx.

A few giggles escaped her.

"Well, at least we've cleared the air," she whispered. "Please, Lord, let it be downhill from here. I really need it."

~~~~~

Finn Roberts stumbled into his office and kicked the door shut. The faulty latch clicked and it swung open three seconds later. He sighed with relief and hunger. The aromas from his reheated carryout cartons made his stomach rumble and ache. He loved late night hours. Easier to get paperwork caught up without a co-worker dropping in to ask for help every ten minutes. He swore every time someone walked in, the paperwork in his in-box doubled, like the stables that filled themselves in the faerie tale of the Mastermaid. His only worry was that someone else working late tonight would be summoned by the delectable aromas and try to mooch. He only shared his Kung Pao chicken and pot stickers with one person, and she was still half a day of driving away.

He nudged aside a carton of report folders and stepped around his desk with a little more care than usual. The ever-present pile of folders, binders, loose papers and file boxes was a foot higher than normal. The last thing he needed was an avalanche at nearly 3a.m..

It took five minutes to re-arrange the workspace on his desk so he could set out the cartons in the precise arrangement for eating while working, without dripping sauce or soup on anything. His boss, Garretson, loved Chinese food, too, but not on official documents.

Just over the peak of thirty, Finn Roberts had settled into his job with a few regrets, but mostly a sense of satisfaction and purpose. His favorite hobbies were worrying about his friends, diving into research for fellow workers, and experimenting with ethnic cuisine. His love of weekend sports kept away his spare tire. His curly, dark hair still had no gray, which sometimes amazed him. His brown eyes were still good enough not to need glasses and when he remembered not to stoop over his desk, his shoulders were still as broad and straight as when he played football in college. Barring the stray bullet that sometimes accompanied the occasional assignment, he looked forward to living to a gray-haired, desk-bound old age.

A sigh of exasperation escaped his lips nearly forty minutes later, dimming his smile a little, when Finn moved aside a stack of papers, excavating his cell phone, and saw the tiny blue light blinking at him. Somebody probably wanted an analysis of some dusty old report by 7a.m.

He almost re-buried his phone, but a chill of worried anticipation traveled down his back, cutting him off before his grumble became
~~~~~

audible. After all those phone calls throughout the day, warnings and unsatisfactory updates and putting together contingency plans, he couldn't just assume anything was business as usual. Finn slid his loose green tie from around his neck, unbuttoned the third and fourth buttons of his rumpled white shirt, and tapped through the various screens to access his voicemail. He closed his eyes and leaned back in his chair to listen.

"Hi, Finn. This is Kathryn again."

She sounded all right. He smiled.

"Aren't you ever in your office?"

That prompted a chuckle from him. Leave it to Kathryn to call the only times he ever left his office, barring bathroom breaks and fetching more water for his coffee machine.

His smile faded as he listened to her admission of trouble. True, she said she thought she had lost the people following her, but that didn't mean anything. Finn knew that rule too well.

Next time he saw Kathryn , he was going to give her a good shaking for insisting on coming to him, instead of digging in and waiting for the Cavalry to come to her for a change. She might even be stunned enough to let him kiss her a few extra times.

"Well, nothing to be done about it right now. Except worry."

An hour later, Finn was bent double, his chair pushed back so he could check a file he had stored under his desk. He only had his head underneath the desk a few inches. He knew better than to put his entire body underneath that rattling drawer with the nail points sticking out in strategic places. But when the alarm on his computer went off, he slammed those few inches against the drawer, banging it hard so it flew open five inches.

Finn winced and pressed one hand against the back of his head while the fingers of the other hand flew across his keyboard. The current screen blanked to make way for the information that went with the alarm. What he read made him forget the tenderness in his scalp.

Momentary alarm changed to determination. Both hands on the keyboard now, he began tapping in commands to set up a decoy program a friend of his had devised years ago.

~~~~~

In the hotel room, all was quiet but for the sounds of two women breathing. Bea lay at the foot of Kathryn's bed, head up, watching the sliver of light where the curtain didn't quite meet the wall and the parking lot lights came into the room. The muffled sound of voices drifted up from the parking lot three stories below, barely penetrating the groaning roar of the air conditioning unit under the window.

Regina moaned, softly, sounding like a sigh. Bea's ears twitched and
~~~~~

her head turned to focus on her. Minutes passed, then she moaned again, a little louder.

Kathryn woke and stayed perfectly still, blinking up into the darkness for a few seconds. Regina's moan turned into a whimper. Kathryn sat up and looked at her companion, waiting. Silence for several minutes. She adjusted her blankets and was about to lie down again when Regina groaned faintly.

The groan turned into sobs. Kathryn slid her legs from under the sheet and went to her knees on the floor between the beds. She put an arm over Regina, and stroked her tousled blond hair with her free hand.

"It's okay," Kathryn whispered. "I'll take care of you. I won't let anybody hurt you. You're going to be okay."

The sobs changed into whimpers almost before she finished speaking. Regina shifted a little, lying on her stomach, and snuggled up against Kathryn. They stayed that way nearly ten minutes.

Finally, she felt the last tension leave Regina's muscles. Whatever dream had been bothering her, it was over. She slowly extricated herself and slid back onto her own bed. Instead of pulling the sheet up and lying down again, Kathryn perched on the side of the bed and pressed the heels of her hands against her eyes.

"Okay, God, You got us this far. Just a little bit longer and I'll stop bothering You," she whispered. A tiny chuckle escaped her. "Okay?"

Sighing, she uncovered her eyes and scooted backwards against the headboard. Bea got up and walked the length of the bed to settle down next to her. Kathryn smiled as the Akita put her head in her lap, and slowly stroked the thick fur.

"You think I'm crazy too, don't you?" she muttered. "Who but a crazy person would put up with her whining all day long and then hold her like a baby when she has bad dreams?"

Silence. Even the air conditioner stopped grumbling. Not a sound came from the hallway or the parking lot.

"I bet you think it's a waste of time, helping her. Yeah, she's a snot. So was I, when I was in trouble. When you're scared for your life and you don't know what's going on, it kind of wipes away all your manners."

Chapter Sixteen

Bea responded with a grumbling sigh and closed her eyes. Kathryn grinned into the darkness and slumped down against the headboard so she was almost lying flat.

Her phone rang. She scrambled off the bed and yanked the phone out of her backpack by the third ring. Her first thought was that Regina would be a pain in the morning if she didn't get enough sleep tonight.

"Anything but that, Lord," she whispered as she flipped open her phone. "'Lo?"

A glance at the bedside clock showed 5:20. Technically morning. But her body insisted there was a long stretch of night left before she was allowed to get up and get moving again.

"It's Finn."

She would have laughed aloud, but she heard the tension crackling in his voice, imagined him sitting at his desk, raking his hands through his hair and nearly pulling it out at the roots.

"Hi, what's—"

"You're in big trouble, sweetheart. Somebody has your license plates and the make of your truck and they're trying to call up all your files. They already have an APB out with the police in eighty different departments. A lot of them are along your route to me. You'd have to go an entire day of driving out of the way to avoid them."

"Okay." She couldn't think of anything to say.

"My system flagged it and I got the decoy program and the maze program going. In time, I think." Finn sighed. "You have got to get out of there, just in case I didn't catch it in time, understand?"

"Perfectly." Kathryn stood and gathered up her clothes that were waiting to be washed. She didn't bother whispering any longer.

"I couldn't trace the request backwards. That means whoever's trailing you, they're pretty high up and powerful. Now's the time to use that package I gave you. Remember that park where we went fishing? Meet me there—that's an hour longer ride. We have a safe house near there and it'll be waiting for us. Got it?"

"Got it." She reached over and grabbed Regina's feet under the covers, shaking until the blond woke.

"Call me when you hit the city limits. I'll probably get there ahead of you. You be careful, kiddo."

"You, too." Kathryn waited a few seconds after the connection broke. She swallowed hard, took a deep breath, and sent up a silent prayer for strength and calm. She tried for a calm expression when she turned on the light on the dresser and faced Regina.

"What's going on?" the other woman mumbled.

"Your friends have our license number and they're using pretty high connections to track us down." She flipped the phone closed and put it back into the backpack, then bent and jammed the rest of their laundry into her duffel bag. Regina's own clothes were dry, even if they needed mending, and she could wear those for the rest of the trip.

"How do you know?"

"I have friends with higher connections." She snatched up her clothes again. "Bea, guard." She pointed at Regina, then at the piece of open floor in front of the door.

Bea jumped off the bed and went to the door, putting her back to it, and stood at attention.

"We have to leave now?" Regina sounded more surprised than disgruntled.

"If you want to stay and wait for them to break down the door, that's just fine with me." Kathryn went into the bathroom.

"How did your friend find us?" A touch of strain entered Regina's voice.

"I called him and let him know our situation and—"

"Why?"

"So he can have everything ready to help us when we meet up with him."

"Are you going to tell me who he is?"

"You'll know when it's time to know," Kathryn said, raising her voice a little over the sound of the running water. She wet the washcloth, rubbed soap on it, and scrubbed her face. Still no response from Regina. Was that a bad sign, or good? "Are you remembering more?"

"What?" Bed springs creaked a little.

"You were having a nightmare. I figured you remembered more about your father and the people shooting at you."

"Oh—yeah."

"Anything helpful?" She sputtered as she got soap in her mouth. That was what she got for talking while she scrubbed.

"A fire. Someone dragged me out of the fire."

"Your father, maybe?" She rinsed and reached for the towel.

"Definitely not."

Kathryn paused, hearing a world of pain in that short statement. *Please, God, whatever happened to her, help her remember before we get to Finn so we don't waste a lot of time. The sooner she's on her way, the better for us all.*

Maybe that was a selfish prayer. Kathryn just didn't care right then. She had too much else on her mind.

"Well, whatever happened," she said as she tugged on her jeans, "my friend knows people who can help you."

When she was dressed she hurried out of the bathroom and snatched up her socks and turned to find Regina sitting on the end of the bed. She hadn't made a move toward her clean clothes sitting on the dresser. Kathryn bit back a scolding. Maybe that nightmare had shook her up more than she wanted to admit.

"Get dressed." Kathryn stooped to put on her boots. "I'll go load the truck and come back for you. And for heaven's sake, don't go looking for the pop machine, okay?"

She grinned, making the words teasing. Regina blushed and looked away. Kathryn scooped up her backpack and crammed her study books inside it. Her sleeping shirt went into the duffel bag. All that remained loose in the room were Regina's own clothes and the toothpaste, deodorant and brush. Kathryn snatched up the duffel bag and took that along, to save time.

"Get a move on," she said as she stepped to the door. Bea stayed with her back to the door, facing Regina.

In the parking lot, Kathryn got in her truck and just sat a few moments, hands resting on the steering wheel, thinking. It was a waste of time to ask why this was happening. She had to trust God would take care of her and Regina.

"Here we go," she muttered, and started the engine. She pulled out of the parking slot without turning on the lights and drove around to a shadowed spot at the edge of the lighted area. Enough light to work by without making it easy for anyone passing by to see what she was doing. She hoped.

Kathryn turned off the engine, got out of the truck and reached in under her seat. Hidden under a flap in the carpeting was a flat package half an inch thick and the dimensions of a sheet of paper, wrapped in brown paper, inside a zipper plastic bag. Kathryn opened it and first pulled out a stack of cards; credit cards, Social Security card, driver's license and vehicle registration sheet. She exchanged them for their counterparts in her wallet and the glove compartment and put the originals in the plastic bag. Then she brought out new license plates.

It was hard changing the plates with only the screwdriver in her pocketknife and not nearly enough light to see by. She had never done this before. She had been carrying that particular packet, courtesy of Finn, for two years now and had thought she would never use it. He sent her updated stickers for the plates, and renewed the second driver's license. She was grateful now for his attention to detail. She never would have thought of those tiny pieces of the puzzle.

Her hands wanted to shake by the time she finished that task. Kathryn put the old license plates in the brown paper wrapper, slid her original identification and credit cards inside with it, and hid everything under the carpeting under her seat again. Now for the tricky part.

All she had was a half-inch roll of masking tape. It wouldn't stand up to a close inspection, but for her purposes Kathryn thought it would do fine. She didn't intend to sit still long enough for anyone to get close enough to inspect the makeshift detailing.

She created racing stripes, angled on the doors and horizontal on the side panels and a double V on the hood of her truck. The lines weren't perfectly straight and the tape kept trying to curl and stick together, but she was in no position to be picky. She stepped back when she finished the hurried application and thought it would get them past any watchers. She hoped the churned texture of the sky as dawn approached meant the day would be overcast and work in their favor.

Last step: she climbed inside the back of the truck and unlocked the storage box. Her fingers didn't want to cooperate, tangling in the early morning chill. Kneeling in the ribbed bed of the truck made her knees ache hard enough she shifted to a squatting position. Maybe this was a sign it was time to get off the road? What good was she, protecting people, when she couldn't move like she used to and had to stop every few hours to rest?

"Later," she muttered. "Think about it later."

A light gray tarpaulin went over the bed of her truck, held in place on the sides with bungie cords. She turned her storage box on its side so it made a hunch in the middle of the cover. That would change the outline of her truck, but not too much. She only needed to make her truck slightly different from what was expected. Kathryn had no way of knowing how much detail was in the report used by her enemies.

"Okay, God, I've done my part. Everything from here on in is up to You." She wrapped her arms around herself, squeezed hard, then turned and headed for the front door of the hotel to check out. As she reached a pool of light in the parking lot, she checked her watch. A little more than half an hour to set up the disguise. Kathryn hoped the time invested would prove profitable. Then she pulled out her phone and dialed.

Again, she got voicemail.

"I'm meeting up with Finn in a couple hours. He has a safe house ready for us," she told Vincent. "You know how to get hold of him. Someone has the cops looking for my truck. Dr. West in Millersburg said two different groups of agents are after Regina. Both sets could be on my tail. I sure hope at least one of them are your friends." She paused, tempted to admit to the exhaustion that hadn't been washed away by three hours of sleep. What could she say that wouldn't sound like whining? "Just—

hurry and catch up with me, okay? Something is really wrong with Regina. More than being a snot." Her voice cracked. "Gotta go."

~~~~~

Carson and Porter walked slowly down the hotel hallway toward the door at the very end. It was too close to a stairwell for the comfort of either man. After spotting Edwards and Cooper at the other hotel, and removing the bug tucked under the front bumper of the 4X4, they had taken their time catching up with the two young women in the blue pickup, to make sure their tails didn't catch them. After four hours, no sign of the enemy, and a growing need for rest, they began to fear the occupants of the sedan might have reached this new hotel ahead of them.

They had conferred less then five minutes before agreeing that even though they hadn't heard from their superiors, they were going to make contact. Too many problematic factors had been added to the chase.

The hallway was too quiet. Even if it was a Saturday, shouldn't travelers be stirring, getting ready for another long day of travel?

Porter knocked. No response. He knocked again, louder. No sounds of movement inside the room. He nodded to Carson, who took up a position with his back to the door, where he could see both ends of the hallway. Porter knelt and brought out a key ring with an assortment of probes, some needle-fine. It was a matter of moments before the lock clicked and the door opened a quarter inch.

"No chain or deadbolt," Porter murmured. "Not good." He met his partner's eyes, traded nods, then he nudged the door with his elbow.

Nothing. No movement in the room. No lights coming on. No sounds of breathing.

It was foolish to stand there in the hall with the light making them targets. Carson reached in and hit the light switch and went to his knees, gun out and ready.

The scene before them was the proverbial tornado's strike. Drawers had been pulled out of the dresser and turned over, a lamp toppled on the floor. Both mattresses were halfway off the frames and the sheets had been torn awry. All the towels were on the floor.

"They got here ahead of us again," Porter muttered.

~~~~~

Fifteen minutes later, Carson left the front desk, crossed the lobby, and hurried outside to the waiting 4X4. Porter tapped the steering wheel and occasionally gunned the engine. He waited for his partner to get into the passenger side and close the door. A raised eyebrow asked his question.

"Two FBI agents got here half an hour ago—get this—with a warrant. They asked for the owner of the blue pickup out in the parking lot, showed them a picture of Regina, and gave them a general description of the girl helping her."

"How did they get it?" Porter added a few curses under his breath. Carson glared at him.

"We'll find out," he promised his friend. "But the good news is, we got a name to work with now. Kathryn. And better news." He grinned and waited until Porter glared at him. "She checked out using the automated system five minutes before the agents showed up."

"How would she know?" Porter shook his head, then cast a suspicious glance at his partner. "Something you aren't telling me?"

"Somebody's helping them."

"Yeah? Tell me who?" He thumped the steering wheel and came too close to the horn. A short, sharp blatt echoed off the glass doors of the lobby twenty feet away. It was doubly loud in the morning quiet.

"Space aliens, for all I know." He grinned at his partner's killing glare.

The ringing of the cell phone startled them both. Porter snatched it up and answered quickly. He closed his eyes, shook his head and blindly handed over the phone.

Carson took it and listened. He grinned, but he had the sense not to laugh aloud.

"Got it. Great. I don't like just sitting and waiting. Isn't there something—" He shook his head. "Okay, I got you. See you there. Thanks."

Slowly, he pushed the power button and slid the phone back into the cup holder. Porter opened his eyes and looked at him, waiting for a ten-count. Carson just shook his head and looked out the side window.

"Well? What's the word?"

"They're heading in to shelter."

"What's that supposed to mean?"

"Someone in the FBI—the real FBI—is helping them, and my friend knows who that is. Pretty soon we'll know where they are. Then we can finish business with dear little Regina."

"I owe her," Porter half-whispered. He smiled, but suddenly he looked nothing but weary.

"We both do."

~~~~~

"Pastor Small? This is Officer Tilby."

The woman's voice sounded unfamiliar at first. Even discounting the fact that the phone had rung at just shy of 6:30 and he picked it up off the bedside table before opening his eyes. Then the minister remembered the chain of events from last night.

"Yes, Officer. What can I do for you?" He considered making a joking comment on the long hours she kept being equal with his own, but the woman sounded tired. She certainly didn't need to be reminded of that.

He reached up and finally turned on the lamp next to his bed. He
~~~~~

winced and blinked rapidly as his eyes adjusted.

"Well, Pastor, you're not going to believe this. Remember how we were going to retrieve that photo of the woman involved in the murders?"

"There's no photo?" he guessed.

"No agents reported in with the local officials, despite people claiming to be agents. Doesn't make sense. Nobody knows anything for a hundred miles in any direction." She sighed, loudly. "Is there anything you can tell me about those two you helped last night? It's easy to see they're in a lot of trouble."

"They didn't say where they were going. Kathryn only said she was taking Regina to someone she trusted in the FBI, who could protect and help her."

"You'd better start praying pretty hard."

"I've been doing that since the moment they drove away, believe me." Pastor Small sat back against the headboard and smiled wearily. He couldn't remember any details, but his dreams had been disturbing, exhausting, and he suspected he had been praying for Kathryn and Regina, wrestling with the powers of darkness the whole time.

~~~~~

Just before dawn, Kathryn's truck pulled onto the highway, three exits further down from the one she had taken to get to the hotel last night. The traffic was sparse enough to let her see any vehicles sitting by the roadside. Her pulse picked up speed when she saw a dark sedan. She tried not to look at the occupants of the car as she drove past. Her palms sweated, and she had a sudden vision of the masking tape peeling off the truck in the morning chill and dew and the friction of the wind.

Regina curled up in the compartment behind her seat, covered with the spare blanket, pillowed on the duffel bag. Bea sat on the floorboards in front of the passenger seat. Kathryn had her hair pulled back tight in two braids and a red bandana wrapped around her head. She studied the traffic in front of her and said a dozen pleading prayers as sweat beaded on her forehead, soaked the bandana and then trickled down from her temples.

The sedan was empty. A grin lit her face.

Maybe she had wasted time, driving out of the hotel the back way and taking back roads to the edge of town. It had been hard on her nerves because she drove without headlights. The rutted, muddy road had been harder on the truck's suspension. Maybe she had been too cautious, but Kathryn didn't dare take any risks.

~~~~~

Harper's desk was clean of everything, including the occasional dust speck. Not a good sign. Lisa hated making her reports when there was nothing on her superior's desk. She hated it when he turned down the lights in his long, plush office and closed the drapes and received his subordinates in semi-shadows. She felt like a prisoner somewhere between trial and the proverbial naked light bulb in the jail cell. She could almost feel a rubber hose whistling down between her shoulder blades.

"All right," Harper said quietly, coldly, studying his steepled fingers. His elbows rested on the leather arms of his chair. "How far can they go without running to someone for help?"

"Someone *is* helping them." Lisa took a breath, trying to regain her usual cool tones. Losing control would not sit well with Harper. "Someone who either knows exactly what we're doing as we do it, or a very good guesser. How else do you explain them leaving the hotel minutes before our people got there?"

"There is that, yes." He nodded and kept his half-lidded gaze fastened on some imaginary point in the air.

That was not a good sign. When he was angry, Harper never looked anyone in the eye until they had crossed the point of no return.

"Sooner or later," he continued, speaking slowly as he would to a mentally deficient child, "they have to contact someone in authority, so Regina can tell her lies. We have to be ready."

"During one of the near-misses, a GPS was attached to the truck Regina is riding in."

"Very good." His voice dropped to a whisper and he nodded twice, staring at a point in the air between them.

"We're triangulating along the path the truck is taking, to forecast where they might be going."

"The identify of the one driving the truck would be helpful. I assume there is no definite identification."

"No, sir."

"What *has* been found out about her?"

"Nothing."

Harper stiffened. For a moment, she thought he was about to look her in the eye. Lisa swallowed down an iceberg of panic.

Chapter Seventeen

"We've done five searches in the system," Lisa continued. "Every time we started to check out the information, it conflicted with what we knew. She's Caucasian, brunette, late twenties. But one report said she was Black and eighty-five years old. The next time we checked, it gave us a different name from the hotel registration. Every time, the data changed. If I didn't know better—"

"You don't know better. Tell me."

"Someone has set up a program to keep people from learning the truth of her identity and her base of operations."

"If that were so, she'd be some kind of federal agent, wouldn't she?" His tone softened just enough that Lisa let herself breathe a little more deeply. He was fair, even if he was demanding, and always recognized when circumstances were beyond the reach and control of his agents.

"That would mean Regina got to the authorities with her story," Harper continued, "wouldn't it? And that would mean someone would be on to us already, wouldn't it?"

"Yes, sir."

"I would prefer to believe we are dealing with someone with powerful connections, but not powerful enough. Certainly not as well-connected as we are. We will ultimately obtain that information. However, believing the worst case has always kept me from being unpleasantly surprised. You know the drill. Prepare to cover our tracks and rid us of those two agents before they catch up with Regina and her friend."

"Right away." Lisa turned sharply on her heel and hurried from the room.

Harper watched her until she vanished through the shadowy doorway. He waited for the solid, dull thud of his heavy mahogany door closing and the click of the brass latch. Then he opened a drawer kept locked with a keypad, and brought out a gleaming silver handgun. The magazine popped out of the bottom at a slight touch on the base. Harper checked the load in a detached way, like another man would check the tobacco in his pipe while contemplating world affairs.

~~~~~

Kathryn remembered the park. She had fond memories of the hiking trail, through the woods and down by the lake, with many convenient benches to stop and rest and think and sneak in a few kisses in private.
~~~~~

At just past 9a.m., she pulled into the long, winding two-lane trail that led from the main street to the center of the park and the gravel parking lot. Four trails led from the lot, to the lake or for hiking or to the picnic areas. She drove down past a stand of trees and over a wooden bridge, and saw two cars in the lot. One pulled out of the parking slot and left as she watched. The other, a green two-door hatchback, was Finn's. Her heart picked up the pace a little as she thought about seeing him again.

"Don't be silly," she muttered, softly enough not even Bea twitched an ear at the sound.

Regina was back in the passenger seat, sound asleep, her mouth open, still wrapped up in the blanket. Kathryn had made sure not to tell her that was Bea's blanket. Why disturb the peace?

She drove around the last curve and the truck's wheels crunched on the gravel. Half a minute later she pulled into the parking slot next to Finn's car. His door opened and he got out before she could shut off the engine. Kathryn rolled down the window. Her face hurt from the wide grin she wore.

"So, that's all the trouble?" Finn asked in a soft voice, gesturing at Regina.

"Find anything?" That was the rule. Get the official business over with and then they could indulge in a little reunion.

"Maybe. Need to confirm some data. Give me the story."

"Beat up. Amnesia. Stumbling around the mountainside in the middle of a storm with people chasing her. Guns. A cabin or house burned down in the middle of it all. She's had nightmares about a fire and her father getting killed. And now someone's been trying to trace my license plates. Thank God for paranoids like you."

"Did you change—"

"Yes, teacher," she said with a groan.

Bea chose that moment to try to wriggle past Kathryn to get to Finn. He grinned and reached past her to pet the Akita, who slobbered all over his hand. Finn still grinned, but not as widely, as he withdrew his hand to wipe it on the seat of his navy pants.

"Hey, Bea," he said, not quite as delighted as he had been a moment ago. "How you doing? Keeping our lady out of trouble?"

"Like she'd ever answer you." Kathryn fought a chuckle. She gestured for Finn to step back and opened the truck door. Bea climbed out after her and dashed off to the grass to nose around.

"Well," Finn said as they walked a few yards away from the truck, "first step is the safe house. For both of you."

"Finn—" she began, and stopped short when he brushed a kiss across her cheek. It threw her totally off balance. Usually she could tell when he was going to try to kiss her.

"I love it when you blush," he whispered loudly. "You glow like a neon light."

"Just great."

"When are you going to let me talk you into settling down?"

"I may let you kiss me once in a while, but—"

"Let?" Finn let out a sharp hoot of laughter. "I think you manufacture trouble just to come see me."

Kathryn wanted to hit him. She wanted to knock him off balance with a kiss that would take his breath away. She wanted him to put his arms around her and not let go for the rest of the day. Now that she was safe, she could admit she had been scared.

"*If* I ever settle down," she finally said, when she couldn't stand him grinning at her any longer, "you're the first on the list. Is that good enough for you?"

"Will you ever settle down?" Finn's grin faded a few degrees.

"Someday. When I finish some things I have to do," she admitted, and could no longer look him in the eye.

Finn shook his head, his smile turned wistful, and he slid his arm around her shoulders. He brought up his other hand and cupped her cheek. Kathryn for once didn't have to think to relax into the warmth of his arm and his support and when he bent his head to kiss her, she wanted him to. She slid one arm around his neck, holding him close.

~~~~~

The safe house sat on a curve in the road, in the middle of a sleepy neighborhood of nearly identical single-story homes. Aluminum awnings over the windows, detached garages, deep back yards, and front yards with at least one big, spreading shade tree each. Except for the color of the brick and the awnings, the houses could have come from a cookie press in the same batch of dough.

Finn put Kathryn's truck in the garage and took the time to cover it with a huge tarpaulin before closing and locking the door. This particular garage had no windows, unlike the other garages on this street. That and the wide vista from front and back, making it impossible for anyone to sneak up on the occupants, as well as the wall of shrubbery that acted as a privacy fence, were probably the main reasons the bureau had bought this house. He double-checked everything, pulled his car up into the driveway in front of the door, and started on one last inspection round outside the house.

When he came inside through the back door, a short flight of steps led up into the kitchen and a longer flight down into the basement. Kathryn was in the kitchen, throwing together an odd mix of supplies into an early lunch while Bea watched. Finn had never had peanut butter and
~~~~~

honey sandwiches on rye bread with tomato soup, barbecue potato chips, and dill pickle slices, but that didn't mean it wouldn't be good. He just wondered how the potato chips had survived so long in the paltry inventory of food supplies kept in the safe house.

He paused in the doorway and leaned against the frame, glad just to know where Kathryn was for the moment, and watch her. She looked good, he decided. She struck him as a little too pale, though he doubted she sat still long enough to get a tan. Her hair was still wet from her shower, pulled back in a ponytail high off the back of her head, making her look like a little girl. She wore spare clothes left by other occupants, agents or protected witnesses; faded denim shorts pulled tight around her waist with a braided leather belt, oversized t-shirt with a big teddy bear on it, and neon pink thongs on her feet. Even though he knew the borrowed clothes were too big, she gave an impression of being thinner than the last time he had seen her.

That had been far too long ago.

Kathryn saw him after a few seconds. She gave him a curious glance, but since he didn't say anything, she kept working on lunch. Bea had raised her head when Finn first came into the house, and now went back to watching Kathryn.

Finn indulged in a daydream for a few seconds, envisioning this ordinary white tile and pale oak kitchen as *their* kitchen. It was a nice enough place with its white eyelet curtains and the table at one end of the room, but try as he might he couldn't make it feel familiar or comfortable. Of course, if Kathryn ever did marry him and this was their home, he knew he had better be helping her with lunch. That made him grin more. Kathryn glanced at him right that moment and stopped short with her hand raised, holding a spoon to stir the soup on the stove.

"Enjoy the domesticity while you can, mister," she said. "It doesn't last long."

"Yeah?" Finn laughed. "I hate to say this, but nice as it is, it doesn't fit. It isn't you."

"Well, hallelujah for that revelation." She wrinkled up her nose at him and continued with the soup.

"Cooking over a campfire, I can see." He stepped over to the stove and casually leaned against the counter where he could see her face as she worked. "How about we take a long camping trip for our honeymoon?"

Kathryn stopped short, just staring into the soup slowly swirling in the pot. The tiniest smile touched one corner of her mouth. Otherwise, Finn would have feared he had hurt or angered her. Sometimes Kathryn willingly indulged in daydreaming sessions, planning their home together. Sometimes she just sighed and changed the subject, or even ignored him when he insisted on staying on topic.

At least this time his reference to marriage amused her. Finn had hope, just like when she had let him hold her for several minutes in the park a little more than two hours ago.

"Who said I was going to marry you?" she said with a long-suffering sigh. Her eyes sparkled more.

"You said I was at the top of the list if you'd ever settle down, right?"

"Right."

"You're the all-or-nothing type, right?"

"Right."

"You're going to marry me, Kathryn. I'm an all-or-nothing guy, too. It may take four more years to convince you, but you will."

Kathryn refused to look at him. Her lips twitched. Finn braced himself for her response, suspecting she was going to use her sharp wit this time, instead of quietly asking him once again to slow down. Her eyes glistened, and she blinked rapidly as she turned her head away.

Regina came into the room, wearing the only robe Finn had been able to dig out of the supply of cast-offs. The color was somewhere between lime and neon green and made her skin look yellow. Her hair was wet. The robe was too large for her and dragged on the floor, and she had rolled up the cuffs on the sleeves to her elbows.

She had removed a few of her bandages, revealing the dirty, fading bruises on her hands and arms. The stitches on her forehead were covered with two strip bandages instead of the somewhat grimy gray gauze pad. She shuffled into the kitchen, sniffing eagerly. Her gaze swept the room, fastening first on the set table and the dishes of food before she looked at Kathryn and Finn.

That decided him. No matter what Kathryn had told him about her assignment, Finn didn't like this woman. Even taking into account her confusion and pain and fear. Everything about her rubbed him the wrong way.

"Lunch soon?" Regina asked. She sat down at the table in the exact middle of the three set places.

That clinched it. He really didn't like her.

"Feeling better?" Finn made his tone pleasant. He had to be nice because for some reason, Kathryn cared about her.

"Much. Are we really safe here?"

"That's why they call it a safe house," Kathryn said. She carried the pot of soup over to the counter and slowly poured it into the bowls waiting there.

"So, what do we do now?" Regina asked as she put two sandwiches on her plate.

"Fingerprints." Finn helped himself to the barbecued chips before they were all gone.

The move was also to give him an excuse to turn his face away, in case Kathryn looked at him. She had an uncanny knack for knowing when he lied, and he wasn't allowed to reveal just yet that he and Garretson and several outside interests already knew everything they needed to know about Dr. Regina Malvern and what happened at her father's isolated lab-house. Kathryn's ignorance was vital to plans even he hadn't been made privy to.

"We'll take a photo of you and put it into the network to see if we can figure out who you are. We'll go from there."

"That easy?"

"Your tax dollars at work."

"I should have known it'd come down to government agencies. You fooled me, Kathryn." Regina pouted.

Finn suspected his intense dislike, which had started before Kathryn gave her much-edited report, could easily blossom into loathing.

"Me? How?" Kathryn squeaked. She winked at Finn and he coughed to cover a chuckle.

"You had me believing there were... other explanations for all your friends and help. Those license plates and Michael and that doctor, and that phone call last night. It's all secret agent tricks, isn't it?"

Regina sounded like a child who had just found out Uncle Jake was inside the Santa suit. Finn resisted an urge to slap her.

"The plates and the phone call," he said, "I admit that's my fault. I have a program to warn me whenever someone tries to trace Kathryn's license plates. I called to warn you two. Other than that, don't blame me."

"But—how?" Regina looked back and forth between them, mouth hanging open.

"You don't really want to know, do you?" Kathryn finished putting the bowls on the table next to their plates and sat down. "Isn't life a little nicer if there's some mystery, some magic left in it?"

"Magic? With all the cloak and dagger you've been dragging me through?"

"Well..." She crunched a potato chip while she considered, then glanced at Finn, a twinkle in her eyes. "Maybe we're a bunch of modern faerie godmothers, riding around in trucks and motorcycles instead of soap bubbles and butterflies."

"That's a sight I'd like to see," Finn muttered. "Michael in a soap bubble or riding a butterfly."

He liked the big, motorcycle-riding troubleshooter who worked for evangelist Allen Michaels' globe-spanning organization, but he wasn't afraid to admit that the less time Michael spent with Kathryn, the better he felt. If the daughters of Quarry Hall had a tendency to fall into troubled situations, Michael had the tendency tenfold. Finn's only comfort was that

Michael was madly in love and planning to get married that winter to a girl named Babby, who worked at AMEA headquarters.

"But—" Regina began, stumbling for words.

"Eat," Kathryn said, "or Bea gets your lunch."

Bea chose that moment to insinuate herself between Finn's and Regina's chairs. Finn gave her a slice of dill pickle, which the dog loved. Kathryn and Finn both laughed when she slurped and chewed with wide bites that showed her teeth and tongue and the blotchy pink and black of her mouth. Regina recoiled in disgust.

"I—have to dry my hair." She snatched up one sandwich from her plate and fled the room.

"What the heck is going on with her?" Finn said in a stage whisper. He listened for the slam of the bathroom door. Come to think of it, he didn't care if Regina heard him or not.

"She doesn't like Bea, for some reason." Kathryn spooned up soup and blew on it before eating.

"Hey, I'm still half-scared of your bodyguard sometimes myself."

"But you like her. You trust her. Regina doesn't like her and Bea knows it."

"Think maybe there's something wrong with her?"

"Nothing more than being a spoiled brat and not getting her way."

"Uh huh." Finn wondered if it was a good sign or bad that Kathryn could admit that about her charge. "And if I know you, you haven't explained anything unless you absolutely had to."

"Maybe." She winked at him without ever cracking a smile. "Now eat your lunch or Bea really does get it."

Silence for a few minutes. Then Finn's phone went off. He sighed and stepped into the other room to answer it.

~~~~~

Four houses down at another curve in the winding street, a dark green 4X4 pulled into the shadows of huge willow trees that hung out over the road from both sides, forming an arch. The two men inside settled in to watch the house that had no windows in the garage and all the curtains pulled closed.

Their vigilance was rewarded half an hour later when a Jeep zipped down the street and pulled into the driveway next to Finn's car. The man who climbed out caught their attention immediately. Round granny glasses perched on his long nose, accentuating his big brown eyes. Balding, he had a long fringe of iron gray hair hanging nearly to the shirt pockets of his Army camouflage fatigues. He yanked two heavy, square black cases from the Jeep and lugged them down the sidewalk to the back door of the house. Finn met him at the door before he rang the bell.

Carson opened a file folder full of photographs and checked both
~~~~~

men against the photos. He nodded at Porter, who picked up the cell phone and started dialing.

~~~~~

Bea took to Zak, the lab technician from Finn's office, almost immediately. She watched him as he came in and set up his equipment in the kitchen, turning it into a laboratory. Fingerprint kit, camera, computer, wireless hotspot and high-power scanner were all set up in a matter of moments, followed by other equipment Kathryn couldn't name. It all linked together like some lopsided spider's web. She had barely been able to watch his hands and trace how everything connected to everything else. She wondered what Zak would have done if there hadn't been enough power outlets in the kitchen. As soon as he finished his work, Bea walked up to him and politely offered her right paw to shake. Zak laughed and went down on one knee and introduced himself, name and job description and even his identification number.

Kathryn heard a snort and turned her head to see Finn watching the exchange, one eyebrow raised higher than Spock's. Their gazes met and he grinned before quickly turning away. She knew Finn had noted how Bea reacted to Regina, how the big dog watched her whenever she came into the room, and the lack of any overtures of friendship between the two of them. Usually after more than a day in Kathryn's company, whoever was in her charge would be friends with Bea and the big dog would at least wag her tail.

At least she isn't getting growling or ears laid back. That would be a definite sign of trouble. Kathryn sighed. *Regina's just a spoiled brat with a high metabolism she definitely doesn't deserve.*

What would she have done if Bea had showed definite antagonism toward Regina? Dump her by the side of the road? Hand her over to the nearest authorities once she got out of the mountains? If Vincent had returned any of her calls, she would have had a better idea what to do. Until she did hear from him, she had to carry through to the end. Whatever that happened to be.
~~~~~

Chapter Eighteen

Kathryn knew continuing in that vein of thought would aggravate the imminent headache that lingered in the base of her skull. If Vincent was silent, it was for a good reason. She tried instead to concentrate on how Regina would feel when they finally had answers to fill the blanks in her memory. The sulky young woman would need all the sympathetic friends she could get when that moment came.

Zak beckoned Regina over to the table where he had the ink pad and sectioned paper ready. To Kathryn's amazement, she obeyed without a murmur. Her face, though, when Zak pressed her fingers one by one into the inkpad and then rolled the tips onto the paper, made Kathryn snort with suppressed laughter. Neither Finn nor Zak seemed to see the wretched, almost nauseated expression of horror on Regina's face as she studied her black fingertips. Zak handed her a cloth reeking of alcohol and lemon and got to work preparing the scanner and computer program that would facilitate matching her fingerprints with a high-security, federal database.

Bea came back into the kitchen. She went over to Zak and rested her head on the man's thigh. Zak took one hand off the keyboard, never missing a stroke with the other hand, and petted the dog's head. That was too much for Kathryn. She scooted out of the room and down the hall to the bathroom and flushed the toilet to cover her giggles.

When she came back, Finn was fixing himself another coffee at the counter and Zak watched the scanner as it hummed and a bright white light ran along the edge of the lid. Regina sat in a chair at the end of the table, watching him work, her chin resting in her fists and her elbows on the table. She looked tired. Kathryn regretted her giggles. Bea lay on the rug in front of the refrigerator, keeping watch over them all.

"Won't that take forever?" Regina asked as her fingerprints appeared on the computer screen. "I mean, all the patterns to cross-check. And what if I'm not even in the files?"

"We've already eliminated a lot of files by using your description and checking the missing persons reports," Finn said. "Plus, somebody thinks you're important enough to kill. That might mean you're important enough to be registered for security reasons."

"Then how come she isn't on the news?" Kathryn wanted to know. She came over to the counter and leaned against it, watching Zak working.

"Or how about a milk carton?"

"I'm a little old for that," Regina muttered.

"Okay," Finn said, and paused to sip at his nearly white coffee. "So she *knows* somebody important, but she isn't in the limelight herself. Satisfied?"

"But what if it doesn't work? What if she isn't in there?" Kathryn pressed.

"We could try hypnotism to get past that block in her memory."

Kathryn didn't like the idea of strangers digging around in her memories. Regina's face lost a little color and her grin faded quickly. Obviously she shared the same revulsion at the concept.

Either that or the stain still on her fingertips drove her from the room a few moments later. Kathryn pulled a chair over into the corner where she could watch Zak at work and stay out of his way. As soon as the sound of running water came down the hall from the bathroom, he started the process to shut down the scanner and the fingerprint recognition program he had explained in sketchy details to Regina.

Kathryn frowned, staring at the computer screen. She wasn't familiar with FBI software, but common sense told her Zak needed to do something more to send Regina's fingerprints to the central database. There was no way all the information for matching and identifying her fingerprints could be stored on Zak's computer. She focused on the corner of the screen where, on her computer at least, the icons for the wireless Internet connection would tell how strong the signal was, and if there was an open connection or not.

The lack of icons bothered her. She slowly rose from her chair and crept up behind Zak, to see more clearly. Maybe she was wrong. She hoped she was wrong, but she had learned long ago to trust that uneasy feeling in the pit of her stomach and the chill up her back.

Finn's arm wrapped around her waist stopped her and startled a squeak out of her. She opened her mouth to protest and he pressed two fingers against her lips. He glanced down the hall, then nodded at the door to the basement before releasing her. As she led the way to the basement, Kathryn caught the glance and nod Finn and Zak exchanged. The lab technician grinned and Finn shook his head.

"You're not searching for her fingerprints," Kathryn whispered, as soon as they reached the bottom of the basement stairs. The pieces came together into a solid picture in her mind, and her temples throbbed painfully for a few seconds in response. "You know already?"

"Wish you hadn't seen that. The less play acting you have to do, the better."

"Finn—"

"Yeah, we know who she is. We just don't know what she is, victim or traitor or dupe or... whatever." He sighed and raked the fingers of one hand through his hair.

Kathryn had a flash of insight. Finn was involved in something far deeper than he was letting on, and apparently so was Regina. He was exhausted, and most important, he didn't like keeping secrets from her. She could tell from the way he couldn't meet her gaze and the stress lines that formed brackets around his mouth. That stopped a few heated questions before they reached her lips.

"All that was for her benefit. Why?" she said instead.

"Playing for time. Can you just keep doing like you've been?"

"I think so. Do you think her amnesia is real?"

"It'd make things easier for us. But do me a favor, don't let her get to the phones."

"I've kept my phone locked from the start, and in the hotels, Bea was set guard on the phones. If she tried to call anyone... that would mean her amnesia is fake. You have reason to think it's fake."

"There's a lot we still don't know, and won't know until all the loose ends get tied up." He gripped her shoulders, staring into her eyes. "Can you trust me and play guard and bait at the same time? Just until tonight?"

"Whatever you need me to do."

Funny, but when he released her shoulders and they headed back upstairs, she wished he had taken time to kiss her. The fact that he didn't showed just how serious things had become.

~~~~~

Harper had papers on his desk and a pen in his hand as he read through them. Lisa took that as a good sign that he wasn't contemplating how to punish those who had failed him, when she stepped into the office with her latest update.

"Something good, I hope?" Harper said in a mild voice. He raised his head and studied her a moment, then sat back and put down the pen.

Today he wore a charcoal suit with micro-thin silver pinstripes that seemed to catch the light in a soft haze. It gave him a supernatural touch that made Lisa shudder. Deep inside, where he would never see it.

"The GPS signal has been stationary nearly two hours now. The local FBI office has sent out a lab tech with mobile fingerprint gear, and our insider can't find out where he went. That tells me it's high priority and higher security. Whoever she has made contact with, they don't know, or they aren't sure who she is. Either she really doesn't remember what happened, like that doctor said —"

"Or she's playing games with whoever is helping her." Harper favored Lisa with a thin smile. Whether he was satisfied with the news or with her work, she didn't know. "Convenient for us, wouldn't you say?"

"Time-wise, you mean?" Lisa would never let herself relax into
~~~~~

Harper's seeming approval. It could be a trap and a weight the next time she made a mistake.

She could, however, relax into the knowledge that he was busy considering the options and not finding fault with her.

"You're very proud of your computer skills, aren't you?" Harper asked in a normal tone of voice. Not the mild tone that could signal trouble, nor the scathing rebuke for stupidity that cut like a whiplash.

"I have a right," she responded quietly.

"You do, indeed. I suppose our mole doesn't know who requested the tech?"

"Garretson is involved. Other than that, nothing."

"You're working on a plan to get around that complication."

"Our insider is already working on it." She held her face impassive, refusing to admit to the tiny flicker of irritation when Harper seemed amused at her wording. She didn't like the word "mole." It demeaned the integral work of the people who risked their reputations and careers, maybe even their freedom, to procure the information Harper wanted.

"Step up the effort to find out about this mysterious young woman with her uncanny talent for predicting our moves. Before our team gets frustrated and takes her out." Harper's eyes narrowed. "You have something on her?"

"Not on her. We're still working around the baffles and rabbit trails the system keeps throwing at us. However... we have a good line on who originated the program to protect her identity. Several possibilities. It's just a matter of tracking down their activities since the lab raid went sour, and eliminating who can't be involved."

"Who do you favor?"

"Agent Finnegan Roberts," she said after a moment of hesitation.

"Why? And why so reluctant to tell me?" Harper's lips twitched. Lisa hated it when he was amused.

"It's all gut right now, sir. I don't like discussing my hunches until I have some evidence to support me."

"McCain, you are where you are because your 'gut' is right more often, and sooner, than others' solid facts." He bent his head over his paperwork, dismissing her. "Don't let it go to your head and interfere with your efficiency."

"No, sir."

Her heart raced as she left the office with a sedate stride and calm expression. Was she excited and pleased and stunned over Harper's backhanded compliment, or terrified because now his standards for her were higher than ever?

Better to be terrified. Safer that way.

~~~~~
~~~~~

Finn had to go back to the office. The story, for Regina's sake, was that he was helping them unofficially, using favors others in the bureau owed him, and he had reams of reports to finish up on a deadline.

A woman agent named Blaine showed up less than twenty minutes after Zak left, to watch over them until Finn could return. With her faded jeans, bulky sweatshirt, and her overall look of a college gym teacher, Blaine seemed nice enough at first. But she had her pistol tucked into the back waistband of her jeans, in full view. Bea took one look and put herself between Kathryn and Blaine with her head lowered and hackles raised.

Bea hated guns and avoided anyone who smelled of guns. Finn knew Blaine and vouched for her, even if he did seem momentarily surprised to see her. Kathryn wondered who he had been expecting. Maybe she was just tired, which made her touchy. Maybe she just didn't want to trust anyone new. The sense of slowly rising tension threatened to bring her headache to the front of her head, where she couldn't ignore it. She had already taken more ibuprofen than was wise.

Blaine only seemed amused by Bea's reaction and quickly made herself at home, getting the layout of the house and a quick run-down on the situation. Then Finn was gone. But not after beckoning Kathryn outside to the back step for a quick kiss. She regretted ruining the brief sweetness of the moment by telling him about Bea's reaction to Blaine, but this late in the game it would be foolish not to share all her doubts.

"Never worked with her before, but I know her face from the office, and others have worked with her. Gotta be the gun." He stepped back, still resting his hands on her shoulders, and searched her face. "I've seen your bodyguard in action enough, I can't dismiss her reaction, though."

"Just hurry back here as fast as you can, okay?"

That earned her another, slightly longer kiss. Kathryn couldn't help feeling a little smug at the very clear regret on Finn's face as he hurried down the driveway to his car.

"Well, that answers one question," Regina said, when Kathryn came back into the house.

Regina was in the kitchen with a package of cookies and a book to read. Blaine was in the hall, making a phone call.

"What question is that?" Kathryn stretched her arms to the ceiling and started on a few bends and twists to loosen up her muscles. Finn did that to her sometimes, making her feel all knotted and jumbled full of energy.

"How you got a Fed to help you out. You're lovers, aren't you?"

"Hardly." Kathryn suspected her idea of lovers and Regina's idea of lovers had a gap the size of the Grand Canyon between them.

"Yeah? What was all that lip action I just caught?" She smirked and looked down at her book again.

"One—okay, two kisses. People do kiss good-bye without planning to jump into bed. Didn't your father ever kiss you good-bye?"

Regina froze. Her hands clenched ever so slightly around the edges of the book, but she never raised her gaze from the pages.

"My father was a good father—as far as I can remember. I didn't need silly demonstrations of affection to know how he felt about me."

"Okay." Kathryn thought about apologizing, but somewhere in the last five or six hours, she had crossed the line of "enough." In another day at the most, she would be rid of Regina. She couldn't make herself feel a little guilty over her eagerness for that deadline.

"What's up?" Blaine asked, stepping into the room.

"I need a nap. I've lost a lot of sleep lately," Kathryn said, and headed down the hall to the bedrooms. Bea got up, claws clicking on the linoleum, and followed her. She made a wide detour around Blaine, nearly pressing against the wall to stay away from her.

~~~~~

The nap helped enormously. Kathryn stayed sprawled out on the bed after she woke, luxuriating in the soft, clean bed and the quiet of the house, and knowing someone else was keeping Regina out of trouble. No aches deep in the strands of her muscles. No nauseated sensation. No sparks around the edges of her vision. For several moments, she considered trying to call Vincent again. If he wasn't responding, he had his reasons. Everything was safe in Finn's hands. She trusted him, even if he wasn't telling her everything he knew or what was going on. He trusted her enough to admit they were keeping her in the dark for the sake of the operation. That had to mean something.

Maybe she could call Sophie? Had the Arc Foundation's computer genius gone home when Vincent got involved in whatever initiated Kathryn's assignment, or was she on the fringes, sharing her skills with programs and searching the Internet? Would Sophie refuse to take her call or respond to her messages?

"Leave it alone," Kathryn muttered, and rolled out of bed. Maybe the house was too quiet?

Even as she thought that, she heard voices, muffled by the bedroom door. It sounded like the speakers were in the kitchen, rather than coming from further away, like the living room. She stumbled her first few steps, but regained her balance before fear could rise up and make her heart race. It was just the lingering remains of her nap, not her illness entering a new phase.

Regina and Blaine played cards at the kitchen table. A pile of wrappers hinted all the snacks left in the house had been demolished by Regina the eating machine.

"Anything left to eat?" Kathryn scooped up two cookie bags, six candy bar wrappers, and the remains of three two-liters of soda. Two
~~~~~

empty chip bags, one corn and one barbecued potato, lay on the counter behind Blaine.

"Courier is bringing groceries pretty—" Blaine stopped and jerked her head in the direction of the kitchen door when the doorbell rang. "Soon," she finished with a grin.

She started to get up from the chair but Kathryn had already looked out the window over the sink and saw the agent with his arms full of grocery bags. She recognized him from department baseball games she had watched Finn play.

"I'll take care of it. Keep playing," she said, and hurried down the short flight of steps to the door.

The agent recognized her, too, and grinned as he put the bags into her arms, then pressed a folded piece of paper into her hand. He didn't say a word, just winked and hurried back to his Jeep waiting at the edge of the sidewalk. Kathryn watched him go and told herself to be grateful he wasn't wearing a suit with his holster visible. Nothing like displaying to the whole neighborhood that something odd was going on in the house.

Kathryn checked the clock. Nearly five. She put the bags of groceries down on the counter and checked the contents. Mostly fresh fruits and vegetables, rice, pasta, cans of tomato sauce and a few paper-wrapped bundles that felt like butcher-fresh meat of some kind. She couldn't repress a grin and knew Finn had done the shopping, either over the phone or the Internet, and picked ingredients for his favorite dishes.

In the note, Finn promised to be at the house by six, and asked her to consider a canoe trip in Algonquin Park in Canada for their honeymoon.

Kathryn had all the ingredients washed and chopped and the rice steaming before Regina and Blaine called it quits with the cards. The agent immediately excused herself to make a report. She went into the next room, pulling her cell phone out as she went. Kathryn wondered what she had to say that had to be kept secret from the people she guarded.

"Need help?" Regina said. She stayed at her place at the table.

"Uh—yeah. Sure." Kathryn managed a smile and went back to checking the cupboard next to the stove for the selection of pots and pans. Why had Regina turned helpful all of a sudden? "Thanks."

"What do you need me to do?" She got up slowly and started around the island unit separating the kitchen area from the dinette.

Bea came into the room, head up, tail wagging the slightest bit. She sauntered over to Kathryn and lay down next to her, effectively blocking Regina from stepping into the kitchen area. She stopped short and glared at the Akita.

"You want to set the table?" Kathryn nudged Bea with her foot in reproof, then stood and turned to reach for the cupboard with the dishes.

It felt like she had just washed the lunch dishes and put them away.

That gave her one more reason to avoid settling down into housekeeping for as long as possible. Would Finn laugh if she told him that?

Silence for a few minutes. Kathryn enjoyed it. Regina fussed with the unmatched placemats and napkins, coordinating and contrasting colors, and setting out the mismatched flatware, two sizes of forks, two sizes of spoons, table knife and steak knife. When she noticed that, Kathryn opened her mouth to tell Regina they wouldn't need that much table service, then stopped to consider.

What did that kind of place setting arrangement tell her about Regina? She ate out in fancy restaurants often? Her family entertained in a posh style? Or was she some kind of servant in a fancy, rich household? Kathryn had to admit the other woman had a way with colors. The table looked inviting even without food. She filed away that thought for later to share with Finn, and went back to cooking.

"Four?" Regina said, stepping away from the table. Bea edged out of her way and settled down on the rainbow colored rag rug in front of the sink.

"Yeah, four." Kathryn finished putting the diced tomatoes and chilis into the rice.

"Just checking." She looked at the table, then at Kathryn, and smirked. "We're going to be seeing a lot of Finnegan for a while, aren't we?"

"Until it's over." Kathryn turned back to the stove and reached for the salt. If Regina was going to start in with more snide remarks, calling Finn her lover again, she should finish with the knife and put it away as quickly as possible.

"That's good," was all she said. She went to the cupboard and started picking through the glassware.

Like everything else in the house, the selection was comprised of the odds and ends in multiple styles, what Kathryn referred to as "Early Salvation Army."

"Smells great," Blaine said, coming back into the kitchen. "Whatever it is," she added with a chuckle, and stepped over to the stove to look at the contents of the pots and pans.

Bea immediately got up and scooted over next to Kathryn. Her hurried movement rumpled the rug under the kickboard of the sink and her claws clicked on the linoleum. She leaned up against the backs of Kathryn's legs and faced Blaine.

Chapter Nineteen

"Hey," the agent said, grinning as she held up her hands in a shielding motion, "when is she going to be nice when I'm around?"

"When are you going to stop carrying that gun?" Kathryn didn't look up from her cooking. Bea only got edgy like that when she smelled blood and guns, but Blaine had a point. The dog never reacted like that to Finn, and he certainly showed up enough times carrying a gun, sometimes even smelling of gunpowder.

"When people stop shooting at me and my friends." Blaine laughed, like it had been a foolish question.

"That's when Bea will be your friend." Now she turned her head to look at the woman, who leaned against the island section of the counter. "And after you take a bath."

"What?"

"You wear that gun so much, you smell of the metal."

Maybe whatever else clung to Blaine would be washed away and Bea would accept her. If not, then Kathryn had to seriously consider making a run for it with Regina, even if it was still light outside. At the very least, keeping Blaine busy with a bath would buy her some time to make a phone call without being overheard. She wished she had tried Vincent or even Sophie before she left the bedroom. Kathryn made a note never to leave her phone sitting around. Blaine could just take her phone to keep her from calling anyone.

The agent frowned and her mouth twitched a little and her eyes were hooded as she visually digested the statement. Then Regina sighed and slid down into a chair at the dinette table. Blaine shook her head and laughed.

Kathryn had the distinct impression the woman had *chosen* to laugh. That bothered her.

Blaine's laughter nearly covered the sound of the kitchen door coming open. She reached back for her gun before the sound died in her throat. Kathryn watched Bea and knew it had to be Finn coming inside. The Akita was too relaxed, despite leaning protectively against her. She would have skidded across the linoleum, teeth bared and a low growl rumbling if a stranger had tried to come inside.

Kathryn turned back to her cooking. From the corner of her eye she saw Blaine slide the gun back into the waistband at the back of her jeans.

"Hi, honey, I'm home." Finn sidled up to the stove past Bea and reached for the stirring spoon. Kathryn slapped his hand.

"Somebody's getting clobbered," Blaine said, shaking her head. She sauntered over to the table and slid into a chair next to Regina. "Don't know how to quit while you're ahead, do you?"

"I have no idea what you're talking about." Finn put his briefcase down on the counter next to the still-wet cutting board, snatched up a glass Regina hadn't put away, and walked over to the refrigerator.

Kathryn gave the rice one more stir with the spoon and turned off the heat under the pan. "You had better be here for some reason other than causing trouble, Mister FBI."

"Depends." Finn took a big gulp of the lemonade he had poured for himself and turned to face the other two. "Anybody want to meet Dr. Regina Malvern?"

Regina froze, her eyes unfocussed as she stared at Finn and seemed to see someone else entirely. Kathryn felt a chill crawl up her back. What exactly had happened, that Finn's superiors had decided to reveal they knew Regina's identity? Something had changed, and something more was about to change. Just what, Kathryn could only guess.

"Doctor, huh? What kind?" Kathryn murmured, helping Finn play the game. She tried to smile, tried to convey support and sympathy when the blond woman looked at her.

Finn pushed aside the placemats and dishes and cleared a spot on the table. He opened his briefcase and brought out a single manila file folder and opened it. The very first item on top was an eight-by-ten glossy of Regina with her hair in a swept-back style that made her look much older. She wore a business-like skirt and jacket, gray and blue plaid, and an emerald green blouse, with a gloss that looked like silk. The gray-haired, sharp-faced man standing with her rested his hand on her shoulder in a proprietary, maybe even possessive manner. The shape of his face, the set of his eyes told Kathryn this was her father.

"But—" Regina shook her head and started over again. "I'm too young to be a doctor."

"Then you're a genius," Kathryn offered. Regina almost smiled at her, then shook her head and looked at the photo again.

Her eyes glazed and she wrapped her arms around herself, shivering a moment. Watching her, Kathryn saw the muscles twitch in her jaw, visibly fighting something negative in her mind or emotions. Memories, perhaps?

What if her suspicions were correct, and Regina had been playing a game with them all along, pretending to be amnesiac and innocent and wounded? What if she had been playing for time? What if "damsel in distress" was just a ploy to get away from enemies or authorities?

Kathryn hated doubting someone under her protection. It made her feel like she had been duped, her time and effort wasted. Especially when her time and energy had limits now.

"You think that's part of the problem?" Kathryn offered, to yank her thoughts away from herself before she got sucked down into another whirlpool of self-pity. She settled down in the chair next to Finn, with Regina on his other side. "Too young, too important, too fast?"

"Sounds like a soap opera to me," Blaine said. Her voice rippled with something that could have been amusement. Kathryn decided Bea was completely right, and not reacting just to the presence of the gun. She disliked Blaine, herself.

"Do you want to hear the story, or do you want to discuss plots?" Finn broke in.

"Grouch." Kathryn slapped his hand lightly.

"You can go back to your cooking. I'm starved if nobody else is." He glared pointedly at the stove. Kathryn wasn't worried. She had turned off the heat under all the pots and pans the moment she guessed what Finn was going to do.

"Regina Malvern," he read, picking up the statistics sheet under the thin stack of photos. "Age twenty-eight, I.Q. of one twenty-nine — close enough for genius without being a pain. Daughter and assistant to Nobel Prize-nominee Dr. Reginald Malvern, noted research scientist."

Kathryn watched Regina from the corner of her eye as Finn read. The blond woman bowed her head and slowly rubbed at her temples, as if the words themselves gave her a headache.

"What did we—what *do* we research?" Regina asked in a slightly breathy voice.

"Well, I'm no scientist," Finn began.

"I knew that a long time ago," Kathryn muttered, trying to lighten the tension in the air. He didn't glare or nudge or rebuke her, meaning all his attention focused on Regina. What did he learn from her reactions?

"You and your father were working on a way to break the physical side of drug addictions," he said, reading through the report.

"By changing the chemical receptors in the addict's body, going down to the nerve synapses and cellular level," Regina said, the words tumbling out.

Was it just Kathryn's imagination, or did her voice, her pronunciation change a little? More assured, more mature?

"We changed the molecular coding of—" Regina stopped short and looked at the other three with widening eyes, her breath coming faster and in shorter breaks. "The unbreakable addictions," she began again. "Like cocaine. That... I think we were more... concerned about the babies born addicted..." She stopped again and rubbed at her eyes where tears began to threaten. "I'm sorry — the rest is missing."

"You're remembering more," Kathryn said, and reached across the table to squeeze Regina's hand. "That's what's important. Okay, so Dr. Malvern and Dr. Malvern are the good guys, trying to help people. What went wrong?"

"Things were going fine up until about five months ago." Finn didn't read from the sheet now. That told her he had read the report enough times he knew it by heart. "Dr. Malvern senior made a few breakthroughs and they predicted they'd have the formula perfected by the end of the year. Then, according to these files, every single advance turned dangerous."

"To them," Blaine asked, "or the addicts they're trying to help?"

"The drug is only stable for storage in a powdered form, and kept between sixty-five and ninety degrees," Regina said, again dropping back to her breathy voice. "It undergoes a chemical change when it gets too warm or too cool, or is exposed to moisture, splitting into alkaloids and acid compounds that attack the nerve sheaths. It could kill the addicts, in horrible pain, before it cured them."

A moan escaped her and she bowed her head, rubbing at her temples. Kathryn got up and went to the sink and ran a glass of water for her, then retrieved the bottle of aspirin she had found earlier that afternoon.

"Sorry," Regina mumbled. "That's all I could remember. Why can't I bring back anything else?"

"You weren't trying to remember," Blaine said. "Once you started working at it, the door shut again."

Kathryn stepped up behind Regina and put the glass and aspirin down on the table. She wondered why it bothered her that Blaine should have the answer to that question so quickly.

"Anyway," Finn said, studying Regina rather than the papers in his hands, "some pretty powerful private parties decided to take an interest in what was happening, either to help them get back on track, or to direct the so-called mistakes into other areas. It gets a little fuzzy after this point." He shrugged and glanced at Blaine, then Kathryn, then looked at Regina.

"Hate to say this, Regina," he said. "You and your father are proud people. You wouldn't take help from anyone and you were stubborn about making reports. Your government contacts were afraid for you."

Kathryn heard the unspoken "afraid *of* you," in Finn's hesitation. How proud, how stubborn were Regina and her father? Enough to get them attacked, her father killed? And by whom?

"Afraid of what?" Regina demanded. "I really *don't* remember that part."

"The lab was broken into, the computers were trashed when someone tried to break the security codes, and according to this report, several attempts were made to either kidnap or kill you or your father."

"When did everything get dangerous?" Blaine asked.

"Last week." Finn glanced at the sheet, then at Kathryn. "The day before Kathryn found Regina, a team of agents responded to a call from her father, asking for someone to come see him. To talk. He hinted that he needed help. The agency was worried because he never *wanted* help before. When they got there—" He rustled the sheets and hunched his shoulders as he read through the reports again. He held the pages so Kathryn couldn't read over his shoulder.

"That bad?" she guessed.

"They walked in on something." He put the papers down. "Whatever it was, it caught them completely off guard because they didn't even get a chance to call in. When a follow-up team got there, they were both dead, along with the team providing round-the-clock security for the lab. One had his gun out, the other didn't even have his coat unbuttoned to get at his weapon."

"I don't remember," Regina whispered, never looking up from her hands.

"They were supposed to notify their team leader that they had arrived, and apprise her of the situation," Finn continued. "She sent another team when they were an hour overdue. When the second team got there, the lab was on fire and the first team of agents had been shot and left to burn in the lab. The security detail was taken out almost a whole day before that, about the time Dr. Malvern made his call."

"What happened to my father?" Regina asked in a clear, even voice.

"They found what was left of his body in the lab. I'm sorry." Finn put a hand on hers and squeezed. Regina didn't seem to notice.

Kathryn moved from her chair to the one on Regina's other side and put an arm around her. She sat still, as unresponsive as clay. Blaine tipped her chair back against the wall and watched the other three in turn, like someone trying to assess their thoughts by their expressions. Kathryn didn't like the silence. She would have welcomed a warning growl from Bea right about then.

"What do those reports say about Regina?" Blaine asked, letting her chair tip forward again with a crack like a gunshot.

Kathryn held her breath. She seriously doubted that was part of Finn's plan. Whatever her doubts about Regina, she wouldn't voice them in front of her. What did Blaine think she was doing?

"Yes," Regina whispered, when Finn just tipped his head slightly to one side and kept watching her, his face calm and unreadable. He didn't react to Blaine's question. That lack of reaction told Kathryn he wasn't ready for it. The other agent's participation wasn't part of the script. Things could go very wrong, very quickly.

Vincent, when are you going to get here and shut things down? I don't need these headaches.

As if thinking that was a signal, that aching that threatened to drop into her stomach sent a few testing throbs through the base of her skull. The aromas of her cooking, which had made her hungry just a little while ago, now threatened to make her nauseous. Kathryn muffled a groan and stayed as still as she could.

"Either she's a victim," Finn said, voice and gaze soft, "or part of one nasty double-cross."

"Double-cross?" Regina jerked. "They think I'd kill my own father?"

The fear blazing in her eyes made Kathryn want to shake her, rather than comfort her. A heartbeat later, she understood — why would Regina think about her father's death rather than the problems with the different groups interested in her drug research? Unless she was in some way responsible for her father's death, and discovery was her greatest fear? Glancing down at the photo of Regina with her father, Kathryn could understand a little how the self-centered child she had come to know over the last two days would chafe against the controlling, possessive, prideful man he appeared to be.

Enough chafing to kill, or just want to kill, to be free?

"Professional rivalry." Finn's voice turned cool, instead of the professional detachment he had maintained until then. "They were — you two were arguing about the next step in the research. Both of you had a reputation for being arrogant and stiff-necked when it came to who was right and who was wrong." He flicked a glance at Kathryn, one eyebrow twitching just a little.

She almost laughed, startled into remembering the part she had been assigned.

"I think the last few days prove Regina is a victim, not a murderer," Kathryn said. *Even if she is a snot, that doesn't make her a murderer.*

"We just have to find out where she was, either who had her prisoner or where she was hiding, between the time the lab was invaded and the security team killed, when her father and the agents were murdered, and then how she got down the mountainside to where you found her."

Kathryn nodded. She glanced at Regina, who looked back and forth between the two of them. For two seconds her face blanked, then she looked angry.

"Yeah, where was I?" Regina sounded belligerent.

"Teams of searchers were following clues up and down the mountainside. One report had someone who could have been Regina in a cabin outside Millersburg the same night Kathryn got her... whatever you call it," Finn added with a nod in her direction.

"Call to action," Kathryn filled in.

"Okay, who *do* you work for, if not for us?" Blaine interrupted.

"The good guys, of course."

Blaine opened her mouth to ask more questions, but Finn jumped in. She was relieved, because she didn't want to go through another cross-examination, with both Regina and Blaine delivering the shots. Especially if Finn made his usual teasing, snide remarks that would just irritate and amuse her simultaneously, and confuse the other two. He loved playing games with people's minds.

"They went in to get a closer look," he said, "and everything literally blew up."

"And that brings us just about to where we are now," Kathryn said.

"Where are we?" Blaine asked quietly.

"Supper, of course." She stood and nudged Finn before heading around the island unit to the stove. "Put the table back the way Regina had it and help me dish up the food, will you?"

"Yes, your majesty. Whatever you say, your majesty," he muttered.

Kathryn wanted to punch him and kiss him, both at the same time. She settled for a glare that stopped Finn before he warmed up to his act.

~~~~~

Finn hated playing mental games. He hadn't lied when he told Kathryn and Blaine he had reports to finish going through at the office, and wouldn't be back to the safe house until midnight to relieve Blaine. On the other hand, he hoped the moles inside the bureau, who had finally revealed their presence with a few tiny mis-steps, would act soon. He wanted to hand Regina over to higher authorities and get Kathryn out of this ugly, tangled web of deceit as soon as possible.

He grinned, thinking about what Kathryn would say if she could hear his worried thoughts. First, she would remind him that she had Bea, and her big guardian was more alert in her sleep than most people when they were awake. Then she would call him a paranoid. A sweet, lovable paranoid, if she was in a good mood. Then she would remind him that he wouldn't worry half as much as he did if he would just pray more.

"You're certainly right about that one, lady, but who has the time to think of what to say, let alone do it?" he muttered at his computer monitor. Finn blinked, rubbed at his eyes, and studied the figures once more. Either the screen was starting to go, or his eyes were.

How much longer did he have to maintain this charade of being preoccupied with reports and paperwork? When would the enemy act?

"Midnight oil?" Garretson, his supervisor said from the doorway. He peered around the door that always hung half-open.

Garretson always looked freshly showered and neat, impeccably dressed and un-creased no matter what the time of day or the situation. Finn wondered if he would pick up that ability when he had put in
~~~~~

another twenty years with the bureau. He admired Garretson and envied how the man had weathered the years.

Finn had the awful suspicion he would develop a potbelly and a slouch and have a perpetually stained tie as he neared retirement age. If everyone could look like a cross between Donald Sutherland and Jason Robards when they got to Garretson's age, getting older wouldn't be so bad.

"Just catching up," Finn said.

He tugged on his tie, which was untied and hanging loose around his shoulders as usual. Garretson wore a deep gray suit, dark aqua shirt, and a tie of matching gray with matching aqua pinstripes.

Finn's lips twitched as he fought a momentary grin. For his supervisor to "casually" wander over to his office and remark on how late he was working had to be a good sign that the suspected traitors were not only in the building, but poised to strike. Garretson had taught Finn the fine points in playing charades and luring the enemy into traps. Neither of them had ever anticipated that they would be trapping their own. He had certainly never expected to put Kathryn in danger to clean up bureau messes.

Finn pounded in the command to print and the printer hummed into life. Paperwork would give him ulcers sooner than dangerous situations that had him looking down the barrel of a gun.

"How much longer are you going to be here?" Garretson tapped the fingers of his left hand on the doorframe, three rapid, two slow, three rapid. Left hand for singular, right hand for plural. One of the two suspected targets of their trap was on the way up to this floor, could even be hiding in the shadows by now, listening.

"At least another hour."

"I'm assembling the team in the morning to go through what you've found out so far. What have you figured out so far about Dr. Malvern?"

"Someone beat her up pretty bad before my friend found her."

"Friend?" Garretson leaned into the office a little more. That was not part of the semi-planned script. "That wasn't mentioned when you reported you had the doctor in custody. What kind of friend?"

"I'd rather not say."

Chapter Twenty

"Oh, *that* friend," the other man said, with another smile and a tone of voice that made Finn's face warm. Which, he knew, only confirmed his boss's suspicions. "She comes in pretty handy. You'd either better marry that lady of yours, or get her trained so she's officially one of us."

Definitely not part of the script. Then again, Garretson had been pushing him for some time now to solidify things with Kathryn, and not just to strengthen connections with the Arc Foundation and the suspected links with information sources that made the FBI, CIA and Interpol seem like amateurs.

"You make her sound dangerous." He winced at the sour tone of his voice.

"Someone who can pull off the stunts she has is either very lucky or unusually talented—"

"Or her guardian angels work overtime," Finn broke in before his supervisor said something he didn't want to hear. And didn't want the unseen watcher to hear.

"The FBI doesn't believe in angels," Garretson said with a half-smile. "They can't be tracked through credit cards, cell phones, GPS, or census figures. But we're getting off the track. What's the next step with Dr. Malvern?"

"Dr. Phillips is giving her a full physical right now." He hesitated, then decided to throw another tidbit at the unseen watcher, in case he or she reported to their employer before the trap closed. "She's got some memory problems, from either physical or emotional trauma."

"Could make things more complicated."

"Makes her a pain in the—neck," he corrected at the last moment. Finn smiled a little, remembering Kathryn's irritation with Regina and the evident distaste Bea had for her.

"Who's with them now?"

"Blaine." Finn frowned at his supervisor. Another variation from the script. What sort of message was he trying to send the mole sneaking up on them?

"Blaine?" The other man frowned. "She's supposed to be on vacation."

"Tell her. She showed up when I was looking for anything female to stand guard. She volunteered."

"Well, some people are workaholics." Garretson shook his head.

"Good job—you and your friend. You'd better marry her before I do."

"Tell her that, would you?" Finn chuckled, but the sound caught in his throat.

He had a flash image of Kathryn dressed all in white, walking down the aisle to meet Garretson. What if something about *him* kept Kathryn putting up a wall in their relationship?

Garretson winked and stepped back into the hall. He pulled the door closed, and had to pull it against the frame three times before it latched. Finn stared at the door until the printer stopped spewing his report. The loud click-bang as the overworked unit let the last piece of paper fall into the tray cut into his spinning daydream of romantic disaster.

Shaking his head, he picked up the papers and shuffled them into order. He turned back to his computer, but the images on the screen made no sense. He was just tired, wasn't he?

Finn gave in to the nagging sense of worry and reached into his bottom drawer — the one where he hid everything when he had an enormous, desk-drowning project in progress. He pulled out a ceramic frame, dark blue with speckles of silver stars all over it. The picture was of Kathryn running across a field, Bea racing along at her side, the wind tugging at her hair, her eyes bright, mouth open in laughter. Just outside the frame was the string of the kite she had been chasing. Finn remembered that day like it was yesterday.

Sighing, he put the picture back in its safe resting place. Soon, this would all be over, including all the paperwork for an operation he hadn't even heard about forty-eight hours ago.

~~~~~

Dr. Phillips was a tiny, silver-haired woman who reminded Kathryn of a bird more than anything else. A bird with eyes as sharp as her wit and tongue, who put up with no nonsense from anyone, no matter what condition they were in physically and mentally. Kathryn liked her.

"Well, you're healing quite nicely," Dr. Phillips said. She stepped back from giving one last long look into Regina's eyes, and wiped her hands on the hem of her long, pale rose sweater. "Despite all your running around," she added, glancing at Kathryn, who lay on her side on the couch, trying to read and ignore the headache that was finally going away. She gave the younger woman a teasing frown. Kathryn smiled back serenely and went on with her book.

The living room was the only place with enough room for Dr. Phillips' various medical bags; room enough to spread out her supplies and let Regina lie down or bend or stretch or do a few jumping jacks to get her heart pumping for the doctor's various tests. Blaine was outside, doing a quick check. Bea waited at the door of the living room. All was right with the world, as far as Kathryn was concerned.
~~~~~

"What about my headaches?" Regina asked, for the eighth time since the examination started, Kathryn noted.

"Mostly psychosomatic."

"I'm not imagining the pain," she insisted.

"I didn't say you were." Dr. Phillips stopped her retort before it settled into its usual track. "Emotions, mental blocks, what have you. It's not rooted in the physical. Once you recover your memory completely, I'm sure the headaches will vanish."

"She gets the headaches whenever she tries to remember, or when she remembers a fragment and then tries for more," Kathryn offered.

"My point exactly."

Regina sighed, more loudly than the last two dozen times. Kathryn hoped the doctor was finished, so she could send Regina to bed. They would all feel better in the morning. She hoped. To her relief, Dr. Phillips started sliding all her equipment back into her bags. Before Kathryn could get up to help her, she was done.

Kathryn walked her to the door and thanked her for her help. She knew nobody else would thank the woman for coming out this late at night. Certainly not Regina. From where she stood in the kitchen doorway, watching the doctor walk down the driveway to her car, Kathryn could see Regina in the living room. A smile touched her lips as her pouting charge tried to leave the room and Bea stepped into the doorway to block her.

"Bea, behave yourself," Kathryn said, coming into the living room half a minute later.

"She doesn't like me," Regina grumbled, as Blaine came in the kitchen door.

"Well, you really haven't had time to make friends, have you?"

"No. I mean, she really doesn't like me. She looks like she's trying to decide if she'll bite me."

Bea moved to stand between Kathryn and Blaine, who paused in the doorway between kitchen and living room, hands braced on either wall, poised like Samson ready to bring down the Philistine temple. Kathryn paused a moment, not liking that ripple of tension that came into the room with the woman agent.

"She wouldn't do that," she said, turning back to Regina. "Unless you were a danger to me, of course."

"I'll take that as a warning," Blaine said, eyes bright, mouth twisted in a smirk that sent a shiver up Kathryn's back. "Sorry, kiddies, but we're moving out."

"Moving out?" Regina dropped down on the couch, her mouth settling into its usual pouting lines.

"They're moving us to a new place. It turns out we've been

compromised. Someone managed to get a GPS on your truck and they're probably on their way here right now."

"Another place? What is with you people? Don't you stay anywhere more than a day?" Regina wailed.

Kathryn wondered why Finn hadn't said anything to her about that discovery before this. If Regina's enemies knew where they were, he should have moved them to a new safe house hours ago, or at the very least removed the GPS from her truck. Or had someone been examining her truck while Dr. Phillips was in here?

All this secrecy threatened to push her over the line of "enough." Kathryn suspected the next person who crossed her was going to get a sample of Vincent's self-defense lessons, whether he, or she, deserved it.

"Fine, if you want to wait here until some goon with a gun comes breaking down the door," Blaine began.

Regina let out a shriek and stomped out of the room. Kathryn should have followed her, but she sank down onto the couch and scooped up the book she had put down only a few minutes ago. Bea climbed up next to her. She whined and shook her head.

"Ten minutes," Blaine said, and hooked a thumb over her shoulder at the back door.

"You're right," Kathryn said, as soon as the woman vanished outside into the darkness. She stroked Bea's head, down to her neck and shoulders. "The sooner we're rid of her, the better."

Bea slurped her cheek. Kathryn shook her head, momentarily disgusted by dog breath. Then she burst out in tired, cracking laughter.

~~~~~

Carson was asleep, slouched toward the open window of the 4X4. Porter had moved the truck three times during their long day of surveillance to different vantage points. Everyone who came to the house had been studied through binoculars, pictures taken, video recorded, and identified. He checked his watch now. Almost eleven. The doctor from the Bureau had left fifteen minutes ago. Soon he could wake Carson and they would exchange places and he could try to catch some sleep in the passenger seat.

The living room lights went out. Porter noted the time again. No bedroom lights or bathroom lights came on. Anyone else watching would think the occupants of the house had gone to bed. He counted to ten. The only light left on was the tiny light over the sink, where the window was too high to reveal anything going on in the house.

He caught movement at the back door. Porter brought up his binoculars and adjusted the night lenses. He made a mental note to get the lens frames repaired; they kept trying to slide off the ends of the binoculars. Then he stopped his grumbling when he caught a glimpse of
~~~~~

Blaine on the doorstep, glancing in all directions. She held her gun low and at ready. The agent stepped down to the driveway and paused at the back corner of the house. Regina came out next, followed by Kathryn and Bea. Kathryn carried a duffel bag and backpack. Blaine kept watch, gun at ready. Kathryn and Regina hurried down the sidewalk to the garage and the four-door chocolate brown Cavalier that had been parked there since Blaine arrived that afternoon.

Porter nudged Carson awake and shoved the binoculars into his partner's hands. Carson grunted acknowledgment and kept the glasses trained on the car and its passengers, less than 200 feet away from them now. Porter picked up the phone and hit speed-dial, still watching the blurs of movement in the semi-darkness. The streetlight directly across from the safe house garage was dead, making it easier to conceal nighttime movement.

Kathryn unlocked the car and held the seat forward for Bea. The Akita jumped in, she threw her bags in and took the driver's seat. Regina took the front passenger seat. The engine started, then Blaine came running down the sidewalk. Kathryn switched into the back seat, Blaine jumped into the car, and two seconds later the backing lights came on.

"They're leaving now," Porter said into the phone the moment the connection came through. The expected order followed and he nodded. "Yes, sir." He hung up the phone and started the engine.

"Just watch?" Carson said. He grinned, yawning, and put down the glasses.

The 4X4 pulled out of the gravel berm in the curve of the residential street and followed the Cavalier. Neither vehicle turned its lights on until they had turned three corners and were nearly out of the neighborhood.

~~~~~

Kathryn hadn't realized how Bea's unfriendliness irritated Blaine until they reached the FBI office building. When she climbed out of the back of the car and held the seat back for Bea to climb out, the agent spoke up, her voice tight, all traces of amusement gone now.

"No way is that beast going inside."

Kathryn just looked at her for a few seconds. Then she looked at the building. It was somewhat typical of the style of the late seventies, with tinted glass and wide strips of painted metal or brick dominating the outside of the blocky structure, a sloped parking lot surrounded by somewhat overgrown trees and bushes, and wide, shallow steps leading up to the front door.

"Finn knows Bea," Kathryn finally said.

"I doubt Security has a pass made up for her." Blaine gestured back into the car.

"He's let Bea inside before."
~~~~~

"Not this time."

Kathryn frowned, not liking the somewhat naked feeling it gave her to contemplate leaving Bea behind, inside the car. But really, what was the problem? They would only be inside with Finn maybe twenty minutes, then come back out and get into another car and drive to the new safe house. This was where Finn worked, after all. What could be safer?

Maybe it was Regina's triumphant little smirk that made the whole situation irritating.

Kathryn sighed and waved her hand at the back seat of the car. Bea jumped back inside. She rolled down the window six inches for air, though the evening was cool and fresh smelling and the car hadn't had a chance to get stuffy.

"Sorry, beast," she muttered, and rubbed behind Bea's ears before stepping back and closing the door. "Satisfied?" she said, turning to face the other two.

"You'd think that mutt was your security blanket or something," Blaine said. Now she wore the same triumphant smirk as Regina.

"Or something. You're just angry because Bea still doesn't like you."

"You're the only one she likes," Regina said.

"No, you two are the only ones she *doesn't* like." Kathryn didn't start walking when the other two did. She wanted to punch someone. Maybe she should worry that her illness had affected her brain. Why hadn't she made the connections until now? She had chosen to believe the smell of the gun made Bea dislike Blaine, but what if it was something more? Had the agent fooled Finn? If she hadn't... definitely, Finn was getting punched. Was this all part of the plan that was so complicated he couldn't even tell her what was going on?

Was there such a thing as a triple-cross? Kathryn mentally slapped herself to get back on track, and resumed walking. She wanted to go back and open the car door to let Bea out, but a chill up her back stopped her. Suddenly, she could believe very easily that Blaine wouldn't hesitate to shoot Bea. Her companion was safe inside the car, for now.

"I know I feel a lot more comfortable without her." Regina glanced over her shoulder at Kathryn and then hurried to catch up with Blaine and walk next to her.

"I don't." Kathryn made no effort to catch up with them.

They didn't slow down, and only paused to wait for her once they got inside the building. Kathryn fought the sensation of watchful eyes focused on her back. There was too much darkness beyond the parking lot lights on tall poles. The fact this building belonged to the FBI no longer made her feel safe.

The lobby had been paneled since the last time Kathryn had visited Finn's office. The deep, red-tinted wood gave the lobby a much darker feeling than the ivory and lavender ribbons in the former wallpaper. The security guard at the round desk in the middle of the lobby hadn't changed and he even recognized Kathryn, picking up and holding out her temporary security badge to her before she reached the desk. This proof that she was indeed expected made her feel a little better.

She thanked him and memorized his droopy, hound-dog face framed by frizzy red hair for future reference. He barely glanced at Regina when Blaine asked for her badge. The agent's presence was enough for the guard. He pressed the electric lock and the gate buzzed and swung open to let them through into the other half of the lobby.

To the right was a discrete wooden sign for restrooms, and an arrow. To the left, an identical sign indicating the stairs. Two sets of elevator doors sat in a shadowy alcove just beyond the lobby and a long hall leading to the first floor of offices. Kathryn wished Finn had his office on the first floor, not the fourth. They headed for the elevators.

"I have to check in before we meet up with Agent Roberts," Blaine said, and veered off their path. "You two want to wait here or come with me?"

"I know the way to Finn's office. We'll go on up," Kathryn said.

"Good." Blaine paused long enough to look them up and down once each. "I'll see you there in a few minutes." She continued on her way to the door for the stairs.

Kathryn stepped into the elevator alcove, then looked back as the door thudded softly closed behind Blaine. "Why couldn't she just ride up with us?" she muttered, more thinking aloud than expecting an answer.

"Who cares?" Regina stepped into the elevator before the doors finished sliding open. "Let's get upstairs and get this over with."

Kathryn felt the same way, but she refused to give Regina the satisfaction of echoing her sentiment.

When the elevator doors slid open on Finn's floor, the hall lights were dimmed enough Kathryn could see light spilling out from under only one door. She shook her head, smiling, as she led Regina down the hall. Finn might tease her about being obsessive-compulsive about her assignments, but he had his own workaholic flaws, too. She didn't have to check the name plaque on the door before she knocked.

Nothing.

She pounded on the door and pressed close against the panel to listen.

Still nothing.

"Finn, you in there?" Something tightened in her chest and she told herself it was just embarrassment at raising her voice in a silent hallway at this time of night.

"Maybe he's in the bathroom or getting coffee or something," Regina offered.

"Probably." Kathryn tried the doorknob.

The door opened easily. She remembered how Finn had complained about his office door once, so badly hung that it always swung open unless he latched it. Kathryn let the door swing open and listened, waiting for… something. That creeping feeling up her back, of every individual hair on her neck and arms trying to stand up, made her want to turn and run. Why would Finn latch his door when he was the only one on the floor at this time of the night? It wasn't like he needed privacy or to block out noise from other offices. She knew him well enough to know he preferred to leave his door open.

So why was it latched?

The computer was on, the usual avalanche of papers all over the filing cabinets and desk and even some on the floor.

A smear of something dark on the edge of the desk, and the lack of papers there, caught her attention. Kathryn saw light glisten on the darkness—it was wet—no, it was blood. Then she saw Finn's shoe sticking out from behind the desk.

Please, God —

She couldn't finish the silent prayer. Kathryn hurried around the desk and found Finn half curled up on his side, fallen papers and books partially covering him, eyes closed and his mouth twisted in pain. The drift of papers didn't hide the glistening red gash on his forehead.

"Finn." Her voice came out as a squeak.

She dropped to her knees in the limited space between Finn and his desk and fumbled at his neck, feeling for his pulse. It felt jumpy. Or was that from her nerves interfering?

Chapter Twenty-One

Gently, she rolled him onto his back and searched for some sign of what had taken him down. He hadn't simply tripped on the mounds of paper on the floor, hit the desk and knocked himself out, had he? She wondered if Finn still had that broken pocketknife in his desk drawer, with a vague idea of using the knife to cut the shirt to make bandages, something to stop the bleeding.

Regina stepped backward and turned her back on the scene. She studied the office like a tourist, then yelped, "Kathryn!" She swooped down on a gun by the door, and reached to pick it up.

"No!" Kathryn thought her heart had jumped into her throat. She almost grinned when her outburst stopped Regina with her hand only inches from the gun. "Don't touch it."

That was one of the first rules Vincent had taught her, when he became head of security for the Arc Foundation and trained Kathryn and the first few recruits in survival on the road. Never pick up strange guns, or knives, or anything that could have been used as a weapon. Never let her fingerprints get on anything that didn't belong to her if a crime had been committed. She would never know until too late if a trap had been set.

This certainly felt like a trap.

Her brain felt like it spun in a dozen different directions as she kept searching Finn for wounds other than his forehead.

"But—" Regina sputtered. "Somebody shot him—they could still be here. We have to protect ourselves."

"Isn't it a little convenient finding that gun just lying there?"

She slid Finn's empty gun holster off his shoulder. Her hands shook a little as she found a bullet hole in his shirt. The cloth looked scorched, like the gun had been close to him when it went off. The racing of her heart made a deafening roar like the sea in her ears, making it hard to think. Her gorge rose as she considered leaning close to sniff for gunpowder.

Why wasn't there any blood?

How did Regina know Finn had been shot?

Her brain skittered away from those questions as she continued searching him.

Why hadn't anyone reacted to the gunshot and come running? Didn't they have any kind of alarm system in this office, in case someone broke in or someone turned rogue and shot up the place without warning?

Regina frowned at her, then turned back to the gun. She picked it up and slid it into her pocket before turning back to Kathryn.

"Convenient," Kathryn said, thinking aloud, trying to wrap her brain around what had happened, struggling to straighten out her thoughts. "Like a frame."

"I don't like how you think," Regina mumbled.

"You do what you have to, to stay alive." That remark woke memories of things Finn had told her for their mutual protection, in case a situation like this ever hit them. Kathryn almost wept in relief, having something to do, something she understood. She patted down Finn, searching for a little black box the size of a cigarette lighter. Finally, her brain had snapped back into gear. She hated feeling helpless and lost. Especially when it came to Finn unconscious and bleeding in front of her. "Come on, you dumb Fed. Where is it?"

"What are you looking for?" Regina backed toward the opposite corner of the office.

"Help, that's what." Kathryn got up on her knees and turned to look at the mess on the desk's surface.

She flinched when she saw the smear of blood where she imagined Finn had hit his head on the desk. It was quite easy to picture how the bullet's impact low in his shoulder had knocked him off balance. Falling, he had struck his head on the edge of the desk and finished the job.

"It's a little late for that," an icy blond woman said, stepping into the doorway. "Hello, Regina, dear." She shut the door and latched it behind her.

"I don't—" Regina stopped, going slightly green when the woman pulled out her gun. It was compact and sleek, and gleamed dull silver. "Cooper?"

"Thank you for picking up that gun." Cooper gestured at it with her gun. "I rather thought you would. What's one more murder after killing your father?"

"I didn't!"

Kathryn turned back to Finn and patted him down again, searching his pockets, going down to the cuffs of his pants. Why wasn't there any blood other than his forehead?

"Get away from him," Cooper ordered. "Now."

"He's bleeding to death." She leaned over Finn to block the lack of blood on his chest from the woman's view, and ripped cloth just to use up time, delay whatever would happen next.

"That'll make three of you." The dark-suited woman stepped closer, holding out the gun in her hand until Kathryn thought she would ram it into her forehead. "Regina," Cooper said with no change of her cold, satisfied expression, "shoot her."

"But—" Regina choked.

"Don't try anything. I'll simply kill you both and say I shot you in self-defense and this one got in the way. Which is true, I suppose. I'm a very good shot—she'll die quicker, with less pain, if you do it my way."

Regina glanced at Kathryn. The look she gave her was clearly a measuring one, calculating her own chances of survival over everyone else's in the room. For half a second, the photo of Regina in her business suit and lab coat flashed before Kathryn's mental eye. Regina Malvern, the mad scientist. It was very believable.

Finn's hand patted her leg. She nearly yelped. She glanced down at him. He had one eye open. His head moved just enough for her to see, nodding at Cooper, and he blinked rapidly three times. Whatever he wanted her to do, she couldn't figure it out. But at least she knew he was alive and conscious.

Too bad he didn't have his gun.

Her racing heart jerked and settled back to nearly normal pace. Kathryn stood, willing her enemy's attention to lock on her and ignore Finn. She backed up another step, pressing her back against the bookshelves. She felt one of Finn's football trophies against her hand and that sparked an idea. Where was the really big one, that almost needed two hands to pick it up? She knew what she had to do. She slid sideways a few inches. Cooper was too busy glaring at Regina to notice. Kathryn swallowed a snort. Regina irritated everyone.

"Now do it," the woman ordered.

Regina started to draw the gun out of her pocket. A thudding sound came muffled through the door Cooper had closed. The woman frowned and looked at Kathryn, then started to turn toward the door.

Kathryn turned, finding the trophy and snatching it up in both hands. She raised it over her head and flung it.

The door burst open and two security guards, male and female, lunged at Cooper. The woman spun and threw herself out of the way, getting clobbered in the shoulder by the trophy, instead of it hitting her dead center of her chest. Regina let out a shriek, stepped backward, and tripped over a stack of papers. She fell and hit her head against the wall, then curled into a shivering fetal ball.

The guards grappled at Cooper. The man went for the hand holding the gun while the woman went for her legs. Cooper let out one strangled growl. She twisted and spun and the man threw his weight into the fight.

Kathryn staggered backward, searching for something else to throw, and papers slid under her feet so she fell against the bookshelves. A tall, gray-haired man in a gray business suit appeared in the melee and stepped around it with an unflappable calm. He held out a hand to help her back to her feet.

"Sir!" Cooper blurted.

As one, Kathryn and the man turned toward her. The guards had both her hands behind her back. The man had her gun, which relieved Kathryn to no end. Cooper no longer looked calmly superior, but frazzled and sweaty, with a bruise on her porcelain cheek and her hair sticking up at odd angles.

"Sir," the woman began again. "They shot Agent Roberts."

"Liar," Finn said. He groaned as he sat up, and pressed the heel of one hand against his bleeding forehead. His other hand opened and a tiny black box with a red button in the middle fell out onto the floor.

"There it is," Kathryn whispered. Her stomach felt like she had just come up from the first awful drop on a roller coaster. That was what she had wanted to find, to call for help.

From the looks of things, Finn had called for help. She felt dizzy and on the verge of tears and wished she didn't have so much trouble keeping up all of a sudden. The two guards hauled Cooper out and down the hall, leaving just her, Regina, Finn, and the man she suspected was Finn's supervisor, Garretson.

"That looks pretty nasty," Garretson said, gesturing with a jerk of his chin at Finn's bloody forehead.

"I've had worse." Finn held out a hand and Kathryn leaped to help him stand. He settled on the edge of his filing cabinet. "You need to brush up on your first aid or bedside manner or whatever."

"But she did shoot you," Kathryn said. She reached blindly behind herself for the toppled desk chair, needing to sit.

"Don't remind me." He tugged open his shirt, revealing a white tee-shirt underneath it, with a hole to match the outer shirt, and ripped it open to reveal a dark vest. "Got me at point-blank range."

"Bulletproof vest. That's why no blood."

"Sometimes the bruises and broken ribs are worse than a gunshot wound," Garretson said.

"Worth it." Finn reached for a stack of what looked like fast food napkins sitting next to his coffee machine. "Did some good housecleaning tonight, Boss."

"Only half clean." He nodded, his smile grim. "Somebody would think you're bucking for a promotion, letting her get that close, then playing dead."

"Easy to play dead when you get the breath knocked out of you, and then slam your head on the way down like I did."

"I ought to punch you," Kathryn muttered, and yanked the napkins out of his hand. She picked up a plastic pitcher next to his coffee machine, with three inches of water in it, wet the napkins, and pressed them against his bloody forehead. "Scaring me like that."

"Necessary," Garretson said. "How about we get our hero here to the infirmary, and then take care of your friend?" He gestured back into the corner of the office.

Kathryn turned. Regina was still in her curled position, eyes wide and staring at something not in the room. She rocked a little, arms wrapped around her middle, and whimpered.

"I wouldn't exactly call her a friend." Kathryn shrugged and stepped around the desk to kneel next to Regina.

"I didn't," the other woman whimpered. "It was an accident."

~~~~~

Dr. Phillips was either still on duty, or she had heard what happened and insisted on coming in to check out Finn personally. The gash on his forehead wasn't deep or long enough to require stitches, but the dark bruise already forming threatened to be a beauty. The doctor patched it together with some antiseptic-anesthetic paste and butterfly tape, covered with a square adhesive bandage.

Regina had followed Finn and Kathryn into the infirmary like a pathetic puppy and dropped into the nearest chair. She ignored the examination, which included getting Finn's ugly, bloody chest bruises iced and treated with analgesic cream. She stayed wrapped up in herself, whimpering every once in a while. Kathryn had lost all patience with her. She suspected that if she thought hard enough, she would find plenty of reasons to blame this night's troubles completely on Regina. How could she sit there and act like that, when Finn had been shot? He could have been hurt much worse than he had been. A bulletproof vest wasn't much good against a bullet in the head or the leg, for instance.

"Well," Dr. Phillips said as she stepped back and turned off the tiny flashlight she had been shining in Finn's eyes, "everything looks fine. I hope this is the last I see of you for a good long time." She gave his hand a tiny slap of mock reproof.

"So do I," he responded with a grin. Then he muffled a groan, which got louder when he raised his hand to his forehead, moving the arm on his bruised side. Kathryn winced in sympathy, imagining just how much his head was throbbing by now, along with his chest.

"You pay close attention to how you feel over the next few days. If you get any headaches— What in the world happened to you?" she blurted as the door swung open.

Kathryn turned to see Blaine come into the infirmary, holding a dripping wad of paper towels to the back of her head. An ice cube fell out of the wad as the woman agent passed the chairs by the door where Kathryn and Regina sat.

"Ambushed in the stairwell," Blaine said with a shrug. She took the
~~~~~

wet wad off the back of her head and examined it.

"Somebody knew we were coming here tonight," Kathryn said, thinking aloud without meaning to.

"Tell me something I don't know. Chief Garretson wants to know if you two are ready to move."

"What about Finn?"

"He wants you two settled and safe, first," Blaine nearly snapped.

"I want to hear it directly from him." Peripherally, Kathryn was aware of the puzzled frown Dr. Phillips wore.

"Hey, don't you trust me?" the woman agent said with a grin.

"Nope. Bea doesn't like—"

"I don't care what that mutt likes!" Blaine held out her hand, beckoning for Regina. "You two are coming with me."

"Not on your life—which I wouldn't give two plug nickels for right now," Dr. Phillips said. She stepped up to Blaine and glared at her. She reminded Kathryn of a Pekinese facing down a Great Dane, but there was nothing humorous in the image. "If the chief wants these two moved, he can tell me, directly."

Through all this, Finn sat silent and stiff, head bowed. His lack of response sent another warning chill up Kathryn's back.

Dr. Phillips strode across the infirmary and reached for the phone hanging on the wall by the door. Blaine held out a hand to stop her and started across the room after her.

Everything stopped for two long seconds and Kathryn couldn't collect her thoughts when the door swung open and Garretson stepped through.

"Ready to go, ladies?" the bureau chief said with a smile.

"But—" Dr. Phillips fluttered for a moment.

Blaine met Kathryn's eyes, shrugged, and slipped out the door before it swung closed again. Kathryn barely noticed at first as she struggled to figure out what had just happened.

"We have to talk," Regina said, finally sitting up straight. Her sudden change from whimpers to speech startled the others.

She looked plain awful; pale and red-eyed from seeping tears and her lips bitten.

"Why don't we talk as we go?" Garretson said. He offered Regina a hand to help her stand.

"No, right now." She let him help her to her feet and stayed there. "I did shoot my father, like she said." Regina swallowed hard and looked at the floor as she hurried on. "But it was an accident—he was pointing a gun at me—and I got scared—and he was yelling—and he was so angry at me—and the gun just went off."

"Wait a second," Kathryn murmured. Pieces were falling into place suddenly in her mind, but they were creating more questions instead of answers.

"There were two of them, Cooper and Edwards. They came to see me and said my father was selling information that belonged to the government."

"Where's Blaine?" Kathryn felt a moment of frustration when neither Garretson nor Dr. Phillips appeared to be paying any attention to her.

"They said the CIA was actually funding our research, not the university, as my father told me."

"How could she get ambushed inside this building, unless Cooper's partner was waiting for her specifically, and knew where she was going to be?" Kathryn demanded.

"They asked me to spy on my father," Regina said, wringing her hands. "I refused because I didn't believe them. Then weird things started happening and when I asked questions, my father got angry and wouldn't tell me what was going on."

"Those kidnapping and murder attempts Finn told us about?" she asked, finally snapping into the conversation.

"I know there were reported incidents," Garretson said slowly, "but no witnesses. Other than the victims themselves."

"It's true!" Regina blurted. "Someone tried to run me down with a car, and someone else tried to grab me at a concert, and then there were chemicals that were moved and mislabeled at the lab, causing explosions."

"Sir," Dr. Phillips broke in. She rested a hand on Regina's shoulder and gently tried to push her back toward the chair. "Maybe you should stop now. She's been through enough tonight."

"Yeah, she has," Kathryn said, feeling a little sympathy again.

"What were you saying about Blaine?" Garretson asked.

"She was just here." She gestured at the door. Was she the only one who had seen Blaine leave? "She said she was supposed to take us to meet you."

"I didn't send her." His voice turned chill. Garretson's gaze locked with Kathryn's, and she knew they were thinking the same thoughts.

"I thought Bea didn't like her because of her gun," she murmured. "Oh, no—Bea!"

"Who?" Dr. Phillips said. She looked unsure whether she should laugh or not.

"My dog. She's in Blaine's car. She wouldn't let her come inside with us."

"Thank goodness," Regina muttered.

Kathryn didn't hear her. She was already halfway out the infirmary door and flying down the hall. Fortunately, it was on the first floor and she knew where she was going.

The security guard stood up as Kathryn darted through the lobby, heading for the front door. He let out a yell as she vaulted over the security gate. She had no idea if he followed her or not as she slammed both fists against the panic bars and shoved both doors open. Blaine's voice raised in curses rang across the parking lot as Kathryn leaped down the steps.

Lights suddenly flooded the scene, half-blinding Kathryn, but she could still make out the image of Blaine face-down on the pavement with Bea sitting on her. The lights came from the headlights of four cars, two on each side, pointed directly at the car. Kathryn stumbled but kept running. She was so busy searching for Blaine's gun, intending to kick it far out of the way before ordering Bea off the woman, she didn't see the tall man who stepped out of the darkness to her right until he caught hold of her left arm.

Kathryn twisted to break the hold and brought up one knee, aiming blindly, but he caught hold of her leg and spun her upside down, catching her by the waistband of her jeans before her head hit the ground. For two seconds she hung in the air, gasping, stunned at having her moves countered almost before she made them.

"Vincent?" Her voice cracked, a mixture of relief and fury and shock. He was the only one who could counter that move, because he had taught it to her.

He turned her right side up again and set her on her feet.

"Good job."

Kathryn shuddered, feeling like she would suffocate for a moment. Then she growled and raised both fists and pounded the wide, hard-muscled chest that made such a tempting target. Vincent let her get in two thumps with each fist before catching her wrists. He pulled her close, tight against his chest, trapping her arms.

"You knew what was going on all this time, didn't you?" she demanded, her voice cracking, caught between fury and tears she refused to let out. "All the calls you didn't answer — you let me work blind!"

Chapter Twenty-Two

"You're not a very good actress." Vincent rubbed her back, rocking her gently from side to side as she shuddered and fought the sensation she would spew. "We needed you to do exactly what you did, and to be entirely believable in all your reactions."

"We?" The hum of gears and wide wheels on asphalt came to her before Vincent turned her to see Sophie drive her wheelchair into the stream of lights.

Beyond her, several uniformed security guards gathered around Blaine, who had finally fallen silent. Bea stayed perched on her back, and it was obvious the guards weren't sure what to do about the big dog.

"Sidarkis brought us in just before everything went down," Sophie said. "It's pretty nasty and stretches a long way, lots of threads in a lot of agencies and corporations and..." She shrugged. "We figured out the Malverns' lab was a target just about the same time everything blew up. You were in the perfect place."

"You couldn't answer one call?" Kathryn knew she was being petty, but she had crossed the line of "enough" so long ago, she couldn't look backward and find it. Fortunately, Vincent still held her tight against him. Otherwise she might just break down crying or do something else to embarrass herself.

"Bea, let the nice people have her," Vincent said, and let go of Kathryn with one arm to reinforce his order with a series of hand gestures. Bea stepped off Blaine and trotted over to them. Then he let go of Kathryn, and she went to her knees to wrap her arms around the big dog's neck and hide her face in the thick, musky, dusty fur.

~~~~~

Kathryn returned to Dr. Phillips' office after Blaine had been hauled away and she watched Finn get into a car with one of his co-workers, who was taking him home. He wanted to go to the new safe house with her and Regina, but apparently Dr. Phillips was one of the few people in the entire FBI who could overrule him. As a compromise, Kathryn promised to come make dinner for him if he was a good boy and slept all day.

"They came to the lab to meet with me and my father caught us talking. He was furious!" Regina said, her words distorted by sobs, as Kathryn walked back into the outer room of the infirmary. "He was screaming about me being a traitor and owing him because he educated
~~~~~

me and made me his lab assistant when nobody else would have me. That was a lie! Lots of people wanted me to work for them!" For half a second, fury peeked through the trembling and tears. Kathryn wondered if anyone else noticed that.

Garretson sat with her, arms crossed, leaning back in a nearly believable casual posture, and just listened. Kathryn caught the tightening and twitching of muscles in his jaw, his half-hooded eyes, the fingers gently tapping his arm. Whatever he was thinking about her story, the FBI chief was not relaxed. Did he believe her, or was he looking for more information to fill in holes and complete the "housecleaning" he and Finn had mentioned?

"Edwards said we should leave," Regina continued after gulping a breath. "He told me to pack. My father tried to stop us. He hit me. Edwards stopped him. That's when he pulled a gun from a supply cabinet. I didn't even know he had a gun. Cooper gave me a gun. To protect myself. Then ... everything's blurry after that."

"You're missing an entire day, from the time your father died until Kathryn found you," Garretson said. "Do you have any memories of what happened?"

"They took me to a cabin," she said in a slightly calmer voice. "There were other people... and I remember someone yelling and more guns. Someone grabbed me, I think. I tried to run away and someone started throwing me around. That's all I remember except for running through a storm and falling, until Kathryn found me."

"And just how do you fit into all this?" he said, turning to Kathryn. For a while there, she thought maybe Garretson was so focused on Regina he didn't even know she had come into the room.

"I was in the area. I got a call. I went where they told me and found someone who needed my help," Kathryn said. She almost added, *Beep! This is a recording.* How many times over the years had she used the same explanation in other situations that always ended with the same questions?

"That's it?" He smiled and shook his head.

"That's all there is to it." She suspected he had been in on the decision to call her. Was he the "old friend" Vincent had been visiting, and had he made the decision to reveal the details of the crisis that struck the mountainside lab and involve him in the search?

"I wish my people were that obedient."

"It's not obedience, it's trust." Kathryn heard Regina sigh.

"I don't suppose you'd like to work for me?"

"My way doesn't use guns."

"Roberts said you'd say that. I told him if you wouldn't join up, he should marry you to keep you out of trouble."

"Oh, please..." Kathryn hated it when her face burned like it did right that moment. She could only imagine how red it was.

"How come you haven't said yes?"

"I can't say yes when he hasn't gotten the guts to ask me yet. He talks about it, but..." She flung her hands upward in frustration. This was not something she wanted to discuss with someone she had only met tonight. And certainly not with Regina in the room.

Just what had Vincent and Finn and Garretson been talking about, waiting for her to bring Regina to them and lead Cooper into the trap? She had the uneasy certainty her relationship with Finn had been part of the conversation. Vincent wouldn't reveal her secret... but what if he didn't realize until too late that she *hadn't* told Finn she was dying?

Sunday

Regina slept in late the next morning, which suited Kathryn fine. She would much rather be restless in solitude, with only Bea to witness when her achy legs made her shift position a dozen times in an hour. Regina's whiny voice threatened to spark a new headache, and there were times that no headache medication seemed to work without triggering an upset stomach.

When she heard Winslow and Pascal, the two agents assigned to the safe house start moving around, Kathryn got up to help them make breakfast. Something solid and warm in her stomach, along with a pot of fresh mint tea, might do the trick and help her relax. She gladly settled in the living room for a leisurely morning of catching up on her reading. The two agents headed outside for a reconnoiter and told Kathryn to make sure she and Regina stayed inside. Just in case.

The ranch-style house was all on one level, with a spacious kitchen in one corner of an L-shaped room that served as family room and dining room combined. The buffet with breakfast sat at one end of the room, with couch and floor pillows and entertainment center at the other. Kathryn stretched out on the couch with a plate piled with sweet rolls, scrambled eggs, and slices of peaches and oranges. She gave the sausages and burnt toast to Bea and she was perfectly happy to lie on the floor alongside her and alternately doze and chew.

Regina stumbled down the hall from the bedrooms with a blanket wrapped around her borrowed sweat suit, her face red and sporting creases from her pillow, and her hair tangled in every direction. She blinked and wobbled a little on her feet and looked at Kathryn for a few seconds before speaking.

"What are you doing up so early after the night we had?"

For answer, Kathryn held up the book a few seconds, then put it back down on the couch to continue reading. Regina was nearly a genius; she could figure out the answer without any trouble and maybe realize Kathryn really wanted some quiet and privacy.

"Where is everybody?" Regina asked after a few seconds more.

"Checking things outside." Kathryn raised her head and checked the clock. It had only been ten minutes since Winslow had told her they were both stepping outside. It felt like longer.

"You mean we're all alone in here?"

"We're never alone."

"Just stop it!" Regina's voice went from zero to sixty in a fraction of a second. The reverb off the glass globes of the ceiling lights put sparkles around the edges of Kathryn's vision. "Stop it, okay? I am sick to death of all your cryptic little phrases and double meanings and how you never answer my questions."

"Yes I do. You just don't know how to listen." Kathryn sat up and marked her place in the book with her finger.

"That's exactly what I mean!"

"Bea is here to protect us, and there are two agents outside. They can hear you. Probably half the neighborhood can hear you. Why don't you use your mouth for eating instead of screaming for a change?" Kathryn nearly choked on laughter at the irony of that statement.

Regina glared at her for two seconds, then spun to face where she had pointed. She made a beeline for the breakfast table, nearly dropping her blanket. Kathryn stretched out on her stomach and tried to read again. With two sweet rolls balanced on her coffee cup, Regina stomped back down the hall to the bedrooms. She almost tripped over her blanket twice before she vanished from sight. Kathryn sighed and looked down at Bea. The Akita lifted her head to look up at her.

"You think something weird is going on here, too?"

Bea put her paws on the edge of the cushion. Kathryn rolled onto her side, making room for her. The dog climbed up next to her and Kathryn wrapped an arm around her. She pressed her cheek against the thick, musky fur and wished she held Finn this close instead. Closing her eyes, she took deep, slow breaths, willing herself into a calm state, relaxing tight blood vessels, the comforting scents of Bea driving away the nausea that threatened to pounce.

Her mind drifted through several dozen questions and concerns about her truck, and when she should call Dr. West and tell him about Pastor Small. Vincent and Sophie still had work to do on whatever brought them out here in the first place, but he said he would make the report to Quarry Hall, so that was one task Kathryn didn't have to worry about. Her truck was somewhere in FBI custody. She had reported what

Blaine said about a GPS and Garretson said not to worry about it, they would take good care of her truck and get it back to her as good as new. Kathryn just hoped they wouldn't decide to fuss with her notebook computer, hidden in the floor of the truck under the passenger seat. Not that she had anything to hide, especially from the FBI, but it was the principle of the thing that bothered her. Surely after all she had done to help them with their "housecleaning," she deserved some privacy?

Slowly, the quiet of the house penetrated her thoughts. It had a waiting feel to it that made the hairs on her bare arms stand up. She felt Bea go tense and alert next to her. Kathryn let go, and the Akita slid back down to the floor and took a few steps toward the hallway leading to the bedrooms. Her ears pricked forward. She froze like she always did when she smelled blood, or guns. Kathryn felt a silent growl rumbling through the air until it reverberated in her chest.

She put her book down on the floor and slid off the couch, moving slowly and smoothly to avoid the creak of the springs and cushions.

Voices burst down the hall, making Kathryn jerk. Then a blare of brass riffs followed, and she realized Regina had turned on a radio.

Yet Bea didn't relax. She took another step toward the hallway and looked back at her.

Okay, God, help me figure this one out, please. This isn't over by a long shot, is it?

Kathryn glided into the kitchen, straining her ears to hear footsteps or anything else through the blare of the brassy music pounding down the hall. It had a muffled feel to it, like it came through a closed door, but it was still loud enough to feel the beats through her stocking feet. Somehow, she didn't think Regina cared for that raucous, pseudo-Big Band sound. She imagined Regina tended toward rhythm and blues and classical in her musical tastes.

There were quite a few things she had imagined wrong, Kathryn decided in that moment.

In the kitchen, she searched for something to use as a weapon. Preferably something no one else would identify as a weapon at first glance. The few knives in the house were of the steak and paring variety, and all too short to be any use as defense. She would have to get very close to her enemy for them to be any good. Kathryn wanted to avoid close quarters, thank you very much.

Under the sink she found a small can of ant and roach repellant and slipped that into the pocket of her jeans, tugging her t-shirt down over it. Further back in the cupboard she found an economy-size can of oven cleaner spray. Kathryn remembered how even the fumes had blinded her as a child, when she had stuck her nose into the oven to see what the housekeeper was doing. A face-full of spray might even incapacitate

Godzilla. At least, for a little while.

Halfway down the bedroom hallway, it turned, and at that corner the bathroom door hung open. Kathryn paused to reconnoiter and listen with Bea at her side. She saw Regina's bedroom door hanging two inches ajar and saw movement. Too much movement.

"Leave me alone!" Regina said in a nearly normal volume of voice. It came clear through the blaring music, now that Kathryn was this close to her door.

"Keep your voice down," a man ordered in a strained whisper. "You're going to give it to me now, before we leave."

"I don't have it anymore. Just take me to Cameron and —"

A dark blur of cloth moved across the opening in the doorway. Regina squealed. Kathryn took a step forward, her hand reaching for the doorknob, not quite sure what she was going to do.

"Look, I called you, just like Blaine told me to do. I did everything just like we agreed. Is it my fault you —"

The sharp retort of flesh against flesh yanked a squeal from Regina, followed by silence.

Bea growled audibly, low and deep in her throat. Kathryn grabbed her, two fingers through her collar, and dragged her backward into the bathroom. She heard the bedroom door creak open. Kathryn retreated into the shower stall, still dragging Bea, and pulled the door nearly closed behind them. She set down the oven cleaner spray to wrap her hand around Bea's muzzle. That was enough to hush her, but she felt the tension pulsing through her body now, a coiled spring ready to launch at the nearest danger spot.

That has to be Edwards, she thought, when she saw a man in a dark, rumpled suit pushing Regina down the hall. Kathryn remembered everything from the sobbing, somewhat disjointed story Regina had told the night before. Cooper had been caught, so Edwards was still at large.

Edwards held Regina by one arm, turned slightly behind her back. It gave him good leverage and control of her. He looked distinctly disgusted and inconvenienced.

Regina, Kathryn decided in that two-second glimpse of her face, looked more angry than afraid. That, and what she had just heard, solidified several suspicions she had been nurturing. One thing she knew for certain was that Regina had lied about the fire at the lab and how her father died. She waited until their footsteps went from tapping on the hardwood hallway to the muffled sound of walking across the carpeting in the great room. Picking up the can of oven spray, Kathryn nudged the shower door open with her elbow and crept down the hall. She kept two fingers hooked through Bea's collar, just in case.

"Where is she?" Edwards demanded in a stage whisper.

"How should I know?" No fear at all in Regina's voice. She was pure, unadulterated spoiled brat now. "She's supposed to be guarding *me.*"

She let out a yelp, and a moment later Kathryn heard the creak-bang of a body hitting the couch.

"Give me the sample."

"I told you, I don't have it," she spat, her voice breaking. "I'll have to make more when Cameron finally comes through and sets me up in my own lab, like he's been promising." The couch creaked and protested Regina's movements. "When we were separated in the storm, I fell and the case cracked. When the drug's wet, it's useless. It could kill you if it touched your bare skin. I threw it away."

"Maybe you're the one who's useless."

"Nope," a new, male voice said from the kitchen, startling Kathryn so she almost let go of Bea. "She's a witness."

The front door banged open. Kathryn stepped down the hall enough to look around the corner. She caught a tableau, frozen for a few heartbeats.

The two men from the diner and the hotel stood on opposite sides of the room and held guns on Regina and Edwards. Sophie had provided pictures from security cameras and identified the men for her. Porter stood in the kitchen doorway and Carson had his back to the front door. Porter held up a tape recorder and smiled at Edwards' stupefied, angry stare.

"It's all on tape," Porter said, "so there's no use denying it."

"He made me!" Regina burst out, standing up. "It was an accident—they lied to me!"

Snarling, Edwards lunged and grabbed her, one arm around her throat. He pulled a gun from under his suit coat and held it pointed at her side as he dragged her down the hall.

Kathryn saw the two men hesitate and realized they hadn't seen her yet, though she could see them clearly. She let go of Bea. The Akita leaped silently and knocked Edwards off his feet.

Regina screamed as she hit the wall. She curled up, arms protecting her head. Edwards scrambled back to his feet, turning to face Kathryn. She saw the gun swing around, blindly seeking her. The hand with the oven spray came up and she fired, hitting him full in the face, holding the spray button down hard enough to turn her finger white.

Edwards yelled. Then his voice changed to a shriek as the cleaner got in his mouth. He collapsed, wiping at his face, shuddering, gasping, writhing, choking and spitting.

Porter dove in and scooped up the gun. Carson yanked Regina to her feet. He was neither kind nor sympathetic. Regina took one look at his face and her terrified act changed back to anger. Both men looked at Edwards, hesitating to act.

Kathryn finally let the can of spray drop. It hit the edge of the carpeting with a dull thud. The fumes curled around like heat-seeking missiles and raced up her nose and down her throat. She staggered backwards, gagging. Bea came back to her side and leaned against her. She tangled her fingers in her fur and looked at the two men with the guns in their hands.

"I sure hope you two are the good guys this time," she said in a strained voice.

"The last time we looked we were," Porter said. He put his gun back into his side holster under his coat.

"Where are—" Kathryn turned, half-expecting Winslow and Pascal to come tearing into the house.

"Knocked out, tied up in the garage." He nodded to his partner and Carson headed out the door, taking Regina with him. She didn't resist him.

"Did you guys suspect her all along?"

"Didn't you?" He almost smiled.

"I just don't know anymore." Kathryn slid down to the floor right there and leaned back against the wall. She wrapped her arms around Bea. "Is it over now? Can I—" Her throat closed up and her shoulders hunched as she fought the heaving brought on by pressure in her temples, her sinuses, and dizziness that tried to turn her upside down where she sat.

"All over," Vincent announced, coming through the front door. The proud smirk on his face fell off when his gaze met hers. "You done good," he whispered, getting down on one knee next to her. "But you don't look good."

"I just wish people would trust me to do my part without... without needing to lie to me all the time." Kathryn choked on the wail sitting like a weight in her chest. At least, she hoped it was a wail and not her breakfast trying to evacuate.

"There's lying with what you say." He sighed as he gathered her up in his arms and got to his feet. "And then there's lying by what you don't say."

"Vincent—" She pressed her face against his shoulder, eyes clenched closed, fighting vertigo as the movement spun the room around her.

"How about some honesty on your part? You and Finn," he said, as he carried her to the front door. She muffled a moan. "By rights, I should put you and Finn together in the same hospital room and lock you in until you have that overdue talk."

Chapter Twenty-Three

Kathryn slept for most of the day, once she got settled in a private hospital room under Dr. Phillips' supervision, and that suited her just fine. She told herself she didn't care what the final verdict was on Regina, if she was victim or dupe or mastermind of the whole ugly scenario. Sophie sat by her bedside one of the times she woke up, and filled in some of the missing pieces Kathryn didn't even ask about. Regina wasn't talking, but the cleanup team had found several email accounts she and her father had both kept well hidden, and at that point it looked like they were both trying to sell out each other, as well as their government sponsors, and leave the other to take the blame. The jury was still out on whether Regina really had suffered temporary memory loss.

"Oh, that makes me feel a lot better," Kathryn said, her voice somewhere between a croak and a moan.

"Liar." Sophie patted her hand.

"Don't you know sarcasm when you hear it?"

"Sister-mine, you obviously haven't spent enough time with Joan. She's the queen of sarcasm. You're an amateur, compared to her." She shook her head until the multi-colored beads in her dozens of thin braids rattled and clattered against each other.

Kathryn wondered how Sophie could get any thinking done with that sound constantly in her ears, or how she could dare make any sudden moves without being afraid of beating herself in the face with her hair. That prompted a muffled bubble of laughter, and she decided maybe she was getting over whatever had knocked her flat.

"I'm sorry," Sophie whispered.

"For what?"

"Keeping you in the dark. Vincent didn't like sending you in blind, but he didn't want you crippled with suspicions."

"He says I'm a lousy liar."

"Actress. There's a difference. He needed you as much in sympathy with Regina as possible, to get her to trust you. And nothing to cloud your perceptions. No suspicions, no second-guessing yourself."

"Did enough of that. And you left Bea out of the equation." Kathryn sighed. "I just thought she was put off because Regina was such a snot, not that she was a murdering Benedict Arnold. When am I going to listen to my guardian angel better?" She sat up, wincing when the sudden movement made the back of her head throb and sent a queasy wave through her stomach again.

"Hey, enough of that." Sophie sat forward, leaning far enough out of her wheelchair Kathryn thought she might fall out, and gestured as if she would push her back in the bed. "We want you out of here as soon as possible. Vincent is the only one keeping Bea from clawing her way through the walls to get to you. That is one unhappy puppy."

"I miss her too."

"Somebody else misses you." She cocked one eyebrow, eyes sparkling as if she had a wonderful secret.

Kathryn groaned softly, and slid down again in the bed. "What did you tell him?" she asked, hooking her arm across her eyes to block out the light that suddenly was too fierce and bright.

"We haven't told him anything, but I caught him trying to listen in while Vincent filled Dr. Phillips in on your problem—"

"Problem?" She snorted.

"Look, I haven't been around that long, but your folks have mentioned Finn and how much they like him with you. If you love the guy, he deserves to know."

"That I have a death sentence?"

"We all do." Sophie caught hold of her hand.

"Not the same thing."

"Well, if you want to get technical—"

"Sophie!" She caught her breath, expecting a lightning-sharp stab from her head to her stomach from the outburst. Strangely, the queasies seemed to give up, pushed away by the jolt of adrenalin.

"We've all been poisoned in our genetics, and we're all dying. And just like you and the Boss, we can keep watching each other's symptoms, but we have no idea how long we have and when we'll go terminal." Sophie squeezed her hand. "You know, it's at times like these I can really see the resemblance between you and Joan. You both want to take the weight of the world on your shoulders and pay for crimes you never committed, and heaven forbid you make a grab for happiness and take a risk on someone getting a little bit hurt by loving you. Don't make me tell you that really hokey story about the guy hanging from the cliff who takes the time to eat strawberries."

"All right," she whispered, and gingerly, slowly sat up. "I won't."

"Wise-guy. The short answer—"

"Hah!"

"Vincent didn't tell him anything, and I threatened to run over his foot when he tried to press me for info, but the guy deserves to know." She squeezed Kathryn's hand and shook it once before letting go. "Here's the thing. Even when you're feeling up to heading home, the Feds want you sitting here as bait for whoever Regina was going to give the drug to. She took a sample from the lab and broke away when the Feds thought they were rescuing her, so chances are good she was trying to meet someone with the sample. Now that she's in custody, there's a chance the buyer will try to find out if you have it."

"So that's why I get the cushy private room. Closed circuit TV goes both ways?" she said, gesturing at the equipment hanging in the corner of the ceiling. Kathryn hadn't kept her eyes open very long once she got settled in her room, but she had noticed what appeared to be a flat-screen TV with a DVD player and a gaming system. Appearances, obviously, were deceiving.

"Got it in one. If somebody shows up — if they get through security and actually get in the room —"

"Play along and pump him for information. Got it." She closed her eyes and lay back in the totally inadequate pillows. "See, I can too act."

"Ethyl Barrymore, eat your heart out." Sophie patted her shoulder. "Oh, and one more thing," she said, the hum of her wheelchair motor indicating she was moving away from the bed. "Jeff West will probably be here tomorrow. We figure if the goons don't make a grab for you, we'll add him to sweeten the pot."

"Why? What does he — they know he helped me and Regina, and they're coming after him?" Kathryn opened her eyes, to find Sophie paused at the door, just about to shove it open.

"Came, past tense. Agent Carson and his partner got him away to protective custody, right after Cooper and Edwards set fire to his house."

"Oh, no…"

"The only thing he regrets is his library. Jennifer made sure he was thoroughly indoctrinated when he signed on, including the part where all of us get a target painted on our backs. The big bosses are considering whether they should pretend Regina accidentally left the drug sample in his office when he patched her up, and see if anyone takes the bait."

"My condolences. I know what it's like, hanging on a hook." Kathryn managed a weak grin when Sophie stuck her tongue out at her.

"Get some sleep." She pushed the door open and wheeled her chair through the gap.

~~~~~

When Kathryn opened her eyes again, Finn sat by the bed, one foot up on the frame, the chair tipped so he rested on the two back legs and rocked slightly. A two-liter bottle of ginger ale, the sides wreathed in condensation, sat on the bedside table with a bag of barbecue potato chips. She smiled and studied his face almost as long as the treats he had managed to sneak in to her. Finn knew exactly what would make her feel good, even if the doctors forbade it. Then again, no one had given her any
~~~~~

dietary restrictions. Was that because they trusted her to know how to take care of herself, or because they had no more idea what was going on with her body than the doctors treating her Uncle Harrison?

"Hey." Finn gave her that tired, achy sort of crooked smile that made her want to drag him home to Quarry Hall and watch over him while he slept. He let the chair drop down onto the front legs with a dull thud.

"Hey, yourself."

"You really did it this time." He shrugged when she just looked at him. "The chief is highly impressed. Won't give up until you work for us."

"I can't."

"I know." He caught hold of her hand and squeezed. "At least he's got a better idea of what you're involved in, after spending the last few days trying to look over Vincent's shoulder. The guy is just plain scary."

"Garretson?" She sighed laughter when Finn scowled at her. "Vincent is a teddy bear."

"Yeah, a seven-foot, five hundred pound teddy bear with razor sharp claws, three sets of teeth, and a scorpion tail."

"I'll let him know you said that. He'll be flattered."

"You're one—" The laughter dropped off his face with an almost audible sound. Finn's hand tightened around hers.

"Sick kid? Yeah, you've told me that before."

"Kath—"

"You know why I turned you down, the few times you snuck up on halfway proposing?"

"You never really turned me down, since I never really asked you. But now that we're on the subject..." He sighed and bowed his head, bringing her hand up to press against his cheek.

"I thought you were teasing, not really serious."

"The more I think about it, the more I like the idea, the more important it is to me. The thing is, we need time to figure out if we'll work, and I didn't want to ruin things, scare you off."

"I've had this crazy idea of not marrying until I was sure I can't live without you." Her breath caught for a moment and she forced her way past the pain that had nothing to do with her body. "Now it's been taken out of my hands. I feel like I don't have the right to marry you, if you ever really ask me, because I don't have any idea how much time we might have."

"Uh huh. That answers a couple questions." He pressed her knuckles to his lips, his gaze staying locked with hers. "Just not the really important ones."

"I don't have those answers, either. The short version is that somebody used me, used my blood, to pass on a genetically engineered time bomb to Uncle Harrison."

"You're uncle has been sick for a while now. Over two years, maybe?" Finn's grip loosened and he sat back, as if he needed distance to see her better, but he didn't let go. "How come you didn't tell me?"

"Nothing you could do. Nothing you *can* do."

"That's a matter of opinion."

"I wish—" She stopped, surprised at the confession that seemed to slip past her conscious mind to her lips. Kathryn swallowed hard, looked away, met his gaze again. She didn't think she saw anger, just hurt. "I wish you had asked me outright."

"Would you have accepted?"

"I don't know. The thing is, everything is… tainted? Everything is different."

"I could get killed at any time, when I'm out in the field." He exhaled loudly, a prolonged sound, and his grip tightened on her hand again. "Maybe that's why I was sneaking up on the big question. Maybe trying to figure out how you felt about the whole idea. If you were scared for me getting hurt, if that would put any pressure on your answer." He slouched a little in his chair and grinned, looking up at the ceiling. "We're both dumb saps. You know that, don't you?"

"Matched pair?" she whispered.

"You got that right. So are we stupid or smart, to grab what time we can have?"

"Finn… I see how my uncle suffers. He has good days when he's perfectly normal, and then he has really bad days, when he's cold and can hardly breathe and can't even sit up in his wheelchair." She swallowed hard. "You know what the worst part is?"

He shook his head and sat forward, leaning in closer to her.

"The worst part is seeing what all this does to Aunt Elizabeth. She suffers with him. I can't do that to you." She shrugged and blinked against the hot, wet pressure in her eyes. "I guess that means I love you."

"Uh huh." Finn lifted his other hand and dabbed with his thumb at the corners of her eyes. "You know how stupid noble it is, not to marry somebody who loves you, just because you want to protect him? Because the thing is, I'm still going to hurt for you, whether we're married or not." He shrugged and leaned closed enough she could feel his breath on her cheek. "The way I see it, we have the right to be happy, as much as we can."

"Stupid noble, huh?" She closed her eyes as he brushed his fingers against her chin, tipping her head to just the right angle to kiss her.

~~~~~

The silent alarm Vincent left for her buzzed in Kathryn's hand, waking her from a half-doze. After sleeping most of the day, she was fully rested at 3a.m. Whether she was ready for action remained to be seen. She
~~~~~

turned over on her side to face the door and pressed three times on the button on the face of the alarm, to acknowledge she was awake and aware.

The door of her room opened just wide enough and long enough to let a slim female shape step inside. The woman's face was curtained by dark hair and she wore dark green scrubs. The door clicked as it latched. Kathryn pressed the control bar for her bed, turning on the light in the wall panel above the bed.

"You're not a nurse, are you?" Kathryn said, sitting up.

The stranger blinked and raised the pistol in her hand in a shielding gesture. For a moment the two traded stares. Then the woman stepped up to the bed and gestured at the clothes laid across the back of the chair between the bed and the curtained window.

"Somebody very important wants to talk to you. Take my advice and give him what he wants."

"No, you take my advice and get out of town."

"If you're depending on someone to see me in here and come running to your rescue, you'll be very disappointed. Right now, all they're getting is a loop of you sleeping." She gestured again at the clothes on the chair, and emphasized her unspoken order by yanking on the blanket to pull it off Kathryn.

Compliance was part of the plan. Kathryn sat up, moving slowly. Maybe Vincent and the others had been right to leave her in the dark so she would be convincing in the deception and trap for Regina's contact. It was hard not to grin right now, thinking about the people getting into position, ready for the last act in this long, involved plan. As oblivious and self-centered as Regina had been, she might have caught on to the tension as Kathryn played her part during the last two days. Pretending to be frightened and sick pushed the limits of her acting talent. Especially since Kathryn wanted so badly to launch herself at the woman and take her down with a tackle worthy of the messiest mud football game Quarry Hall had ever seen.

She pulled on her sweatshirt and jeans over the long tee-shirt and loose shorts she had been sleeping in. Kathryn mentally penalized the stranger for not noticing or reacting to the lack of hospital gown. Shouldn't she be suspicious that Kathryn was ready for something to happen?

"Mind telling me who you are? Since you seem to be planning on us spending a lot of time together. That's what kidnapping means, doesn't it?"

"Lisa. That's all you need to know," the woman said. She backed up to the door, keeping the gun trained on Kathryn.

Lisa searched her duffel bag and backpack, reinforcing the theory that Regina's contact believed someone had the sample of the stolen drug. Kathryn couldn't fathom why anyone would expect her to have it, especially when she and her possessions had been in FBI custody for more than a day now. She speculated on what Lisa's reaction would be if they had followed Finn's suggestion and put a plastic cube of fake drug powder in her backpack for the enemy to find. Would Lisa have shot her and left her for dead, or would she still have taken her prisoner?

Kathryn mentally worked through the different possible scenarios as they started down the stairwell, which was conveniently right next to her hospital room. Lisa made her carry both her duffel bag and backpack, keeping her hands full. It took all her self-control not to glance up at the tiny video cameras that had been installed that afternoon in preparation for Regina's contact to strike. Kathryn envisioned Sophie keeping watch, controlling a wall full of computer screens, keeping track of her progress. Vincent and Finn and Carson would be waiting, backed up by other agents from several different agencies, ready to take custody of the mysterious, powerful person who could convince self-centered, rich Regina Malvern to betray her overbearing father and her country.

A car pulled up to the side door of the hospital as the stairwell door opened and no alarm went off. Kathryn wondered if she should be impressed at the connections this man had, to disable hospital security, or if she should be disgusted at how easily they were duped into thinking they had gotten around hospital security.

The back door on the driver's side of the car opened and a sleek, dark-haired man climbed out. The interior light of the car illuminated him just enough for an impression of square-cut features and athletic figure in a black three-piece suit. He studied Kathryn, standing in the open doorway with his hands clasped behind his back, and she returned the measuring glance. She imagined him in several dozen super-spy movies, always playing the lying, double-crossing leader of the villains. An athletic Asian man in a dark suit got out of the front passenger seat and approached Kathryn with a gun focused on her. She felt slightly disappointed that she wasn't facing a Bond-type villain. Or was that just the medication Dr. Phillips had whipped up to try to combat her symptoms?

"Cooper and Edwards worked for you?" Kathryn asked, before the silence went on too long. Her voice rang softly against the wall behind her and then died, muffled by the darkness and the emptiness of the lot behind the hospital at this time of the morning. She cast one sideways glance at the darkness where Vincent and Finn promised they would be waiting, and said a quick prayer for steadiness and protection.

"They used to work for me." The man's voice sounded cool, confident, rich, with a touch of boredom. "You and I have some unfinished business."

"We never had any business." She flinched, twisting sideways, sensing the barrel of the gun aiming for her ribs before Lisa could jab her.

"She doesn't have it on her," Lisa said.

"Have what?" Kathryn let the duffel slide down, keeping a grip on the straps, letting the bag become a barrier between her and the woman. Her backpack stayed on her shoulder and she raised her hand to take a firm hold on the strap, ready to twist and swing it around to hit or distract an attacker.

A flicker of movement turned into moonlight reflecting on a sleek, dull silver gun in the man's hand as he raised it and aimed it at her. Kathryn couldn't take her eyes off that gun. It looked like a prop in a near-future movie.

"The sample. Where is it?" He sighed, followed by a *tsk*ing sound when she just stood still and stared him down, her face as blank as she could manage.

"Sample of what?"

"Regina Malvern was to bring a sample of the drug to our rendezvous. She had absolutely nothing on her when she was taken into custody, so logic says you have it. And if you turned it in to the authorities…"

Kathryn muffled a sigh of her own. The trailing words, the silence, the little flicking movement of the gun all belonged in a bad spy melodrama. She hoped someone was close enough to listen and pick up on the implications: someone had searched Regina's few belongings and reported to this man that she didn't have the sample of the drug on her. Probably Blaine, or maybe there was another mole within the organization.

"Oh, didn't you get the memo?" she said. "I guess Edwards couldn't talk with a mouthful of oven cleaner. Regina told him she dropped it and it melted in the rain."

"Oven cleaner?" The man chuckled. The warmth of the sound sent prickly chills up her back. Someone as evil as she imagined him to be had no right to have such a pleasant-sounding laugh. "Your handiwork?"

"You use what you have at hand." Kathryn stayed focused on him when she wanted to look in all directions for the first sign of rescue closing in, ready to spring the trap.

"Somebody," he said slowly, his voice thoughtful, "has made sure nobody can find out anything about you. Your background, your training, your real name."

"My real name?" She nearly laughed at that. Kathryn had always been her name, though what went with the label had changed greatly in the last ten years.

"I don't like that," he continued. "It makes me think you're a bigger danger than you appear. Who are you really, Kathryn?"

"Who I am doesn't matter," she said. "It's *what* I am that counts."

"Ah. A philosopher." He tipped his head toward the woman standing beside her. "What do you think, McCain? First impressions. A worthy member of our team?"

"Sir?" The woman took half a step back, and even in the shadows cloaking them all, her momentary surprise was clear, no matter how quickly she schooled her face back to watchful calm. "Blaine basically said she was an arrogant smart-mouth."

"Blaine's opinion means nothing," the man said. "Her performance was so far from satisfactory, it doesn't bear discussion. But you, mysterious Kathryn, you are more than worthy."

"I don't think so," Kathryn said. What was taking Vincent and the others so long? Were they trying to make the man hang himself with his words? Lull him into complacency? Or did they want him to take her to his headquarters before they captured him?

"That's the question, isn't it? Worthy of hiring, or such a worthy opponent that a wise man would eliminate you?" He raised the gun a little higher and his finger slid across the trigger.

Kathryn flinched—she couldn't help it—as she imagined a click of the trigger moving, the gun cocking, ready to fire.

"Talents like yours are priceless," he continued. "I wonder about the reach and power of your employer. What will it take to hire you away to my service?"

"Is this where you offer me the world in exchange for my soul?"

"Is that what it will take? The price of your soul?" Again that warm, amused chuckle.

"You're too late. My soul is already claimed and no way of getting it back. There's nothing you can offer me."

"Wrong answer. How sad." He nodded to Lisa. "I do hate to waste resources."

Kathryn turned, swinging her duffel back, directly into Lisa's gut at the same moment the woman raised her gun. She swung the backpack at the Asian man before he could take more than one step. The only place to go was down and take cover under the car. Flares arched across the sky. Light exploded all around the car as she slid across the asphalt, bracing for the first bullet to scream past her.

Shrill, rapid-fire bursts penetrated the thunder of her pulse and gasping breaths. The man cursed. Lisa shouted something. The car rocked and Kathryn envisioned the three jumping in and racing away—with her caught underneath it. Before she could do more than wordlessly send up her soul in a desperation prayer, the car rocked again.

Silence.

Running feet pounded the asphalt, men racing up to surround the car. Then Bea whined and the clatter of her claws on the pavement turned into a skidding sound as she tried to slide under the car to reach Kathryn.

"It's okay," Finn called, somewhere overhead. "Come on out."

For a few seconds, Kathryn felt frozen. She shuddered from the adrenalin rush. Part of her wanted to burst out laughing at the sudden image of being stuck under the car. She couldn't seem to get her arms and legs to move in the right way to crawl out. Then a pair of dark brown boots came within sight and stopped next to Bea. A moment later, knees hit the pavement, and Finn was there on his hands and knees, looking under the car with a flashlight in one hand, the other hand stretched out to her. She started shaking, but that didn't get in the way as she crawled out and he hauled her to her feet again.

Finn gave her just enough time to turn and see Lisa, the Asian, the driver, and their mysterious employer—hopefully the man Regina called Cameron—all sprawled unconscious on the pavement or across the seats of the car, with tranquilizer darts embedded in their flesh. Then he led her away, keeping his arm tight around her waist as they went around the side of the hospital, with Bea right beside them, to the windowless service van that served as a command center for the operation.

"Well, did you have fun?" Sophie asked, as the door in the side slid open.

"Depends on your definition of fun." Kathryn shuddered, and gripped Finn's sweatshirt just a little tighter.

"Hey," he murmured. "It's okay. It's over." He offered her a shrug and a crooked smile, and he didn't let go of her.

Something clicked inside, answering questions she had only begun to put into words. A sense of calm washed over her, in odd, almost amusing contrast to the shivers still controlling her flesh. Kathryn smiled, swallowing hard against giggles.

"It's over," she echoed and pressed her face into his shoulder. If he asked her to marry him, if he didn't, if they had years together or only a few months or never moved on from the understanding they had reached today… none of that mattered. They had right this moment, and she was grateful.

The End

THANK YOU!

Thank you for reading this book from Mt. Zion Ridge Press.

If you enjoyed the experience, learned something, gained a new perspective, or made new friends through story, could you do us a favor and write a review on Goodreads or wherever you bought the book?

Thanks! We and our authors appreciate it.

We invite you to visit our website, MtZionRidgePress.com, and explore other titles in fiction and non-fiction. We always have something coming up that's new and off the beaten path.

And please check out our podcast, **Books on the Ridge,** where we chat with our authors and give them a chance to share what was in their hearts while they wrote their book, as well as fun anecdotes and glimpses into their lives and experiences and the writing process. And we always discuss a very important topic: *Tea!*

You can listen to the podcast on our website or find it at most of the usual places where podcasts are available online. Please subscribe so you don't miss a single episode!

Thanks for reading. We hope you come back soon!

About the Author

On the road to publication, Michelle fell into fandom in college and has 40+ stories in various SF and fantasy universes. She has a bunch of useless degrees in theater, English, film/communication, and writing. Even worse, she has over 100 books and novellas with multiple small presses, in science fiction and fantasy, YA, suspense, women's fiction, and sub-genres of romance.

Her official launch into publishing came with winning first place in the Writers of the Future contest in 1990. She was a finalist in the EPIC Awards competition multiple times, winning with *Lorien* in 2006 and *The Meruk Episodes, I-V*, in 2010, and was a finalist in the Realm Awards competition, in conjunction with the Realm Makers convention.

Her training includes the Institute for Children's Literature; proofreading at an advertising agency; and working at a community newspaper. She is a tea snob and freelance edits for a living (MichelleLevigne@gmail.com for info/rates), but only enough to give her time to write. Her newest crime against the literary world is to be co-managing editor at Mt. Zion Ridge Press and launching the publishing co-op, Ye Olde Dragon Books. Be afraid … be very afraid.

And please check out her newest venture: Ye Olde Dragon's Library, the storytelling podcast. Interspersed between the chapters will be interviews with authors of fantastical fiction. Listen to the podcast on your favorite podcast app or listen on the website: www.YeOldeDragonBooks.com, and click on the Ye Olde Dragon's Library link.

www.Mlevigne.com
www.MichelleLevigne.blogspot.com
www.YeOldeDragonBooks.com
www.MtZionRidgePress.com

NEWSLETTER:
Want to learn about upcoming books, book launch parties, inside information, and cover reveals?

Go to Michelle's <u>website</u> or <u>blog</u> to sign up.

Thanks for reading!
If you enjoyed this book, would you help Michelle by posting a review on Goodreads?

Are you a member of Book Bub? If so, please follow Michelle on Book Bub, and you'll get alerts when new books are coming out.

As a way of saying thanks, Michelle invites you to the Goodies page on her website. It will change regularly, offering you a free short story, a sample audiobook chapter, sneak peeks at new cover art, inside information on discounts and new release dates, etc.

Please go to: Mlevigne.com/good-stuff.html

Also by Michelle L. Levigne

Guardians of the Time Stream: 4-book Steampunk series
The Match Girls: Humorous inspirational romance series starting with **A Match (Not) Made in Heaven**
Sarai's Journey: A 2-book biblical fiction series
Tabor Heights: 18-book inspirational small town romance series.
Quarry Hall: 11-book women's fiction/suspense series
For Sale: Wedding Dress. Never Used: inspirational romance
Crooked Creek: Fun Fables About Critters and Kids: Children's short stories.
Do Yourself a Favor: Tips and Quips on the Writing Life. A book of writing advice.
To Eternity (and beyond): *Writing Spec Fic Good for Your Soul.* A book defending speculative fiction.
Killing His Alter-Ego: contemporary romance/suspense, taking place in fandom.
The Commonwealth Universe: SF series, 25 books and growing
The Hunt: 5-book YA fantasy series
Faxinor: Fantasy series, 4 books and growing
Wildvine: Fantasy series, 14 books when all released
Neighborlee: Humorous fantasy series
Zygradon: 5-book Arthurian fantasy series
AFV Defender: SF adventure series
Young Defenders: Middle Grade SF series, spin-off of *AFV Defender*
Magic to Spare: Fantasy series
Book & Mug Mysteries: cozy mystery series

Quest for the Crescent Moon: fantasy series
Steward's World: fantasy series reboot and expansion
The Enchanted Castle Archives: fantasy series